A Hero's Heart

By Sylvia McDaniel

Books by Sylvia McDaniel

Contemporary Romance

Standalones
The Reluctant Santa
My Sister's Boyfriend
The Wanted Bride
The Relationship Coach
Her Christmas Lie
Secrets, Lies, and Online Dating
Paying for the Past
Cupid's Revenge

Anthologies
Kisses, Laughter & Love
Christmas with you

Collaborative Series

Magic, New Mexico
Touch of Decadence

Western Historicals

Standalones
A Hero's Heart
A Scarlet Bride
Second Chance Cowboy

The Cuvier Women
Wronged
Betrayed
Beguiled

Lipstick and Lead
Desperate
Deadly
Dangerous
Daring
Determined
Deceived

Scandalous Suffragettes
Abigail
Bella
Callie
Faith

The Burnett Brides
The Rancher Takes a Bride
The Outlaw Takes a Bride
The Marshal Takes a Bride
The Christmas Bride

Anthologies
Wild Western Women
Courting the West
Wild Western Women Ride Again

Collaborative Series

The Surprise Brides
Ethan

American Mail Order Brides
Katie

A Hero's Heart
Published by Virtual Bookseller
Published originally by Kensington Publishing Corporation: 1998

Cover Design by Melody Simmons
https://ebookindiecovers.com/

Editing by Kensington Publishing House
www.kensingtonbooks.com/

Formatting by Laurelle Procter
laurelleprocter@gmail.com

Short Description: While searching for his brother, Wade
rescues a woman and her younger sisters, and ends up
pretending to be her husband while he escorts her and her family
to Oregon.

ISBN: 978-1-942608-22-6 (paperback)
ISBN: 978-1-942608-23-3 (e-book)

{Historical Western Romance – Fiction}

www.SylviaMcDaniel.com

Synopsis

Wade Ketchum is searching for his only surviving sibling when he finds a ready-made family.

Rachel Cooke is stranded on the Oregon Trail with three orphans and a rebellious sister, until gambler Wade Ketchum rescues them. The hardened cowboy is searching to find his long lost brother, is out of cash and has no time for a praying spinster.

When Rachel runs out of options, she makes a deal. Wade must pretend to be her husband and help her reach Oregon.

But somewhere along the trail, pretending becomes real. Can she help Wade realize that he still has a heart capable of love?

Table of Contents

Chapter One

1846 Indian Territory

Death spiraled toward the sky in a hazy plume of thick black smoke, spreading its raucous odor across the hilly countryside. From his chestnut mare, Wade Ketchum gazed upon the burned wagons, scattered furniture and littered bodies. The sight seemed unreal in the early morning light, but the woman kneeling beside a freshly dug grave, shoulders shaking with grief, made the scene painfully real.

Wade slid from his saddle, the creak of leather echoing in the deadly quiet. Alert, he walked towards the woman, his boots crunching on the hard ground. As she bent over the grave, her sunbonnet rested against her slender shoulders, exposing a soft mass of mahogany tresses at her nape.

Her head was bowed her hands clasped together.

"Please, Father, I need your help. Guide us through Your wilderness."

Wade hesitated. The woman was praying.

"Send someone to help us. I can't do this alone." She sobbed. "Our lives are in Your hands. Amen."

Wade cleared his throat.

She jumped up, whirling around at the sound. Her gaze collided with his, and her shoulders seemed to sag with relief.

"I was afraid it was the Pawnee returning," she said, her voice filled with relief, her eyes wary of him.

"Are you hurt?"

"No, just terribly frightened," she answered, her voice shaking with suppressed emotion.

Wade glanced at the camp. Smoke drifted across the area giving it a ghostly appearance, nothing stirred. The attack had been recent, and even one survivor was a miracle.

A feeling of unease crept up his spine. Why was she still here, vulnerable to another attack? "What happened?"

"The Pawnee ambushed our wagon train late yesterday evening. I've been trying to hitch up our wagon." She rambled nervously on. "I was beginning to wonder if we were going to all die here in this barren country." The woman held out a shaky right hand. "I'm Rachel Cooke."

"Wade Ketchum, ma'am." Gripping her cold palm, he realized the woman was skittish as a wild horse.

She withdrew her hand from his, wrapping her arms around her middle as if to protect herself. She stared at the destruction of what once had been fifteen or more wagons, and seemed to sag before his eyes. One wagon stood apart from the others, the canvas singed and ripped, but otherwise still intact.

"We were fortunate," she whispered, as a sob escaped her throat. "Somehow our wagon was spared." She wrung her hands fretfully. "But the oxen were spooked by the raid, and I haven't been able to hitch them, to take us away from here."

"Ma'am, I'm surprised you still have oxen."

"They were down at the creek being watered when the attack occurred. We heard the noise and hid in the bushes."

Wade wanted to reach out and touch her, reassure her somehow. Knowing he had to be in Fort Laramie in three days, knowing she would only slow him down, and yet knowing he couldn't leave her behind, he said, "I'll hitch your wagon and help you reach the next town."

"Just get us out of here. Away from all this. I don't care where you're going," she said, her voice trembling with fear.

"I won't leave you, ma'am," Wade said, trying to dispel the fear from her eyes, nervous about the possible return of the Pawnee.

His gazed wandered to the single grave. "Your husband?"

She followed his gaze. "No, it's Miss Cooke. The grave is my father's." She choked up momentarily. "I couldn't stand the thought of animals or Indians desecrating his body. So I spent the morning, burying him the best I could. But the others, God rest their souls, I couldn't help them."

While not a classic beauty, she was pretty, in an unusual way. There was a wholesomeness of face and spirit that Wade was not accustomed to in a woman.

He sneaked another glance, his gaze taking in the delicate profile and lush curves. Those curves would be a definite distraction.

Wade picked up the hitch and approached the oxen. He slipped the yoke around their necks and proceeded to fasten it on the animals. "I have to be in Fort Laramie in three days. I'll take you that far, but then you're on your own."

She wrapped her arms around herself, as if a chill had passed over her. "I'm so grateful you came along. We were on our way to The Dalles, Oregon, to my father's new church."

"You should be able to catch up with another wagon train in Fort Laramie, Miss Cooke. They'll see you on to Oregon." He checked the ropes one last time. "Are you ready? I don't want to linger here any longer than necessary."

"I agree. Just let me get the children," she said.

"Children?" Wade heard himself blurt the word. "I thought you said you weren't married? That no one else survived."

"Just my sister and three orphans. My father was a minister. We ran an orphanage back home, in Tennessee."

Suddenly, a small army crashed through the brush. Wade whirled around and pulled his gun, expecting to face Pawnee and came face-to-face with a beauty. The young woman held a small baby in her arms and a little girl of about seven tugged a freckled-faced adolescent boy behind her. They all stopped, wide eyes fixed on him and his gun.

Wade stared at the group in disbelief. "What the hell?" He shoved the weapon back in his holster.

"Mr. Ketchum, please watch your language!" Rachel exclaimed.

He didn't have time for children. They were little creatures that cried or whined most of the time and had a way of getting under your skin, twisting your heart. He didn't need the aggravation, or the memories they evoked.

The little girl looked wide-eyed at him, and Wade growled, "I don't know, Miss Cooke. I didn't bargain for this."

Catching sight of Rachel, the baby started to fuss, holding out his arms. The young woman carrying the infant grimaced with distaste. She hurried over to Rachel, her long skirts swishing, and shoved the baby into Rachel's arms. "It's your turn to take care of this wet, fussy brat."

With a toss of her blond curls, the other woman informed Rachel, "We couldn't stand waiting in that ravine any longer. The children had to see you were all right."

"I'm fine, Becky. This is Mr. Ketchum. He's going to see us to the next town."

Becky carefully assessed him from head to toe. For a moment he felt like he was sized up, tagged, and numbered. Trouble was etched in her smile, in the way she walked and in every line of her seductive body.

"Nice to meet you, Mr. Ketchum," she cooed.

Wade shook his head in bewilderment. These two women couldn't possibly be sisters. They were about as much alike as a skunk and a porcupine.

"Rachel, the wagons – they're all burned," the little girl cried.

She knelt with the baby on her hip, putting herself at the child's level. "Yes, Grace, I know."

"Where is Papa Cooke?" the child asked.

"Remember what we talked about last night?"

"But I want to see him."

Tears filled Rachel's eyes. "We won't see him again until we get to heaven. Let's say a prayer for Papa and everyone else before we leave."

Wade swore beneath his breath. "Miss Cooke, we don't have time for a prayer service. Those Indians could return any time."

She looked at him the way a schoolmarm would gaze at a misbehaving child.

"Please, Mr. Ketchum, the children and I need just a few moments to say good-bye. We'll make it quick."

How could a woman who looked so soft be so damn stubborn?

He watched Rachel gather her small brood around the lone grave. She pulled a Bible from her apron pocket and read a passage as unfamiliar to him as Greek. Then bowed her head and led them in prayer.

Not for the first time, Wade wondered what he'd gotten himself into. He shook his head, mentally chastising himself for getting involved. Three days from now the biggest card game west of the Mississippi was being played in Fort Laramie, and he intended on winning that money. He had to win a decent amount in that card game or find himself stranded, unable to continue the search for his brother.

But he couldn't just leave them here. And more importantly, the sight of Miss Cooke bending over that grave had touched a memory he'd rather forget.

"Thank you, Father, for sending us Mr. Ketchum," Rachel said. "Amen."

"Good Lord! Now she thinks I'm a damned saint," Wade mumbled his thoughts out loud.

Immediately, Rachel turned to face Wade, sending him a puzzled look. "What did you say, Mr. Ketchum?"

"I don't have time to cart a bunch of kids around," Wade said, running a hand through his hair as he gazed upon the children. "I have to be in Fort Laramie by Saturday."

Becky twittered with laughter. "Oh, I don't think a strong man like you would leave three small children and two helpless females all alone in the wilderness."

Helpless? Maybe they appeared vulnerable, but any woman who survived an Indian attack and buried a man, was anything but defenseless.

"Mr. Ketchum, I would like to leave here as soon as possible," Rachel asserted suddenly. "Are you going to help us or not?"

Everyone turned to him expectantly. Only the baby seemed uninterested in his response. The blonde-haired little girl looked so much like his sister Sarah, her gaze felt like a knife gouging his heart. They were wasting precious time.

He cursed under his breath. "Of course, I'm going to help you. But I'm not going to spend another minute waiting for the damn Pawnee to return. Let's go."

~

Rachel drove the team of oxen, just like she had for the last three months. The dust was still incredible and the heat intolerable as the wagon bounced along the rutted trail. But Rachel knew that yesterday's Indian raid had changed everything, and she was frightened.

"If he ain't the best-looking man we've seen since we left Tennessee!" Becky said as her gaze devoured Wade.

Rachel barely comprehended her sister's words. Her mind and body were weary. She was grimy. And even though she had scoured the blood and dirt from her hands, she felt stained. Stained with her father's blood and that of other members of the wagon train.

"I'd bet the trail he's traveling is littered with broken hearts," Becky prattled on as if this wasn't the day after their father's death. "How could any woman resist a man who looks as fine as he does."

"Becky!" Rachel exclaimed, finally unable to ignore her sister's comments any longer. She peeked over her shoulder, worried the children were listening.

"I know you're young, but must you always be so interested in men?" Rachel asked wearily, knowing she wasted words on deaf ears. "The soul is more important than physical beauty."

"You think about his soul. I'll admire the way he sits a horse, that spark in his eyes and the muscles in his forearms." Her voice was barely audible over the rumble of the wheels and the creaking of the wagon.

Gripping the reins, Rachel guided the oxen up the steep incline as she sneaked a glance at the stranger who had aided her. His hat rested low on his forehead, shielding his gaze from the late afternoon sun. Reluctantly, she admitted her sister was right. Rachel had not failed to notice his powerful good looks, or the way his pants fit snug across his muscular buttocks.

His emerald eyes were dark and seductive and she knew Mr. Wade Ketchum was the type of man women acted like fools over. The type of man Becky attracted. The type Rachel avoided.

"We don't know him," Rachel warned her flirtatious sister.

Becky laughed, a satisfied sound. "Give me twenty minutes alone with the man, and I'll give you his life story," she promised, a smug smile pasted on her beautiful face.

"Please, Becky."

Her sister frowned in irritation. "I'm not going to sit back and let an opportunity like him pass me by. You may be happy being a spinster, but I will be married."

Spinster! How could one word dredge up so many awful thoughts and gloomy feelings? Rachel took a deep breath to lighten the sudden heaviness in her stomach. Silently she acknowledged the truth of Becky's words. She was plain and had spent the last four years taking care of her father's orphanage.

"'He that trusteth in his riches shall fall, but the righteous will flourish as a branch.' Proverbs 11:28." Rachel cited the Bible for her sister, hoping its message would penetrate her lovely, shallow skin.

Becky rolled her eyes. "Please! Papa's dead. There's no need to continue quoting scripture."

"Just because Papa is gone doesn't mean anything's changed."

A pout clouded her sister's beautiful face. "For eighteen years, I've been preached at until the stuff is oozing out my pores. Not anymore. I don't care if I ever step inside another church."

"Rebecca!" Rachel exclaimed.

"And I'm not helping you take care of those brats anymore, either," Becky said, her rebellion building with each word. "As soon as we reach Fort Laramie, I'm taking the stage home."

"There is nothing to return to, Becky."

"This is all your fault."

"I didn't ask Papa to move."

"Maybe not, but Papa knew how much you pined for Ethan. He thought you needed a fresh start.

Rachel sighed. "I do not pine for Ethan."

"Ethan wasn't interested in you, or he would have stayed," Becky said.

Rachel gripped the reins tighter. The memory of Ethan Beauchamp opened a wound in her heart, one that should have healed years ago. "I know that now. But I was younger than you when I met Ethan. And he left me after making promises I realized later he had no intention of fulfilling."

Becky sighed. "I know. You've told me a thousand times."

"And you still haven't heard me. I don't want you to get hurt, the way I did."

"Don't worry about me," Becky declared as she gazed at Mr. Ketchum. "I'm the one breaking hearts."

"Don't you dare throw yourself at that man," Rachel whispered, horrified at the thought.

"I'm a grown woman. I can do what I please." Becky turned her back on Rachel, clearly indicating the conversation was over.

Rachel sighed. The belle of Memphis, while Rachel played housekeeper. The social life Rachel craved, Becky took for granted.

It hadn't always been that way. At eighteen, Rachel had fallen in love; then Papa caught Ethan kissing her. She'd been old enough to be courted, old enough to be kissed, even old enough to be married. Or so she thought, until the day Papa discovered them. Soon after, Ethan disappeared and Papa became angry at the mention of Ethan's name.

The man she'd hoped to marry had gone away, and along with him, any chance for a family or a life of her own. For four long years, she had cooked and cleaned for her father, putting her needs aside.

Then six months ago, Papa had decided to move west, and now here she was alone in the wilderness with three orphans and a sister that couldn't even boil water.

Wade slowed his mare, pulling alongside the wagon. His muscular shoulders were clearly outlined through his chambray shirt. His strong hands held the reins. In the late afternoon sun, Wade's long ebony hair shimmered with brilliance and fell to his shoulders in shiny waves. He was a handsome man, who would never be interested in a homely spinster like herself.

As if knowing her thoughts centered on him, Wade turned in his saddle and smiled, sending her pulse to pounding.

~

Wade watched orange rays from the setting sun streak across the purple shadows of the evening sky. The towering rocks of Scott's bluff cast long silhouettes over their campsite m as the wind softly rustled the pine needles in a gentle motion.

After a cold meal of dried fruit and meat, Rachel had hurried the children off to bed. Through the open tent flap, he could see her cradling the baby in her arms, rocking him to sleep. Pleasant memories of a woman who smelled of roses and flour pervaded his mind and drained his heart.

The vivid recollection brought an ache as fresh as the day his mother had died. Seventeen long years ago, he'd promised to take care of his brothers and sister, keep them safe from harm. But promises could be broken as easily as fine china, and even now, the memory of his failure wrenched his soul.

Wade paced away from the campsite, away from Rachel and the children. He couldn't help but feel anxious. She and the children were dredging up painful memories from the past. Memories of Walker and the rest of his siblings.

He had to win that money, to continue his search for Walker. Separated from him for sixteen years, Wade worried he wouldn't recognize his brother when he saw him. The last clue he'd received was that Walker had gone west, to Oregon, with his new family.

Now all he needed was to lose the women and children, and earn enough money playing cards to continue his journey. For, more than anything, the women were distracting. And if he was completely honest with himself, it wasn't both of them, but one woman. He found his gaze searching out Rachel all day, making sure she was well, watching her with the children, admiring her strength as she pulled her group together and kept on going.

Forcefully, he reminded himself that there was no room in his life for a woman, especially a preacher's daughter. The sooner they reached Fort Laramie and parted, the better for everyone.

"Mr. Ketchum, are you busy?" Becky's sultry voice called from the shadows.

Wade reluctantly strode back toward camp. The younger Miss Cooke was a practiced charmer, who had sharpened her wiles on him all evening. Becky was as predictable as the ticking of a clock, and Wade had known it was only a matter of time before she sought him out. "What can I do for you, Miss Cooke?"

He stared as she strolled toward him, a coquettish smile on her lips. "I hope I didn't disturb you, but I wondered if you would mind moving some boxes around in our wagon."

He watched as Becky deliberately ran her tongue across her bottom lip and sidled closer to him.

"I'll move the boxes for you, Miss Cooke," Wade replied, impatient to put distance between himself and this flirt.

She reached out and laid a hand on his chest. Gazing up at him with adoration, she pouted. "Don't hurt yourself moving those big, heavy boxes."

Looking from the hand on his chest, into the most calculating blue eyes Wade had seen this side of Papa's saloon, he felt a chill all the way to his bones.

"I'm sure it's perfectly acceptable to touch a man where you come from. But I was raised in a saloon with a brothel. And when a woman touches a man, she's usually drumming up business."

He almost laughed as her blue eyes widened in horror.

Becky jerked her hand back as if she'd been scalded. Even in the near darkness, her cheeks burned a brilliant pink.

"Are you suggesting that I'm a whore?" she challenged.

"No, ma'am, not in the least. I just think you should know what I'm used to," he replied. "I'll move those boxes for you."

As he strode off, he could feel her gaze burning into his back. Women like her had tried to seduce him since he was fifteen. Growing up in a saloon, he'd quickly learned what was going on upstairs. A different game, called poke-her.

In his younger years, he'd taken advantage of every opportunity available in his father's saloon. But now he was choosier. While no one would ever call him a saint, at twenty-nine, he'd become bored with easy women and tired of the sleazy side of life.

Hoisting himself into the wagon, he gazed around at the neat stacks of crates. A few had indeed been knocked over. While he was moving the boxes back into place, curiosity overcame him at spotting writing on the outside of a crate: Bibles.

Shaking his head, he sat back on his heels and counted the crates. Four boxes of the Good Book took up precious space. Quickly, he shoved them back into position, thankful Fort Laramie would see the end of this bunch of greenhorns.

Bent over, he turned to leave and almost bumped into a large, draped object occupying the back corner of the wagon. With growing suspicion, he lifted a corner of the quilt, half expecting more Bibles. Instead he found an intricate wood-carved case with ivory keys. An organ. He dropped the blanket back into place, laughing until he realized he was stuck with this group of fanatics till they reached Fort Laramie.

Was she planning on playing the blasted thing all the way to Oregon or straight into heaven? Whoever had convinced them to make this trip had never crossed the rugged trail awaiting them. With a chuckle, he crawled outside to the waiting Miss Cooke.

"Good night, Miss Cooke," he called, before strolling off.

They would never make it over the mountains with the extra weight of an organ and Bibles. He was surprised they'd made it this far. Every greenhorn deserved one warning, and hopefully this pious, stubborn female would listen with the God-given sense she had and lighten the wagon load.

Strolling to the tent, he yanked the flap open. Rachel glanced up at him, clearly startled, then returned her attention to the children.

He watched as Rachel moved to each one, kissing their cheeks in a good-night gesture. The girl wrapped her arms around Rachel's neck and hugged her. "I love you," the child said.

"And I love you, sweetheart."

Rachel crawled to the tent opening. "I'll be outside if you need me, Toby."

"Yes, Ma'am," the boy called into the night.

The words of warning Wade had been ready to sling at Rachel died away as he watched her with the children. The long-forgotten memories of tucking in his brothers and sister assaulted him, bringing back the searing blade of guilt.

He strode away from the tent, taking deep breaths. The sound of Rachel's footsteps alerted him she followed. He'd been too young when his mother died, leaving his younger siblings in his care; with a father who was too busy working his saloon to concern himself with children. He'd worked hard to keep them all together, and in the end, his efforts had been for nothing.

Pushing the dreaded memories away, he willed his thoughts back to the present. Dusk covered the camp area, wrapping it in the coziness of twilight. Until he was certain they had traveled safely away from the Pawnee, there would be no campfire.

Even the fading light failed to hide Rachel's exhaustion. Her eyes, had lost their sparkle. Her voice lacked its earlier vitality.

"Did you want something, Mr. Ketchum?" Rachel asked.

Her voice, low in the darkness thrummed his nerve endings, like a soft guitar.

In her present condition how could he berate her about the impossibility of traveling across the mountains with a wagon load of Bibles and an organ?

"It can wait, Rachel. You look like you need to rest."

Rachel rubbed the back of her neck. "I slept very little last night. I don't know if I'll be able to sleep tonight, either." She ducked her head and said softly, "I keep seeing their bodies."

An incredible urge to shield her from the nightmares – to protect her, to enfold her in his arms – overcame him. But his hands remained at his side.

"Don't think about it. You and the children are safe." His voice sounded gruff, even to his own ears.

"I know, but so much has happened." Her small shoulders sagged as if the weight of the world rested upon them. Without thinking, he stepped toward her, placing his hands on her neck.

She jumped at his touch. "Mr. Ketchum…I appreciate your concern, but…"

Her voice quivered, yet she didn't move away. The tenseness in her shoulders seemed to relax under his fingers' gentle massage. Soft wisps of hair curled alluringly on the back of her slender neck. He wondered how she would taste there.

"Can't you call me Wade?" he whispered.

A heavy sigh escaped her lips. "Wade…" She faltered and stepped out of his reach. He watched her chest rise and fall in rapid breaths. "We should talk."

What had possessed him to touch her? His rough hands tingled from gliding over the warm calico of her dress, leaving him yearning to feel her skin.

"My sister…" Rachel paused. "My sister can be…"

Wade couldn't help but grin. He stood back, folded his arms across his chest and waited for her to complete the sentence.

"Please don't misunderstand Becky's actions. She's young and used to getting her way."

The urge to pull her into his arms was strong. All he'd done was touch her. How could one small caress of a woman who'd probably never been touched by a man leave him aching for more?

The months of being without a woman had certainly caught up with him if he was responding to a prim and proper preacher's daughter. Women like Rachel were never interested in men like himself. They wanted marriage, babies, stability. Not that he was interested, but if he were, a gambler didn't have anything to offer a woman, especially one like her.

"Don't worry about Becky. She can take care of herself," Wade replied.

But the way he burned after touching the prim Miss Rachel Cooke, who in the hell was going to take care of him?

Chapter Two

Dear Diary,

Three days have passed since Papa was taken from us. Though Mr. Ketchum has been a Godsend, I miss Papa so. Mr. Ketchum said it was unusual for the Pawnee to actually attack a wagon train, since they usually only steal livestock. I wonder what we did to provoke the savages.

Today, while Becky reluctantly drove the team, I went through Papa's belongings. Six hundred dollars doesn't seem like much to buy supplies, take us to Oregon and get us settled and fed through the winter. I can't help but wonder, will it be enough?

Rachel breathed a sigh of relief. The children were finally asleep. Grace had found every possible excuse to avoid bedding down, until Rachel had lost her temper and scolded the child. What was wrong with her? She'd snapped at everyone all evening after finding Mr. Ketchum teaching Becky and Toby to shoot while Grace watched. The children had looked at her like she'd grown an extra head, and from the way it pounded, she wondered if it were true.

When she stepped out of the tent, the scene that greeted her was enough to make her want to crawl back in and hide until morning.

Becky hovered around Wade with a coffeepot in hand, refilling his cup and smiling flirtatiously. Her hair gleamed in the firelight, her apron was spotless as if she'd just stepped from someone's parlor.

Rachel felt like her sister's exact opposite. Strands of hair curled around her cheeks and neck, having escaped their knot earlier in the day. Her apron looked as if it had gone off to war and lost. Maybe it was better this way. After all, she wasn't looking forward to confronting Mr. Ketchum.

Apprehension guided her footsteps to the glowing fire where Becky played hostess. Her sister smiled and flirted, the tinkle of her laughter resounding in the night air. Rachel cringed. The giggle grated on her already tightly strung nerves.

Wade leaned against his saddle, a smirk on his face as he sipped his coffee and watched Becky. Rachel had to give the man credit; he never seemed to get overly excited about the girl. Then again, Papa had warned her that men acted on urges more often than feelings.

Rachel stepped into the light of the campfire, and Becky glanced up. "Why don't you go on to bed, Rachel? You look worn out."

When had Becky ever been concerned about her health before?

"No. I want to talk with Mr. Ketchum."

Becky sighed, her eyes clearly sending Rachel the leave-us-alone message. "Can't it wait until tomorrow?"

"No," Rachel said, spreading out a blanket to sit on.

"If this is about my shooting that gun—"

Wade interrupted. "Go to bed, Becky."

Becky's spine stiffened and she turned upon Wade, giving him a glare that should have singed his hair all the way to its roots. "You want me to leave?"

With cool authority, Wade replied, "Yes, you."

Her hands grasped the skirt of her peach muslin dress, and she raised it, flashing an ankle. "I was bored with the company anyway!"

As Becky flounced off toward the wagon, Rachel tried to suppress the smile that came naturally at her sister's childish gesture, but somehow the corners of her lips turned up.

"I've never had a lady call me boring before. But it was worth it, just to see you smile," Wade said.

Embarrassed, Rachel felt herself blush. "I shouldn't. But Becky is often difficult, and you handled her so well."

"Becky is a kid in a woman's body."

"Mr. Ketchum!" Rachel exclaimed indignantly, then sighed. "I must admit you're right."

"I just tell it like I see it, honey."

Tension spread around the campfire, different from the tight ache that lay coiled in Rachel's body. She watched Wade stretch his long legs, crossing his right boot over his left ankle, and settle back against his saddle. Self-consciously, she touched a hand to her straggling hair and waited. Silence filled the camp, and he bestowed on her a patient grin.

Unable to stand the silence any longer, Rachel blurted out, "About this afternoon. I know you know how to use a gun, but Toby is too young to be handling guns."

"Most boys his age are out hunting with their fathers."

"He's only twelve," she argued.

"He should know how to take care of himself." Wade said as he took a sip of coffee. "You've coddled him."

"I have not!"

"Then why can't the boy start a fire, hitch up the wagon, saddle a horse or shoot a gun?" Wade picked a blade of tall grass growing close by and chewed on it. "What happens the next time someone attacks you? Who's going to protect you, Rachel?"

Rachel jumped up and paced around the campfire. "Papa did all those things."

"He's gone," Wade quietly reminded her.

Tears welled up in her eyes. She wouldn't allow herself to cry in front of him. "I know."

"All of you should be able to hitch the wagons, as well as start a fire and shoot a gun," Wade stated.

Tears burned the corners of her eyes. "Toby is a child."

"Like hell he is." Wade tossed the grass aside and rose to his feet. "He's a young man."

Rachel walked to within inches of Wade, her chest heaving with suppressed tears. "I don't want to see him hurt."

"Then let me teach him," Wade countered.

Rachel shouted, "I don't know you. I don't know what you'll teach him?"

Wade resisted the urge to throttle the woman. "What kind of a man do you think I am?" He lowered his voice, restraining the memories of a little boy scorned by fellow parishioners. "I'm a gambler, a card shark and the son of a saloon owner. But I don't make my living by killing men." He took a calming breath. "That's the problem with you Bible thumpers. You're too busy looking down your noses at us sinners."

"Just because I'm a preacher's daughter doesn't mean I look down at other people," Rachel said defensively, her voice high.

"Then why am I not good enough to teach Toby?"

Her bottom lip trembled. She closed her eyes tightly as if trying to block out the truth. "Until two days ago, I had a father to protect me, hitch the wagon, start a fire, hunt for food. Now I'm alone in the wilderness, hundreds of miles away from Oregon, with three children and a useless sister."

As if all the strength left her body, Rachel sank to the ground, tears streaming down her face. "I'm scared! I don't know what to do!" She wept, gulping sobs coming from her throat.

A curse escaped Wade's lips. What now? He had a hysterical woman on his hands, and he'd never dealt well with tears. The only medicinal thing he had in his saddlebags was a bottle of Kentucky Red whiskey, guaranteed to wash the dust from his throat and soothe her pain. He picked up the cup Becky had left on the ground.

Strolling over to his saddlebags, he pulled out the bottle and poured himself a half-cup, Rachel a quarter-cup of whiskey. Then before Rachel noticed, he added a dose of coffee to hers. One quick glance at Rachel's sobbing form was enough to convince him he was right in giving her the alcohol.

She sat on the ground, her head cradled in her hands, crying. Her sobs weren't as violent, but her shoulders still shook. He sank down beside her and placed an arm around her. "Here, this will make you feel better."

She lifted her head, her large hazel eyes glittered gold in the firelight. He ached with the grief he saw reflected in the depths of her stare, and wondered if his eyes had looked the same way. For the first time in many years, he had a sudden urge to protect someone, to take care of her.

"What is it?" Rachel asked as she moved away from his arm.

"Coffee." Wade didn't want to lie to her, but if he told her the truth, she would never touch the drink.

She sniffled and took a sip of the hot brew. Immediately, she coughed and sputtered. "Why can't Becky learn to make a decent pot of coffee? It's so strong."

"I made this pot. It's a different kind. They brew it in Kentucky." His conscious twinged.

"This is awful." She took another sip and grimaced.

"Sorry," he muttered.

"I'm sorry, too for my outburst." She wiped her eyes with the tail of her apron. "But I miss Papa so."

"You've been through a lot these last few days." Leaning back against his saddle, he watched the firelight's shadows flicker on Rachel's flushed face.

"Papa was taking Bibles to his new church in Oregon."

"I know." Wade sipped from his whiskey. "But loaded down the way that wagon is, it'll never cross the Divide. What was your father thinking, dragging along an organ?"

"I insisted." She hiccupped. "The organ belonged to my mother." Her voice rose with fierce determination. "I won't leave it behind."

He watched as she finished the coffee in a single gulp. For a woman who had never tasted whiskey before, she was catching on quickly. "Let me pour you another cup."

She sniffled, but appeared calmer. "All right."

Wade poured the coffee into the cup and then went to his saddlebags. With his back shielding the bottle from Rachel's view, he poured more whiskey into the cup. Hopefully, this would be enough to send her into peaceful oblivion for a little while.

Handing her the cup, he sank down on the grass beside Rachel. In the flickering firelight, her features seemed more relaxed. There was a softness about her expression that made her…pretty.

If only her chestnut hair was not drawn back in that tight little bun. How would she look with her hair falling past her shoulders? Would her tresses feel as silky to the touch as they appeared?

Until tonight, he'd never noticed how lovely she was. Her drab dresses, schoolmarm bun, and the stress of the last few days had disguised her beauty. But tonight, with the glow of the campfire in her eyes and the light of the moon reflecting on her hair, she had rocked his senses all the way to his toes.

Hazel eyes beseeched him. "Wade, about Toby…" Her words slurred through her full lips, beckoning him to kiss her.

"Yes, Rachel." He sighed as his eyes wandered over her body, taking in her ample breasts and small waist. How could he ever have thought of her as plain?

"He looks up to you. Please don't let him get hurt."

"I give you my word, Rachel." Wade lay down in the grass, his head supported by his arm. The whiskey had relaxed him except for the lower half of his body, which suddenly sprang to life, pushing against the buttons of his pants.

He turned his attention to the night sky, hoping that concentrating on the twinkling stars would ease the hardness between his thighs. "Have you ever seen a prettier sky?"

Rachel leaned her head back, and losing her balance, fell backward. "The stars were never this bright in Tennessee."

Wade held his breath. She was so close. He could reach out, touch her, hold her. "Did you ever take the time to notice them?"

Rachel sat up, her body swaying. "You probably think I'm a dried-up old maid, who's never sat under the stars with a man before."

Wade chuckled and pulled her beside him. "No, you're wrong." They were lying face-to-face, body-to-body. He ached to touch her intimately with his hands. "If you're an old maid, it's because you've been hidden from sight, taking care of your family. Some man out West will snatch you up for himself."

Rachel sat up and for a moment he thought he'd said too much. Reluctantly he rose beside her.

"Everyone depends on me," Rachel murmured. "It's been that way since Mother died." She gazed into his eyes. "That's why I'm so protective of Toby and the children."

They were mere inches apart. A soft, musky smell tickled his nose. He reached out, and without meaning to, caressed her cheek with the back of his hand. "You're a good woman, Rachel. But you've got to learn to let go of them so they can grow up."

"It's my duty to protect them. Keep them safe."

He became bolder, running his fingers through her silky hair. He had to know how she looked without that wad of hair on the back of her head. His searching fingers found the hair pins and he pulled them out, one by one. Mahogany curls tumbled, around her, flowing past her shoulders almost to her hips.

Wade stared in wonder. What had he done? The transformation left him stunned. He'd uncovered a gold mine right beneath his nose.

"What are you doing?" she breathlessly asked.

"Seeing how beautiful you are," he whispered in the night.

The hardness between Wade's legs pulsated in rhythm with his heart. His head was fuzzy, but the sensation was so pleasant, so warm. He couldn't resist his need to touch her.

Hands still tucked inside her hair, he pulled her closer to him. Her lips were full and sensuous, and he watched as she nervously ran her tongue across them. He couldn't help but wonder, would she taste as sweet as she looked?

Hazel eyes widened as his mouth descended onto hers. Warm, full lips met his as he gently tasted her. His tongue traced the outline of her mouth as he wrapped his arms around her, pulling her closer. She moaned, a soft little sigh, and opened her mouth beneath his as he savored her sweetness.

Like a delicate blossom, she unfurled beneath his caresses. His lips never left hers as he pushed her onto the ground. Her soft, full breasts were crushed against his chest, driving him wild. He wanted to touch them, kiss them, and see how her nipples looked in the moonlight.

God, she felt good; she tasted good. But somewhere in his dazed mind, the voice of reason whispered this was Rachel, not one of his father's saloon whores.

He broke the kiss and stared down at her. Slowly she opened her golden eyes. He couldn't tell if the fire within was from the campfire or was an inner blaze he'd ignited.

Her breathing was heavy, strained, as she whispered, "Oh, Ethan, don't stop."

Chapter Three

The whistle of a meadowlark seeped through the fog of sleep, slowly awakening Rachel. A delicious sense of warmth lay coiled around her, enveloping her in a soft cocoon. Her head was cushioned against a firm pillow, its musky smell secure and comforting. She shifted her weight and stretched, her hand brushing against something warm, lightly dusted with hair.

Rachel's eyes popped open. The sight of a masculine arm wrapped around her waist sent sleep scurrying from her consciousness. She scarcely moved, afraid of waking the man radiating the warmth she lay enjoying.

His body was molded around her back, his legs and arms curled about her. The realization that more than just his stomach was pressed against her buttocks was enough to make Rachel jump. She disentangled herself from Wade, breathing a sigh of relief when she didn't wake him.

As she sat up, blood seemed to gather in her temples and pound in a fierce tempo. She raised her hand to her face, groaning.

The last thing she remembered from the previous night was sitting around the campfire drinking coffee and crying. With a start, she realized her hair was loose and flowing around her waist. The memory of Wade taking down her curls, one pin at a time came rushing back. He'd run his hands through her locks and called her beautiful.

What else had he done?

With sudden recollection she remembered Wade's lips caressing hers. He'd kissed her, but worse she'd returned his kiss enjoying the way his lips felt on hers.

She glanced down noticing her worn muslin dress and dingy apron, the same clothes she'd worn the night before. Every button was buttoned, every lace was laced. There was no evidence of any impropriety having taken place.

She couldn't resist glancing at Wade. Lying on his side, he slumbered on, unaware of the volcano brewing beside him.

Noise from the tent drew her attention, and she knew the children were awake. Becky would be coming out of the wagon at any moment, and here she sat beside a sleeping Wade.

Before she could scramble away, her thoughts of Becky seemed to conjure up her sister, who walked around the back of the wagon. When Becky saw Rachel sitting beside Wade, she paused, her eyes widening in a stunned expression.

As white hot lava flowed over rock, Rachel's face burned with embarrassment. Becky hurried to her side.

"You look like you just woke up." Her tone was accusing.

The high pitch of her voice made Wade jump. His emerald eyes opened wide.

Not for the first time, Rachel wanted to wrap her hands around her sister's fragile neck.

"I don't know," Rachel said as she glanced at Wade. "I think I fell asleep outside last night."

Wade stretched his taut body and rose, his full lips turned up in a smile.

"Beautiful morning, isn't it ladies?" he asked as if he woke every morning with a woman at his side.

"If our Papa were here, you'd be looking down the barrel of a shotgun right now," Becky warned Wade.

He stood, his height overshadowing Becky. "What for? Sharing body heat with your sister?"

Becky glanced down at Rachel, shaking her head in disbelief. "What did this scoundrel promise you to entice you into his bed?"

Rachel rubbed her temples, her headache increasing in intensity. "Nothing happened." At least, she didn't remember anything happening.

"Oh, honey, how could you forget last night?" Wade teased his voice low and seductive.

"Please don't, Mr. Ketchum. You're only making things worse," Rachel pleaded. She willed the previous night's memories to reappear. "Nothing happened."

"Well, it doesn't look that way to me," Becky snapped. "Just look at you. Your hair is hanging down around your waist, your lips are puffy and swollen."

Rachel jumped up, unwilling to listen to another word of Becky's tirade. Her stomach reeled from the sudden movement. She felt as if an army had tramped through her head and mouth last night, and this morning they were holding drill practice.

Two quick steps later, she embarrassed herself by losing everything in her stomach. "Oh," she moaned.

Becky followed across the short distance, her voice anxious. "Rachel what's wrong with you?"

"Please Becky. Get me a dipper of water," Rachel managed to gasp as she drifted over to a willow tree and eased herself down upon the soft ground. She laid her head against her bent knees.

Distantly, she heard Becky ask Mr. Ketchum, "Why did you lay with my sister? Rachel's not experienced with your type of man. She'll expect marriage and you're not the marrying kind."

"I suggest you mind your own business, Miss Cooke," Wade said matter-of-factly. "What I do with your sister is between the two of us."

Rachel heard Becky's outraged gasp. Footsteps alerted her that someone approached and she moaned. Why didn't everyone leave her in peace? Maybe then she'd die a quick death from whatever had poisoned her system.

A wet cloth appeared before her eyes. "Here hold this against your forehead." Wade's voice was gruff, but his hands were gentle.

"My head is pounding, my stomach is sour and I feel like the British army invaded my body last night." Rachel wiped the cloth across her face. "Why, Mr. Ketchum?"

"Last time I checked, Kentucky was not owned by the British," Wade joked.

"Here's your water," Becky said as she returned, handing the dipper to Rachel.

She drank greedily from the ladle as Becky continued: "The kids are awake and wanting breakfast."

"I just need a few moments, and then I'll be all right," Rachel replied, her hands shaking.

"Honey, what you've got is going to take longer than a few moments," Wade said, experience evident in his voice.

"Just exactly what is it that I've got?" Rachel asked.

Wade pushed his hat back and crossed his arms, a bemused expression on his face.'

"You didn't give my sister alcohol to trick her into your bed, did you?" Becky asked.

"I don't have to trick women into my bed," Wade replied.

Becky glared at him, then turned her attention to Rachel. "Are you sure you don't have a hangover?"

"I don't know what a hangover feels like," Rachel retorted. "I've never had a taste of the devil's brew n my life." The expression on his face reminded her of a guilty child's. "I didn't drink alcohol, did I?"

"Well..."

"Did you give me alcohol?"

"Just a little," Wade replied sheepishly.

"What happened last night?" Rachel was seething.

Before Wade could explain, Grace and Toby ran up beside Wade, silencing their conversation. Grace glanced at

Rachel, a worried expression on her face. "You don't look well. Are you sick?"

Rachel sighed. What could she say? I suspect Mr. Ketchum got me drunk last night and I don't remember what else happened? She simply replied, "Yes, I'm not feeling too good."

Grace asked, "Where were you this morning? When I woke up, you weren't in the tent."

A quick glance at Wade, revealed he was fighting a losing battle to hide his grin. Rachel wanted to smack the smile off his handsome face. Clearly, he was enjoying the trouble he'd caused.

Wade knelt beside Grace. "Rachel fell asleep by the fire last night, and I didn't want to wake her. I gave her my blanket."

The little girl smiled at him. "That was nice."

"Not to mention a hangover and several other unmentionable things," Becky muttered with a smirk.

"Please," Rachel interrupted. "I suggest we pack up and get on the trail. I'd like to be in Fort Laramie this afternoon."

Wade glanced at Rachel a moment longer, as if he wanted to continue the argument, before he turned to Toby. "Come on, I'll help you take the tent down."

"Take Grace back to the wagon," Rachel told Becky. "I'll be there in a few moments."

With a sigh Becky took Grace by the hand. "That man's a devil, Rachel. You best be careful."

Rachel watched her sister practically drag poor Grace across the grass. For once Becky was right. Wade Ketchum was definitely no saint.

～

Wade rode alongside the wagon, yet far enough away to discourage conversation. He didn't want to talk with the

Cooke sisters. Becky was a narcissistic female whose thoughts were only filled with getting a man, and last night Rachel had left him hard and wanting like a schoolboy. At least, until she'd called him Ethan.

His pride still smarted this morning at the memory of her whispering the man's name with such passion. Who was he, and what had he meant to her?

Pale and forlorn, Rachel sagged against the canvas of the wagon, holding the wet cloth to her forehead. She gazed at him with a hurtful, questioning expression, making Wade feel smaller than a pine sapling.

Sometime during the night, he realized Rachel trembled with cold and he'd wrapped his body around hers, torturing himself with the feel of her body snuggled against his. And when she rolled over in the night, he'd placed her head against his chest, his arms cradling her.

He'd dreamed all night long of taking her, right there on the ground, under the stars, but Rachel was no whore. And he knew, sober and awake, she wouldn't be willing.

Becky was right. Rachel was the kind of woman who wanted marriage, respectability; and he was not the kind of man who offered those things. In fact, he had nothing to offer a woman. No home, no money.

A home meant stability and family, neither of which Wade was qualified to provide. Money was something that flowed through his hands at the drop of a card.

Besides, he'd vowed to settle his past once and for all by finding his brother, not acquiring a wife in the middle of nowhere.

But damn, Rachel Cooke had turned out to be a surprising woman. The memory of her kiss was still fresh on his mind and on his lips. She'd responded to his touch in a way he never would have suspected. She appeared so cool, so devout, and plain on the outside, but beneath the surface lay a passion sweet and pure.

Wade glanced at Rachel. She leaned against the wagon, swaying with the rhythm of the oxen, the wet cloth pressed against her temple, her face pale, eyes closed.

Fort Laramie was the end of the trail with the Cooke sisters and as far as he was concerned, it wouldn't come too soon.

~

Crossing barren rolling hills, Rachel caught her first sight of Fort Laramie and felt an enormous sense of peace. Civilization and humanity all in one place.

Built by the American Fur Company, the fort, molded of sun-dried bricks, had clay blockhouses at two of its corners. Pointed wooden stakes formed a fence, with two gates that swung wide at the entrance. The fort was a busy place, with Indians in tepees and an emigrant wagon train camped alongside each other outside its walls.

Rachel glanced at Wade Ketchum, his broad back swaying gracefully with the rhythm of his horse. The memory of waking up in his arms had stayed with her all day. Yet she had slept soundly for the first time in days. It was the first night she'd felt safe and secure since her father's death. It was the first time, since Ethan, she'd wanted more than a kiss from a man.

Bits and pieces of the night before had slowly returned, along with a burgeoning sense of shame. It was a good thing Mr. Ketchum was leaving them at Fort Laramie.

She watched as he pulled on the reins of his horse, stopping just outside the walls of the fort. He motioned for Becky to halt the wagon, not far from the other emigrants, several of whom waved in friendly acknowledgement.

"We'll set up your camp here. You'll be safe next to these people," Wade called out to Rachel.

She purposefully ignored him as Becky set the brake and tied the reins to the handle. The children scampered around the wagon, glad to be exercising their stiff limbs.

"Mr. Ketchum, would you be so kind as to help me unhitch the oxen before you leave?" Becky asked.

Wade glanced at Becky, then hesitantly responded, "Sure."

Together, they unhitched the team while Rachel climbed down from the wagon and slowly started setting up their camp. Before Mr. Ketchum left, she intended to find out exactly what he'd given her last night and if anything had happened between them. Like nasty mosquitoes, the questions had plagued her all day. Telling all was the least he could do after the comments he'd made that morning.

Toby and Grace were busily setting up the tent when Wade walked around to the back of the wagon. Her senses on alert, Rachel was aware of his presence even before he spoke.

He cleared his throat. "Rachel?"

She turned and gazed into the emerald green eyes that engulfed her, drowning her, while her heart leaped in her chest. The air seemed thin as her lungs expanded and she gasped for breath. He was so close, she could smell the musky scent of him, and her clothes suddenly felt constricting and heavy.

"Yes, Mr. Ketchum?" she responded, her voice steady.

"I'm leaving," Wade announced.

No explanations, no apology and no remorse for his actions of the night before. Rachel tensed.

"I need to know what happened between us last night. How did I end up sleeping…?"

She couldn't say the words. Wade smiled, the corners of his mustache curling up in response.

"You were upset. I wanted to calm you down, so I put a little whiskey in the coffee."

"How could you?" Rachel demanded, appalled at his lack of consideration.

"I was trying to help you. How was I to know you'd want a second cup?"

"Mr. Ketchum, you could have had the decency to tell me." Rachel replied, hands on her hips. "What else happened?"

Wade smiled, a quick little grin. "Nothing. Except a kiss." He paused, watching her closely. "Which I enjoyed until you called me Ethan."

The relief she'd felt was quickly nullified at the mention of Ethan's name. Oh, God! Had she really called him Ethan?

"Who is he, Rachel? Did you kiss him like you kissed me last night?" Wade asked his voice low and deep.

"Ethan is none of your business."

Wade stepped closer to her, trapping her against the wagon. "You might want to thank Ethan, next time you see him. Otherwise, something more would have happened between us last night." Wade stroked the hair away from her face. "The stars, the whiskey, and you by my side. I wanted to lay you down and—"

"Mr. Ketchum!" Rachel whispered urgently, stopping him from saying the words she was afraid of hearing.

Wade gazed down into her hazel eyes. Witch eyes. He'd wanted her with a single-minded passion last night, and even today she'd stirred his blood every time he looked at her. He ached to feel her mouth beneath his once more.

He stepped in closer. His hand moved from her cheek to the back of her head as he pinned her against the back of the wagon, pressing his body into hers. He watched her eyes widen as she licked her full lips, enticing him, bewitching him. With a groan, he sank his lips to hers and kissed her with all the pent-up passion from the night before.

But this time neither were woozy from the alcohol. This time they were both very sober, and quite aware of what was happening. Wade wrapped her in his arms, deepening the kiss, feeling her breasts crushed against him. She didn't fight him, but leaned into him, opening her mouth fully for his kiss.

Her body molded against his, the sweet scent of lilacs and Rachel filling him as his blood pounded in his ears.

The realization that they were both enjoying this sneaked into his consciousness. She tasted fresh, clean and he wanted to drink of her until he'd had his fill, until she was crying out his name. No woman before had ever enticed him this way; it both scared him and intrigued him. She was sweetness and sunshine blended together, and she wasn't meant for him. He broke the kiss off.

If only they had more time. For one brief moment, he wished he was the type of man who deserved Rachel.

Stunned, she touched her fingers to her lips, rubbing them in amazement. Then, suddenly as a lightning storm, her eyes flashed, her body tensed and she shoved him with all her might, sending him stumbling away from her.

"Get away from me, you son of Satan," she hissed.

Wade rubbed his hand against his chin, his whiskers making a scratchy sound. "I've been called a lot of names, but never that one. Come to think of it, Rachel, my father could have been Satan."

Wade donned his hat and took Rachel's hand. She tried to withdraw it from his grasp, but he held on tight and turned her palm face up. Reaching into his pocket, he pulled out her hairpins and dropped them one by one into her hand.

"Whoever Ethan was, he was a lucky man to have a woman like you. If you need me, I'll be at the Mountain Dog Saloon. Good bye, Rachel."

~

Dear Diary,

We arrived in Fort Laramie only to discover that Mr. Jordan, the wagon-train master, will not take on single women. I came close to begging, and even agreed to hire a man to help us, but still the stubborn man refused to budge. One of us must be married in order to travel with his train.

Though the summer is quite young, the snow closes the passes early in this part of the country and I fear we'll be stuck in the mountains of Oregon if we do not leave now.

So how does one go about finding a husband in a matter of days? There is one man I know in town. One man who is on his way to Oregon. But, dear God, this man looks like Lucifer, and could charm the scales off a rattler.

Chapter Four

"Afternoon, ma'am," The stranger tipped his hat, his eyes traveling the length of her body. Rachel flashed him her meanest scowl, sending him scurrying into the saloon.

Two hours of blazing sun, odd looks and a few leering grins from men entering and exiting the Mountain Dog Saloon had left her on edge. She felt as if she were on display, marching back and forth in front of the tavern, her parasol shielding her from the sun, her boots clicking on the wooden sidewalk. The black brocade of her dress radiated heat absorbed from the hot afternoon sun. Beneath petticoats and stays, Rachel's body seemed to be melting.

This was not part of her plan. She had no more prepared for a long wait than a snowstorm. All morning she'd rehearsed her speech to Mr. Ketchum, without considering the possibility of how to get him outside the saloon to hear it.

Respectable ladies did not enter saloons, for any reason. Behind those swinging doors the brotherhood of man met, and the only females welcomed were women true ladies did not recognize.

She'd considered sending Wade a message, but the men who approached the door frightened her.

The sun slipped below the horizon, leaving the street in darkening shadows. Rachel shuddered. She'd stood out here for hours. How long could a man play cards and how safe was a lone woman on the streets of Fort Laramie after dark?

"Hey, lady. Want to go inside with me?"

A trickle of unease raced up Rachel's spine. The man was bigger than a grizzly bear and looked as if his last bath had been given to him by his mother. With a sweeping glance, he sized her up like she was dessert. Warning bells rang in Rachel's mind. Common sense said run, yet she stood fast.

"No, thank you. I'm waiting for Mr. Wade Ketchum. Would you mind going in and asking him to come out?" she requested, the approaching darkness making her bolder.

"You wait right there," the big oaf commanded.

What if Wade refused her? What if this burly man wouldn't go away and leave her alone? Rachel waited, impatient to see Wade, yet reluctant to put her proposition before him. Her head was beginning to ache from the tension, and she didn't feel comfortable leaving Becky with the children this long.

As the doors swung open, Rachel looked up to see the mountain man standing in front of her, his large body overshadowing her. His arms were as big as her waist, each of his hands large enough to wrap around her throat.

The big oaf scowled down at her. "The man's busy. He can't come out." He took a step closer to Rachel; she shivered with fear. "Little lady, why don't me and you go grab a bite to eat? I bet you got enough in that coin purse to buy us a nice dinner."

Before she had a chance to reply, he wrapped his hand around her arm and started to pull her away from the door. Rachel dug her heels in, but the wooden sidewalk refused to hold her. She stumbled toward the man. "I can't. I don't think my husband would approve."

He grabbed her wrist and brought her hand up before his eyes. "I don't see no ring."

Rachel swallowed. She was a terrible liar and this grizzly bear either didn't care or wasn't fooled by her attempt at falsehood. "My husband gambled my ring away."

The man sent her a dubious look, but while he was trying to decide if she'd told the truth, another monster man shouted at him from the sutler's store. "Pierre, get over here." The man waved at him. "I need your help."

Pierre glanced at Rachel with longing and then at his friend. Reluctantly, he turned to Rachel. "You wait here. I'll be back."

He took off with a rush and Rachel felt a surge of relief. The time for inaction was over. Squeezing her eyes shut, she said a quick prayer.

When she opened her eyes, she took a deep breath, and plunged through the doors of the saloon.

~

Wade sat at the table, his back to the wall. A whore stood beside him patient and waiting. For a saloon girl, she was nice-looking, but she didn't have hazel eyes, she didn't blush easily and she was not petite or heart-tuggingly fragile. The lust he'd been so eager to be rid of seemed to have dried up the moment he walked into the saloon.

Not only had his lust dried up, but so had his luck. Nothing had gone right today. The cards were colder than a snowstorm in January, and he was down to the last of his cash, the last of his reserves. Soon his horses would be up for bid and he'd be flat busted. The biggest card game of his life was cleaning out his pockets faster than a whore on Saturday night.

It didn't help that his mind had strayed continuously to Rachel. The queen of hearts had hazel eyes and bore a slight resemblance to the preacher's daughter. He'd been beaten twice by the damn card, and each time it seemed as if she'd smiled.

The dealer dealt him new cards.

"Mr. Ketchum?" The shaky, familiar, feminine voice called, sending the piano player's fingers astray. A sour note brought the music to a halt. The voices of the patrons fell silent and the clatter of glass stilled. A hush descended upon the room, as all attention focused on the respectable woman, who dared enter the forbidden zone, standing at the door.

"I'm looking for Mr. Wade Ketchum," she said, her voice stronger, more determined.

Wade froze. The woman who'd haunted his dreams last night, who wouldn't leave his mind today, stood at the door, calling his name. What in the hell was she doing here, in the Mountain Dog Saloon? He watched as she glanced about the crowd, her chin up, her shoulders squared. She held her parasol like a weapon.

She spied him sitting at the card table, and Wade watched her advance upon him, a determined march to her step. Her bottom lip quivered.

There was something about her quiet dignity and strength that Wade admired. But why was she here?

He watched as Rachel stood before him, trying to appear undaunted by the crowd of onlookers. But her hands shook. Her eyes grew large as they roamed over the scantily-clad woman beside Wade, taking in the short skirt, the barely concealed bosom. She swallowed convulsively and quickly averted her eyes, focusing instead on him.

Wade couldn't help but smile at the stubborn woman's spunk.

"Nice to see you again, Rachel." He leaned back in his chair, sending the whore scuttling out of the way. "I'm rather surprised you're here."

Their parting had been both pleasurable and painful. The kiss they'd shared had remained on his mind and on his lips.

"Mr. Ketchum, I must talk to you. Could I please see you outside for a few minutes?" Rachel asked, the alabaster color of her skin turning a delicious shade of pink.

"I'm kind of busy right now." Wade fanned out his cards. She had waltzed through the door and lady luck seemed to smile in his favor. Two pairs. Aces and jacks. It had to be a sign. He couldn't leave now. "We can talk right here."

"I think it would be best if we spoke in private."

Wade looked around at the crowded saloon. Men stood watching and waiting to see what would happen. A voice in the crowd yelled, "Is this your wife, Ketchum?"

Rachel's spine stiffened until he thought it would surely crack from the tension. She pulled a handkerchief out of her pocket and fanned herself. "Please, Mr. Ketchum, I sent you a message I was waiting outside."

The cards in his hand were a winning combination; the last of his money lay on the table. Two minutes more would see the hand finished. He couldn't get up and walk away now. "No one told me."

Wade frowned. Something must have happened for her come inside a saloon looking for him. Something dreadful. "What's wrong? Is one of the kids hurt?"

He watched her twist the handkerchief in her hands, her eyes downcast. "The children are fine."

"Then why are you here?"

"I have to..."

"Tell me, Rachel," Wade demanded, realizing she wouldn't have come here if it wasn't urgent.

Her face was pale against the stark black mourning gown she wore. She put the handkerchief up to her nose and inhaled deeply. "I must – get married."

Laughter resounded through the saloon. Wade stared in shock. Married? Had he heard her correctly?

A booming voice yelled from the crowd, "You got the lady in the family way, Ketchum?"

Rachel's mouth dropped open. Her eyes widened in fright and her pale face suddenly turned scarlet. She put the handkerchief to her lips and hurried for the door, bumping any man who was in her path, with her parasol.

Wade stared in disbelief at her retreating figure.
"Damn! What in the hell is she talking about." He threw
down his cards and hurried out the door.

She ran as fast as her long skirts would allow, but he
easily caught her as she reached the front gate of the fort.

Grabbing her by the arm, he whirled her around to face
him. "What in the hell are you talking about?"

Rachel stood before him, tears streaming down her
face, her shoulders shaking. "I should never have gone in
there. I should never have considered this would work. I'm
crazy for believing you would help me."

"Slow down, woman. I can't understand a word you're
saying. Tell me what's happened."

He watched as she took several deep, calming breaths.
"I've never been so humiliated in all my life. Now,
everyone thinks that you and I..."

Wade grinned completing her thought with relish. "I
have to admit you created some scene back there." He took
a deep breath. "Did you say what I think you did?"

"Yes, Mr. Ketchum. I must be married by day after
tomorrow."

"Why? I know you're not...ah...in the family way."

"Of course not!" Rachel exclaimed, her hazel eyes wide
in her distress. "How could you think such a thing?"

"You're a damn good-looking woman. Any man would
be stupid to turn down..." Stunned, he suddenly realized
she had come with the express purpose of asking him to
marry her. He released her arm as if he had touched a hot
iron and started to back away.

"Oh no. I'm not interested in getting married. You're a
fine woman, but marriage..."

Rachel held up her hands, as if in anguish. Words
began to pour from her lips at a rapid rate. "The wagon
train will not accept Becky and me unless one of us is
married. I thought if you married me, we could get it

annulled as soon as we reached Oregon. It wouldn't be forever. Just a couple of months."

"One little slip and those months could turn into years. We'd be stuck with one another."

"There will be no slip, Mr. Ketchum," Rachel assured, him her tone indignant at the very suggestion.

Frustrated, Wade tossed her an icy glare. "Just what do you have against my name? You want me to marry you, yet you can't even call me Wade."

Rachel stared at him, clearly embarrassed. She stammered, "I...don't know. It seems to fit you."

"It should; it's my name. Find someone else to get hog-tied to. I'm not getting married for any reason."

She looked crestfallen. She wrung her hands in desperation. "I must find someone or we're going to be stuck in this fort. What kind of life could I provide for us here?"

Wade gazed around the small complex. It was teaming with people, mostly men and Indian squaws. He imagined Rachel and Becky stuck here, and knew that eventually they would be forced to work in the saloon or marry some randy soldier boy and bear him five or six kids.

"Could you at least help me find someone?" she pleaded.

Wade bristled. She wanted him to help her find another man to marry?

"I'm not going to help you go through with this foolhardy plan of yours," he responded angrily. "What if I talk to the wagon train's leader? Maybe I could convince him."

Rachel laughed a derisive sound. "I don't think so. He was adamant against single females. And if he did change his mind, it wouldn't take Becky long to convince him he'd made a mistake."

Wade sighed. She was right. "Maybe you could hire someone."

Rachel shook her head. "No. He said hired men have been known to leave when the trail became too rough."

They were standing just inside the palisades; the guard tower loomed over them. Wade stared past the tower, towards Laramie Peak. He was broke. He would have to sell one of his horses, find a job or...

He grabbed Rachel by the arm and spun her around to face him. "I have an idea."

She pulled back in fear, but he gently placed her arm in his and proceeded to stroll along the inside of the fence, as if they were a couple out courting. "What if you hire me to see you to Oregon for six hundred dollars and we pretend we're married."

Rachel stopped and pulled her hand away from him. "That's outrageous. Not only is it lying, but six hundred dollars is an excessive amount!"

Wade grinned. "The idea's not bad though."

Hands on her hips, she glared at him through the twilight. "You're suggesting I play the role of your wife, lie to everyone we meet and then, when we get to Oregon, pay you for escorting us? What do I tell people after we get there?"

"I'll leave before we reach The Dalles. You tell everyone I've gone ahead to prepare our place, and then you receive word I've been killed."

"I can't lie." With a stomp of her foot she turned and started to walk away, leaving Wade behind.

"Rachel," he called after her. "That wagon train leaves day after tomorrow. If you don't go out with this train, you'll have to wait until next year or return home to Tennessee. How about five hundred dollars?"

She stopped, her back to him. The mention of the wagon train's leaving seemed to have sunk into her consciousness, and Wade watched and waited for her response. A coyote howled in the distance, echoing Rachel's apparent frustration.

Just when Wade was sure she was going to walk away, she said, "Four hundred dollars, take it or leave it."

Four hundred dollars would do a lot to help him locate Walker and get back on his feet. Wade strolled up to Rachel, took her hand and shook it. "It's a deal."

The flag flapped in the breeze directly above Rachel. She glared at him, "Before you start counting your money, I have several conditions for this false marriage."

Wade grinned, knowing without her having to say, what they would be. "I'm waiting."

"No one will know, including Becky and the children, that we're not truly married." He nodded in acknowledgement. "Our marriage will be in name only. You will sleep outside."

"Rachel," Wade said with disbelief, "no one will believe we're newlyweds if we aren't bunking together."

He moved in, closing the distance between them until they were mere inches apart. She trembled and pulled her shawl closer to her.

Wade wanted to pull her into his arms and warm her. But he wasn't sure if she shivered with cold or fright, and the thought of her soft curves against him rejuvenated the passion he'd thought had disappeared.

"Are you sure you don't want to try this union of ours, like a real marriage?" he asked mockingly.

Rachel gasped, her parasol coming up between them. She put the tip of it in Wade's chest and gave a slight push. "Don't even think about it, Mr. Ketchum. No kisses. No touching. Nothing. Am I making myself perfectly clear?"

"Don't make promises you can't keep, Rachel," Wade said, his voice deep and low.

In the twilight, her eyes smoldered. "I'm not, Mr. Ketchum. We'll sleep together, but you will not have the privileges of a husband."

Wade noted the stubborn set of her chin. "We'll see."

"If you want to find some saloon girl along the trail to take care of your baser needs, go right ahead. It won't bother me," she said her voice indignant.

Wade frowned. "Saloon girls don't tempt me like you do."

Rachel shrugged her shoulders. "As long as you understand I'm not taking their place."

He pushed back his hat. When was the last time a man had courted the preacher's daughter? Maybe it was time someone showed her what really went on between a man and woman.

Maybe pretending to be married to Rachel wasn't going to be as easy a job as he'd first suspected. If he made it all the way to Oregon without touching this woman, then he'd have done more than earn his four hundred dollars.

"So when do we start this game?" Wade asked, trying to stop his treacherous thoughts.

"The sooner, the better. I'm sure Becky will be upset I didn't tell her, and I'll need to reassure the children," Rachel replied, her voice shaky. "But more than anything, we'll need to talk to Mr. Jordan."

"Are you sure you can lie and play this game all the way to Oregon, Rachel?" Wade asked.

Rachel cast him a sharp stare. "What choice do I have?"

At the edge of camp, they stopped and watched the tranquil scene. Grace sat, her doll at her side, as Toby taught her the intricacies of checkers. Daniel chased moths around the fire, his toddler's steps awkward and unsure. Becky sat close to the flames, sewing in hand.

The complexity of what he'd agreed to struck Wade. Escorting a load of gold would have been easier than taking on the responsibilities of seeing two women and three children across the mountains safe and sound.

Rachel gazed at the children and sighed. "I swore on Papa's grave I would get them to Oregon, that I would help his church." She looked at Wade. Her full lips were tightly drawn. Her chin had a determined set. "God forgive me. But yes, Wade Ketchum, I can pretend to be your wife, if it will get us to Oregon."

Chapter Five

"You're what?" Becky screeched, her voice piercing the night air. She laughed, a high contemptuous sound, as the fire flickered shadows across her face. "What kind of trick are you playing, Mr. Ketchum? Rachel would never marry a man like you."

"It's true, Becky," Rachel interrupted.

A quick glance at Wade confirmed her worst fears. Mischief sparkled from his eyes, provoking Becky's ire. His arm snaked around Rachel's shoulders, clasping her close to him.

"I know it's hard to believe, Becky, but after the other night, we decided it was best we marry," Wade said.

A coyote howled in the distance, and Rachel wanted to echo its sentiments. Who did Wade think he was fooling? Becky would never believe this ridiculous story. Rachel pinched the inside of Wade's arm in silent warning.

He glanced down at her, his green eyes twinkling with laughter. "She swept me right off my feet."

Rachel resisted the urge to swipe the mocking smile from his lips and quiet his forked tongue. Couldn't he see he was only making the situation worse by feeding Becky this yarn? And from the skeptical scowl on her face, Becky wasn't fooled.

"We were married this afternoon," Rachel said, her voice tight and controlled.

The cool night air blew across the fire, sending ashes and sparks shooting upward. Rachel stepped away from Wade and pulled her shawl closer to her. She was cold, but she didn't know if it was from the chill in the air or the frostiness Becky exuded as she realized they were serious.

Her sister shook her head in denial. "Tell me this is a joke."

Rachel's conscience twinged with guilt. "It's no joke." No matter what, she loved Becky and the children. They deserved the truth. But they also deserved a chance at happiness, and that likelihood lay in Oregon.

"How could you marry this man?" Becky advanced on Rachel until she stood mere inches away, her blue eyes flashing with fury.

"I know what you're thinking. We should have waited longer. But like Wade said, the thought of leaving Fort Laramie without him was too much." Rachel paused, her stomach quivering. She hated lying.

Becky laughed. "The man is a heathen, Rachel. He drinks, curses and takes advantage of women. You're crazy if think you're going to reform him."

The idea of changing Wade was so funny, Rachel would have laughed except for the lump that seemed to enclose her throat. "I'm not planning on converting him."

"Were you so desperate to get married that you accepted the first proposal that came your way?"

"No! But can't you see we needed a man to help us reach Oregon? I did what I had to do."

Becky marched on Wade, who had remained quiet during her tirade. "What do you get out of this?" She paused, stared him straight in the eye and poked her finger in his chest. "If you're looking for money, you're going to be sorely disappointed. Church mice are rich compared to us."

Even in the dim light from the campfire, Rachel could see Wade's face tighten in anger. "I don't want anything from you. After the way you found us the other morning, I thought you'd be happy I married your sister."

"That wasn't love, Mr. Ketchum. Possibly lust, but even that's unlikely."

Wade pulled Rachel into the safety of his arms, as if to shield her from Becky's venomous tongue. The unexpected move left Rachel feeling warm. Why was he protecting her?

"How do you know what I find attractive?" Wade paused. "I think you're upset that I didn't take the bait and come sniffing around your skirts."

Her sisters pale skin turned a rosy shade. Her blue eyes dilated until Rachel thought they would pop out of their sockets.

Becky raised her chin. "I would never have accepted your attentions. Rachel has been blinded to your obvious faults."

"If Rachel has been blinded by anyone, it's you. And if you don't like me, you're welcome to find your own way to Oregon."

"Please, Becky." Rachel said. "I don't want to leave you behind, but Wade is my husband."

She looked at Wade, who sent her a secret smile and squeezed her closer. Merciful heavens, what had she gotten herself into? Those two little words, "honor" and "obey," were woven into the marriage vows, and even though they weren't legally binding, she would have to obey him or at least give the appearance of obedience. As for honoring him, well, that was something that had to be earned.

"Humph!" Becky said. "You've made your bed and I really don't care. But I don't have to obey anyone's rules anymore. I'm eighteen, old enough to make my own decisions."

Becky stalked off to the wagon, her skirts swishing.

Rachel took a deep breath and glanced at Wade. He raised his brows, a questioning frown on his face, yet his embrace gave her a sense of security, of safety. He released Rachel as if he realized he was holding her and strolled toward the fire.

Daniel started to fuss. It was way past his bedtime and he rubbed his chubby hands across his drooping eyes.

Rachel picked up the toddler, cradling him in her arms. At eighteen months, he was heavy, and she sank down in the rocking chair Becky had occupied earlier. The baby laid his head against her shoulder, his soft little body conforming to hers. Rachel kissed the top of his head, gaining strength and comfort from holding him.

When she looked at the children, she realized she would do whatever was necessary to safeguard them.

Grace wandered over to Rachel, a rag doll cradled in her arms, and stood watching her rock Daniel to sleep. "Rachel?" she finally asked her face serious, concerned.

"What is it, Sunshine?"

Grace glanced at Rachel, her big brown eyes full of worry. "Will you send me and Toby away now that you're married?"

The child's words pierced her heart. Rachel shifted Daniel over to one hip and made room for Grace. She reached down and lifted the child onto her lap. Daniel fussed at the intrusion.

"No, Grace. You, Toby and little Daniel are my family. I would never let anyone split us up."

Toby's voice cracked the evidence of his rapidly changing hormones. "Mr. Ketchum, I'm glad you married Rachel. I don't care what Becky says."

Wade glanced at Rachel, his eyes warm and soft, laughter in his voice. "Thanks Toby."

Rachel couldn't take the strain any longer. She stood up. "It's time for bed."

The longer this night went on the harder it was going to find it to crawl into the tent with Wade. Becky had put it bluntly. She'd made her bed, now she must lie in it. "Put the checkers up, Toby. Grace, gather your dolls."

A round of moans from Grace and Toby followed her announcement. Daniel was fast asleep in her arms as she carried the toddler to the tent and gently laid him down.

Whatever happened, she had to remember the children. They were her biggest reason for taking part in this farce.

Inside the tent was filled with shadows from the campfire. She smiled in secret triumph. Their wedding night! How would Wade respond when she told him they would be sleeping in the tent – with the children?

The fact that she knew Becky would never relinquish the wagon had led her to believe she'd still be chaste when they reached Oregon. She and Wade would spend the entire trip sleeping in the tent, beside Toby, Grace and Daniel.

But what would it be like with Wade resting by her side?

The children were gathered around Wade, watching as he made hand puppets in the shadow of the fire. Yet another sign of the man's contradiction. How could a man who disliked children be so good with them?

"Where is Mr. Ketchum going to sleep?" Grace blurted out the question Rachel had wanted to avoid voicing as long as possible.

Rachel couldn't contain the self-satisfied smile that overtook her lips. For once, she knew she had the upper hand, and while she tried not to overreact, the advantage felt good. "He's going to sleep in the tent with me and you, Grace."

Wade frowned, his brows furrowing with disapproval. "It's our wedding night, Rachel."

"You know Becky sleeps in the wagon, and the children and I take the tent," Rachel innocently replied.

"That was before," Wade calmly announced. He strode away, his determined steps carrying him to the wagon. "Becky, pack your things. You're moving out to the tent."

The tightly closed canvas curtain of the wagon suddenly snapped open. Becky stuck her head out. "Absolutely not! I will not sleep with those brats. You and your bride can sleep in the tent."

Becky yanked the canvas closed. Wade jerked it open. "Let's get this straight. You'll sleep in the tent with the children until we reach Oregon. Or you can sleep by the fire. I don't care which you choose."

Becky's mouth dropped open in surprise. She glanced at Rachel. "You've made a colossal mistake, big sister. And I hope I'm around when you realize it."

She marched off to the tent, her shoulders straight, her nightgown flapping in the breeze. The image she presented reminded Rachel of a fat hen strutting across the barnyard, squawks coming from her beak, her feathers all ruffled.

Toby led Grace to the tent, following behind the queen hen at a safe distance.

"Well, Mrs. Ketchum, we're alone." Wade said as he sat down on a stool by the fire, his voice as chilly as the night air.

Rachel sighed. "I'm sorry Becky took the news so badly. I had hoped she'd be more accepting, since I am twenty-two years old and considered and old maid by most people."

Wade laughed, his voice deep and resounding. "You make twenty-two sound like a hundred. A beautiful woman like yourself, I'll bet you could have been married many times before now."

"Me, beautiful? I think you've been out in the sun too long."

"No! You've listened to that nag of a sister of yours for too long. You're better looking than she is, Rachel."

Rachel raised her hand to her chest. Her heart pounded so loudly, she was certain Wade could hear it. Was he serious or was he trying to sweet-talk his way into her arms?

"I suggest you go prepare our bed, Mrs. Ketchum," Wade announced, his eyes twinkling with merriment in the flickering shadows of the fire.

Rachel felt as if the earth was starting to tremble beneath her. She had depended on sleeping with the children. Could she resist the man and his charm for the next three months while sleeping in his bed?

"What are you waiting for, Rachel?" Wade asked. "I thought women liked a few minutes alone while they prepared themselves for their husband?"

"You're not my husband," she hissed.

Rachel turned and stalked off, her feet quickly carrying her to the wagon, his mocking laughter in her ears. She scrambled inside the small, dark space and waited for the trembling to subside. Somehow she had to get through this.

She glanced around the inside of the wagon. There was barely enough room for one person, let alone two people. The boxes of Bibles, the organ and their supplies took up most of the space. They would be sandwiched together tighter than meat and bread, unless she found a way...

Scrambling out of the wagon, her long skirts almost tripped her. Wade was busy extinguishing the fire. She looked underneath the bed of the wagon to where her father carried the spare boards for repair. Pulling a wooden plank free, she dusted it off and put inside the wagon.

Crawling back in, she lit the lantern and quickly made up their bed. With the sheets, blankets and pillows all neatly arranged into two separate sleeping areas, she placed the board between them, lodging it between two boxes.

With a swish Wade opened the canvas covering and crawled into the wagon, his head bent his hat brushing the top.

"What's this?" Wade asked, pointing to the board that lay between their pallets.

"I believe it is referred to as a bundling board," Rachel informed him.

Wade laughed, his voice ringing in the close confines of the wagon. Rachel felt claustrophobic, engulfed by him, by his presence. He had consumed what little space was left inside the tight wagon. There was no place to move, no place to escape. Even the air she breathed held Wade's scent, overwhelming her with his intensity.

"Did you want me to help you undress?" Wade asked, his eyes twinkling with mischief, his voice silky smooth.

"Absolutely not," Rachel replied horrified. "I'm sleeping in my clothes."

"You're going to sleep in the same clothes the rest of the trip?"

"No. But neither am I going to sleep in my night rail," Rachel said with definite purpose as she climbed under the bedcovers on her half of the pallet.

Wade shrugged. "Suit yourself."

He pulled his shirttails out of his pants and started to undo the buttons lining the front.

"Mr. Ketchum! The light, please," Rachel demanded.

Wade smiled and continued unbuttoning his shirt until the garment lay completely open. A light smattering of hair grew across his muscled chest, in a vee that disappeared beneath his pants. Slowly, he shrugged the shirt off his bronzed back and down the hard ridges of his arms.

Paralyzed, she watched him undress, staring at the hard expanse of his chest. She observed the rippling effect of his muscles as he laid the shirt on a box close by. Sitting down, he proceeded to tug at his boots, until they slid from his stocking feet. She took a deep breath, trying to still her racing heart, knowing she should roll over.

But she couldn't look away.

When he reached for his pants, she gazed up into his eyes and noticed the laughter emanating from their depths. She burned from the tips of her toes all the way to her cheeks and quickly rolled over, facing the inside of the wagon. The audacity of the man! The least he could do was turn the lamp off.

Wade chuckled and extinguished the flame. The wagon was suddenly enshrouded in darkness. But the darkness only heightened the sounds, as Rachel heard the jingle of his belt and the rustle of his pants when he slid them from his body. She felt the creak of the wagon as he lay down beside her.

"Mrs. Ketchum, if you think that board, all those clothes, and your virginity are going to keep me away from you, you're mistaken. If I had a mind to bed you tonight, nothing would stop me." Wade paused, his words lingering in the air. "You're starting to become a challenge, Rachel. And I love a good challenge."

Rachel lay as still as a church mouse, her heart pounding in her ears.

"Why, Mr. Ketchum? So that in three months you could leave me in Oregon with a baby in my belly? So that I could become just another one of your women?" Rachel sighed in the darkness. "No, thank you. I want a man who will stand by my side, who will love me and the children through the good times and the bad. I don't think that's what you want."

"Go to sleep, Rachel. You're safe tonight. But I won't promise not to try to seduce you somewhere along the trail. I'm no saint, just a man. A man who thinks you're a hell of a tempting woman."

Chapter Six

Bleary-eyed from lack of sleep, Rachel stared absently at the dirty diapers swirling in the tub of hot water. Wade's handsome face swam before her eyes, his voice reverberated through her head.

She had awakened this morning to an empty pallet. Where he had gone, she had no idea, though a pesky voice whispered that last night's promises to deliver them to Oregon were all a sham.

But she had to believe he would keep his word. Tomorrow, the wagon train was pulling out, and somehow she and the children would be following that caravan.

She took a deep breath to calm her unsteady nerves. He was probably out taking care of his horses or seeing to personal business and would soon return. But that tiny voice of doubt, wondered about his whereabouts.

Pushing back a loose strand of hair, Rachel whisked the diapers about in the tub of water. The night before had stretched on endlessly, with only short periods of rest, and today exhaustion seeped into her every joint.

Each time her eyes closed, she could hear Wade's deep voice, in the dark, "I won't promise not to try to seduce you."

Hot and flushed, she had been plagued by his statement all night long. Her experience with men was limited, but never before had any man, not even Ethan, said such scandalous things to her. Worse, Wade's husky whispers in the dark didn't seem dishonorable. Somehow they seemed deliciously wicked, leaving her warm with curiosity.

The memory of those full lips, caressing, covering hers, made her shiver with remembrance. But how many women had he rehearsed on before he mastered the skill of making her insides feel quivery, her breasts ache to be touched?

She would have to be on guard every moment to keep his devilish lips from performing their magic on her. For surely, the way she felt when he touched her, there had to be a spell at work.

Rachel dipped the swirling diapers from the water and put them in the cool rinse pan waiting nearby. Though early, the morning sun beat down upon her unmercifully, promising a scorching day. She turned to retrieve her bonnet from the back of the wagon and almost bumped into Becky.

"Good morning, Becky," Rachel said, in an effort to be cheerful, despite the tension from the night before.

"Where's the happy bridegroom?" Becky asked.

Rachel's fears and anxieties over Wade's whereabouts tripled. What if he had deserted her? "He had business to take care of."

Becky's eyebrows rose. "I would have thought he'd want to spend the morning in his wife's arms."

"Unfortunately, time didn't permit that," Rachel lied.

Becky watched Rachel swirl the diapers, her mouth pinched tightly. Finally she asked, "So how was it, sister dear?"

The blood pounded in Rachel's veins, rushing to her face. Appalled, Rachel replied, "That is none of your business."

Becky laughed shrilly, a wicked smile on her beautiful face. "Maybe so. But I still wonder why my pious sister would marry such a wicked man." Her voice dropped to a whisper, "Does he possess some hidden charm that makes you lose all control?"

Rachel's face flamed in embarrassment. "That is also none of your business."

Becky scoffed. "The real question is why in the world would a man like Wade want to marry you? You're an old maid, and he's the most virile thing we've seen east of the Mississippi."

Rachel gripped the wash stick fiercely in her hands. "I don't have time to listen to you criticize me."

"I'm trying to help you, Rachel. The man is using you."

If she hadn't been so angry, Rachel would have laughed, since Becky had the situation backwards. She was using Wade. Using him to reach Oregon.

"No matter what he says, he doesn't love you Rachel."

"Leave it be, Becky," she warned.

It didn't matter that Wade didn't love her. That she knew and accepted. But she was tired of being told how homely, colorless and dull she looked. And now, like a pot over the campfire, she was close to boiling over.

She stirred the diapers, trying to soothe her wounded pride, trying to ignore Becky's spiteful remarks, wondering when her sister had become so hateful. With the wooden wash stick, she pulled up another wet diaper.

"He's probably in town right now saying good-bye to one of his whores," Becky jabbed.

The words reminded Rachel of the scantily-dressed woman standing next to Wade the night she'd asked him to marry her. The memory cracked Rachel's resolve to remain calm. As with a teapot, her pressure reached the boiling point, but instead of whistling, she watched her hand pick up the sopping diaper from her paddle, and with a flick of the wrist, send it flying through the air.

With a smack, it hit Becky's face.

Becky squealed, her voice full of outrage, as she peeled the dripping cloth from her nose and mouth. "A diaper! You hit me with a diaper!"

Rachel was almost as shocked as Becky. Never before had she reacted so quickly without thinking.

"I have tolerated your sharp tongue and your hateful remarks for the last time," Rachel stated her voice shaking with anger.

"Just look at me! You ruined my dress, my hair." Becky dropped the diaper in the dirt as if the clean cloth would give her leprosy. Disbelief radiated from her blue eyes. "What is the matter with you? Has Papa's death driven you crazy?"

"Of course not! But I will no longer tolerate your viciousness to myself or anyone else. Grow up, Rebecca. We're on our own now!"

Becky gazed at Rachel as if she'd lost her mental capacities. "Since Papa died, you've changed."

"I didn't have much choice," Rachel replied, annoyed. "Someone had to take care of us."

As Becky stood beside the wagon, tears welled up in her eyes. "I miss Papa. I want to go home." Tears ran down her already wet face. Her spun-gold hair hung in shambles.

A long, pent-up sigh escaped Rachel. "I wish Papa were here, too, but he's not."

"Why do we have to go on? Why can't we go back? With Papa dead, there's no reason to continue," Becky whined.

"My husband is going to Oregon." Rachel said the words quietly, but their effect was evident.

Becky's sobs quieted, turning into soft hiccups. With the back of her hand, she swiped her tears away. "Nobody cares about what I want."

"It was Papa's will that we continue on to Oregon," Rachel said.

"No, Rachel. It was your will. You didn't have to marry Wade. We could have gone home."

Rachel picked up a wet diaper and wrung the water from it, twisting it into a tight rope. "We're going on to Oregon, Becky."

Becky sniffed loudly. "Speaking of the devil, here he comes." She picked up her sodden skirts and stalked off, her shoulders squared, her head held high as she marched to the tent.

Rachel glanced up from her laundry. Wade ambled across the prairie, his horses trailing him, Mr. Jordan beside him. She couldn't contain the smile of relief.

The corners of Wade's mouth lifted in greeting.

Rachel went forward, wiping her hands on her apron. "Hello, Mr. Jordan."

The man cleared his throat, obviously nervous. "Miss Cooke. I'm sorry. Its Mrs. Ketchum now, isn't it?"

"That's all right. I'm not used to being called Mrs. Ketchum quite yet either."

"Frank wanted to come by and talk to you, Rachel," Wade announced. "He wanted to ask you if we were really married."

The man stammered in obvious embarrassment. "That's not exactly why I came by, Mrs. Ketchum."

"It's okay, Mr. Jordan" Rachel pointed back to the wagon, hoping he wouldn't call her bluff. "I can get you the certificate if you'd like?"

"No. That's not necessary. I mainly wanted to stop by and say congratulations. And let you know the wagons leave at daylight. You folks will need to pull in as soon as possible."

"Frank, you wouldn't know of anyone interested in buying an organ would you?" Wade asked.

Rachel cut in before Frank could answer. "The organ is not for sale."

The man glanced from Wade to Rachel. "Ma'am, you're not thinking of pulling that organ across the mountains, are you? I'm surprised you've made it this far with that heavy thing."

"That organ was my mother's. I will take it across the Divide, even if I have to leave behind every ounce of food we have," Rachel said with determination.

"Ma'am, I'm advising everyone to lighten their wagons as much as possible. From here on, the trail gets rough. We'll cross Laramie Peak in the next few days."

"I understand but, I need that organ and those Bibles for a church in The Dalles."

"If your oxen die, that organ and those Bibles won't do you a bit of good," Frank warned.

"I'll not leave the organ or Bibles behind."

Wade shook his head. "Our first day of married life, and already my wife is more stubborn than any mule I've ever owned."

Mr. Jordan smiled in understanding.

"Rachel, you can take the organ and the Bibles, but the first time we get stuck or the oxen are overworked, we leave everything," Wade said, flatly.

"I disagree, Mr. Ketchum. People are waiting for those Bibles in Oregon. And that organ will bring lots of joy during the long winter months."

Wade sighed, a sound of frustration if ever Rachel had heard one.

"Sweetheart, my horses are not pack animals, and I won't walk the rest of the way to Oregon. If the wagon gets bogged down, the cargo is gone."

"Well, at least you're not throwing them out yet," Rachel answered.

The wagon-train master shook his head. "You folks are going to be dumping that stuff further up the trail. I guarantee it."

"You're probably right, but at least I've tried to make my little bride happy," Wade said with a wink.

Rachel resisted the urge to throw a wet diaper at Wade.

"I'll see you folks in the morning," Frank said as he walked out of their camp, toward his own wagon.

Rachel ignored Wade and went back to wringing diapers and hanging them on the wagon. She could feel his eyes on her, watching her every movement, yet she resisted the magnetic pull.

Wade strolled over, his thumbs hooked in his belt. He stopped mere inches from her, and she had to tilt her head back to meet his gaze. He stood so close she could smell his musky scent, feel his breath upon her face.

His fingers felt rough as he brushed a stray lock of hair back from her jaw. Bewitching emerald eyes sparkled with amusement. "Sleep well last night, Mrs. Ketchum?"

"Like a lamb," she lied.

He laughed. "Lambs need protection from big bad wolves." His fingers lifted her chin even higher. "I'll be sure to sleep close by your side tonight, to protect you."

Before Rachel could reply, his lips brushed hers in a gentle kiss that left her aching for more. When he broke away, she took a deep breath, gasping for air.

Rachel stared dumbly after him, as he strolled off. If this was how seduction felt, how in the world was she ever going to resist?

~

For the next two weeks, they followed the Platte River, the trail ascending slowly as they traveled parallel to the Laramie Mountains.

Time seemed to pass in a blur of sunrises and sunsets. Three weeks had passed since the Indian attack. Three weeks since her father's death. A mere two weeks since she and Wade had agreed to their 'pretend marriage.' During which she had seen little of her husband. It seemed he was always busy taking first or second watch.

The wagon jostled a sleepy Rachel on the seat beside Becky.

"Yah! Get a move on," Becky yelled to the oxen.

Rachel opened her heavy eyelids and noticed they'd stopped in the knee-deep water of a shallow stream. The oxen bellowed in fright as Becky snapped the whip, cracking it across their backs.

"Get on, Elmo," she called to the lead ox. The wagon swayed from the animals' efforts, but the wheels didn't budge.

The huge beasts strained, the wagon rocked, its wheels sinking deeper in the mud. With rising alarm, Rachel knew her worst fears were about to be realized.

Wade had promised the first time this happened he would leave the organ and Bibles behind. Panicked, she started unlacing her boots as quick as her nimble fingers would unhook the lacings.

Becky glanced at her in shock. "What are you doing?"

"I'm going to help them," Rachel replied as she slid over the side of the wagon, trying to hold her skirt up with one hand. The water came almost to her knees, the muddy stream swirling from the oxen's efforts.

The slippery ooze squished between her toes, as she crept to the back of the wagon. The rocking chair was tied to the feed trough, which Rachel leaned against.

"Now, Becky. Get the oxen moving now."

At Becky's command, the animals strained and pulled at their yoke. Rachel pushed with all her strength, but the wagon only rocked back and forth.

Toby sloshed through the water to Rachel's side and put his back against the wagon. Together, the two of them shoved, but the wagon only sank deeper.

Rachel let her skirt drop and reached into the swirling water, to feel for the wheel. With her bare hands, she tried digging the wagon wheel free – anything to keep Wade from finding them in this dilemma.

Scooping the mud away from the wheel, she yelled to Becky. "Try again."

Becky snapped the whip. "Get on, Elmo."

"Push, Toby, push!" Rachel cried. The two of them strained while Becky called to the oxen.

The sound of a horse splashing through the creek sent Rachel's heart plummeting. Instinctively she knew the rider was Wade and refused to acknowledge him.

"Having trouble, Mrs. Ketchum?" His mocking voice sent a chill up her spine.

Rachel glanced up to see Wade sitting astride his sorrel mare, his green eyes twinkling with I-told-you-so amusement.

"No. We're just trying to get the wagon out of a little hole it sank into."

Wade laughed. "Admit it, Rachel. You're stuck."

"I'm not stuck," she denied.

"Okay, you're not stuck. Your wagon is."

Rachel stood up and sighed. Her voice heavy with resignation, she admitted, "Just a little. But I think we can get it free."

Sliding off his horse into the stream beside her, Wade reached down and pulled her upright to face him. Gently, he wiped a spot of mud off her cheek.

Rachel took a deep breath, trying to control the butterflies that took flight in her lower body.

"Move over and let me help," he said as he nudged her aside. He called to Becky, "Okay, give 'em the signal."

"Giddyap," Becky yelled.

Wade put his shoulder to one side of the wagon, and Toby took the opposite side. Rachel slogged through the water to combine her weight with Toby's. Together, the three of them pushed the wagon forward until the back wheels rocked fruitlessly.

Finally, Wade yelled, "Stop. We're only sinking deeper."

He stood up, pulled his hat off, and wiped the back of his arm across his slick forehead. The muscles beneath his shirt rippled with the movement and Rachel swallowed the knot building in her throat.

He gazed at her, his expression serious. "You know what's next, Rachel."

"No. Wade, please. Let's try again," she pleaded.

"I told you the first time the wagon got stuck, the organ was gone."

"No!" Rachel cried. "Not my organ, Wade. Let me go through the trunks. I'll get rid of some of the household goods before I'll let my organ go."

"The blasted thing is too heavy," he insisted. "It's got to go if we're going to make it across the mountains."

Rachel felt tears welling up. "No. It was my mother's."

Wade grabbed her by the arm and pulled her through the creek, sloshing water past their knees. Out of the water he tugged her up onto the bank, into a small grove of cottonwood trees.

"I told you that instrument or the Bibles would have to go."

"Don't make me give it up. I can't bear to part with it," she implored.

"Rachel, the animals can't pull the heavy load. Something has to go. Now choose something or I'm going to pick for you."

Hot tears scalded her eyes. He was right; she knew it, but the organ had belonged to her mother, the Bibles to her father.

Frustration and anger welled up inside her, combined with her chafing at Wade's absence of the last two weeks.

As defeat and sorrow overwhelmed her, she turned her disappointment on Wade. "Why are you doing this? Can't you understand how much those things mean to me? Why did I ever let you into my life, Wade Ketchum?"

He stared at her, his emerald eyes soft with an understanding she refused to acknowledge. His voice was tender. "Because you needed me, Rachel. Though your stubborn pride would never admit it."

She was stunned by his words. Her stubborn pride! The very idea of the man. "I needed my father. Not some two-bit gambler who waltzes in and out of camp just long enough to eat a meal, and then disappear again. Don't you dare stand there and tell me I'm stubborn, or I'll rattle off a list of your faults that will keep us here all afternoon."

"So, you've missed me!" he teased.

"I didn't say that," Rachel snapped her cheeks reddening.

Wade smiled a confidently, cockily. He stood so close she could see the laugh lines gathering around his eyes. The next thing she knew, he was hauling her in his arms. He pushed back a stray lock of her hair, brushed her cheek with the back of his hand, sending tingles all the way to her toes.

"It's been hard to sleep beside you each night," he said so low his voice was almost a whisper.

Rachel's mouth opened in surprise. He pulled her in tighter. Through her wet, thin petticoat she felt the hard muscles of his thighs pressed against her legs, his rigid manhood solid and hard against her belly. A sliver of fear raced down her spine, mingling with anticipation. She watched as he lowered his lips to hers.

"Why do you make me feel this way, Rachel?"

His lips covered hers, and the anger that had moments before coursed through her veins changed to liquid fire as he caressed first her top, then her bottom lip.

Rachel moaned, amazed that the sound bubbled from her. She loved the way his lips made her feel so warm, so hungry. She wanted him to continue kissing her until...Until what?

She slipped her hand between them and pushed him away. "Wade, stop. We mustn't."

He opened his eyes and Rachel shuddered at the passion reflected from their depths. "Why, Rachel?"

"It isn't proper," she whispered as she watched his chest rise and fall with ragged breaths. "It isn't right."

Wade sighed with frustration and released her, putting distance between the two of them. "It might not be right to your way of thinking, but it feels damn good to me."

With that, Wade turned and strolled away, leaving Rachel behind in the grove. She had only kissed one other man in her life. And for some reason the memory of Ethan's kisses didn't compare to Wade's.

A sudden noise, the scrape of wood against wood, sent her scurrying from the grove. She ran out just in time to see Wade drop the third box of Bibles on the ground.

"What are you doing?" she cried.

"I'm dumping the Bibles."

Rachel watched as he went back into the water and sloshed to the wagon to retrieve another box. She chased him into the stream and grabbed at his arm. "Stop. You can't do this. We must have these Bibles for the church."

Wade pulled his arm free and climbed back into the wagon. He lifted the box and started to shore. When he reached the bank, he dropped the box onto the ground. Rachel ran to the waterside and tried to lift the heavy box to lug it back to the wagon.

Several wagons pulled up at the edge of the bank to await their turn to cross the small creek. One of the men yelled at Wade, "What's in those boxes, Ketchum?"

"Bibles."

Mr. Drake, one of the immigrants, laughed. "Your wife thought she was going to get 'em all the way to Oregon?"

Wade frowned at the man. "My wife's father was a missionary who was killed on the trail by Indians. He was going out West to start a church."

The man abruptly quit laughing. Wade popped the wooden lid off the box, reached down and lifted out five of the brand new books.

He handed Drake one of the bibles, "Here, maybe you could use one."

Exhausted by the strain and emotion, Rachel watched in disbelief as Wade walked down the row of waiting wagons and handed each woman a Bible, coming back to the boxes time and again until he'd emptied every one. From the expressions on their faces, she knew Wade had just won the heart of every female on this train at the expense of her father's Bibles.

It was hard to accept, but she had to give Wade credit. It was better to give the books to their fellow travelers than to leave them by the trail where they would only rot in the hot sun. They would serve people's spiritual needs as her father had intended. And at least she still had her mother's organ.

But Wade's actions confused Rachel even more. She didn't know whether to thank him or curse him. Then there was that small part of her that just wanted him to hold her.

~

Struggling with the wagon in the mud had already delayed them over an hour. Rachel watched the men gather to help Wade free the wheels.

From the corner of her eye she glimpsed a masculine blonde head bobbing in the crowd. His build caught her attention. Somehow he seemed familiar. She hadn't seen him previously with the group, and his back was turned to her, but something about the way he carried himself, the shape of his body told her he wasn't a stranger.

The man turned and headed toward the wagon, and Rachel saw his face clearly for the first time.

She did a double take and stared unable to believe her eyes. For the first time in four long years she gazed in disbelief at the man she had loved so long ago.

"Oh, dear," she murmured, stunned.

Rachel jumped up, her previous discomforts forgotten as she ran towards the wagon calling, "Ethan Beauchamp, is that you?"

The man stopped. His gaze shifted to Rachel. The clear blue eyes she had cried for stared back at her in disbelief.

"Rachel?"

Ethan ran towards her and grabbed her, sweeping her up in a spin, hugging her regardless of her wet, muddy state.

"Oh, Ethan, it's been so long. I can't believe you're here!"

Chapter Seven

Wade stared, his jaw clenched. Rachel wrapped her arms around this stranger, hugging him as if he were the prodigal son returned. He watched in irritation as the man stepped back from his wife's embrace and scrutinized Rachel. Though he couldn't hear their words, Rachel's laughter sounded joyous, and her face beamed, bright with excitement.

Wade had never seen her truly happy. It rankled him that another man had brought that smile to her face.

He tried to tell himself that he wasn't jealous, that he didn't want any gossip or speculation about their marriage. But damn, he didn't like this man pawing Rachel.

A loud splash drew Wade's attention from the couple, and he watched in disbelief as the priggish Miss Becky waded through the creek as fast as her long, wet skirts allowed. When she reached the happy couple, she stepped between Rachel and the man to throw herself in his arms. Whoever he was, both women were delighted to see him.

The women hooked their arms in the man's and proceeded to the bank, where Wade purposely positioned himself. Rachel demurely met his gaze, her hazel eyes uncertain, as her hand rested in the crook of the man's arm.

She cleared her throat nervously. "Wade, I'd like you to meet a friend from home. Ethan Beauchamp."

The name hit him like a fist in the face. Wade struggled to remain nonchalant in front of the man whose name Rachel had murmured that night when she'd kissed him by the fire.

The insidious cord of jealousy wound its way around Wade's heart, strangling the organ. The urge to throttle the man was strong. But instead he offered Ethan his hand. "I'm Rachel's husband, Wade Ketchum."

Ethan turned to Rachel, clearly ignoring Wade. "You're married! Why didn't you tell me?"

A blush stained Rachel's face. "It's only been two weeks. We were married in Fort Laramie."

It had been difficult for her to say those words, her yearning to tell Ethan the truth all too clear.

The man turned back to Wade, and shook his outstretched hand, his grip soft but firm. "Ethan Beauchamp. Nice to meet the man who stole these two lovely ladies from me."

Wade nodded in acknowledgement while he scrutinized Ethan.

"Well, you're not the only ones with news. I, too, got married before heading out West," Ethan proclaimed.

Wade thought he was going to have to hold up both women as they absorbed this new information. Becky dropped Ethan's arm as if it were a red-hot poker, and Rachel's turned whiter than the snow-topped Rockies.

Rachel gulped. "How nice."

The stunned look on Becky's face dissipated, only to be replaced with a pout. "Whom did you marry, Ethan?"

"Someone you've never met. Her name is Mary," he replied.

"My, my, you always were impulsive." Becky glared at Ethan with open hostility. "I guess we just weren't good enough."

He reached out and lifted Rachel's hand to his lips. "Oh no. I never forgot my two favorite girls. But it's a lonely life being a circuit preacher, and I couldn't bear to be alone."

Wade snorted with disgust. Did women really fall for this sappy foolishness?

"We'd better get that wagon moved, so the rest of these people can cross," Wade said, ready to be rid of Mr.

Beauchamp. Of all the people in the world, he had to wind up traveling with Rachel's old beau.

~

"Rachel, I'd like you to meet my wife, Mary," Ethan said later that night. Rachel set her sewing aside, and stood up to greet the petite woman with a cherubic face.

Her sweet smile, blonde curls and sapphire eyes gave her the look of an angel. "It's a pleasure to meet you, Mrs. Ketchum."

She couldn't have been much older than Becky, Rachel thought, watching her stand in the flickering firelight, expectant and unsure, while Ethan disappeared to speak with the rest of the men.

The two women eyed each other dubiously. "Please, call me Rachel. While the men go off to talk business, why don't you sit here with me beside the fire?"

Rachel had been prepared to dislike Ethan's wife, to resent the woman who had taken the place she had once hoped to occupy. But it wasn't Mary's fault Rachel's father had objected to her marrying Ethan. It wasn't Mary's fault fate had ended their courting.

"Thank you. I thought it so gallant of your husband to give the women Bibles this afternoon. I know you didn't want to lose them, but you must be awfully proud of him."

A twinge of guilt pricked Rachel. "Yes, it was better than leaving them to rot by the trail."

"I made a note in mine, so that my great-grandchildren will look back and see his name," Mary proudly proclaimed. "Your husband must be a wonderful man."

Rachel picked up the sewing that she'd momentarily laid in her lap. "He's…unique."

Every woman on the train must think that Wade a hero for giving out the Bibles, but none of them knew he was really a bullheaded gambler down on his luck, who had taken her and the children under his wing. The only reason Wade had agreed to their proposition was money.

Mary took out her own needlework and sat on the stool beside Rachel's rocker. "How long have you been married?"

Rachel bit her tongue, trying to control the sense of uneasiness that question always seem to bring. She gazed intently at the button she was stitching on Toby's shirt. "We were married a little over two weeks ago, in Fort Laramie."

"Oh, my! How exciting!" Mary exclaimed. "Ethan and I have been married for six months."

Rachel lifted her head to gaze at Mary, her curiosity overcoming her. "Where did you meet Ethan?"

A tender smile graced Mary's delicate face. "At a church social. He was the visiting preacher. We had a whirlwind courtship, and two weeks later we were married."

"You married him two weeks after you met him?" Rachel exclaimed.

A soft smile touched Mary's lips. "It was rather sudden, but as a missionary, he would be leaving to continue his work. I had to go with him."

Rachel frowned. Ethan had been visiting her father's church when they'd fallen in love. Yet he'd left Rachel after her father found them kissing. Had she misconstrued their relationship four years ago, or did he find a woman at every church he visited?

"How did you meet Mr. Ketchum?" Mary asked innocently.

Rachel told her the unfortunate details of the attack on the wagon train, her father's slaying and Wade's rescue of them. Telling the story always reminded her of her loss.

"You were fortunate Mr. Ketchum came along and rescued you."

"Where are you and Ethan heading?"

"Oregon City. Ethan is going to settle down and teach. And preach when he has a chance," Mary replied softly. "How about you? Where are you and Wade going?"

Rachel frowned. Their final destination would also bring about Wade's departure. A sense of uneasiness crept through her at the thought of parting, leaving her perplexed.

"We're going to The Dalles. My father intended to help a young man named Ben Marshall with his church. "

"Oh, well, now you have your husband."

For a moment, Rachel was stunned. Mary had only seen Wade handing out Bibles. The side of him Rachel had found in that saloon back in Fort Laramie was hidden, safely tucked away until the next time the gambling fever took him away.

The baby started to cry, and Mary glanced at Rachel. "Would you mind if I picked him up?"

"Go ahead. It's his bedtime and he's starting to get fussy."

The longer she spoke with Mary, the more she liked the woman. Yet she couldn't help wonder why it didn't bother her that Mary and Ethan were together. Ethan looked the same, yet she didn't feel that spark of attraction she'd once felt. It seemed his image had been replaced by a tall, dark-headed man with emerald eyes, whose laugh was deep and throaty.

It wasn't long before Ethan returned for his wife, a somber Wade at his side. Becky trailed behind them, a pout upon her rosy lips.

"I think I'll turn in for the night," Becky said, retreating to the tent.

"Good night, Becky," Ethan called to her his deep baritone voice warm and pleasant. "I'm glad we found each other again."

Becky turned around, a frown gracing her pretty face. She hesitated, staring at Ethan as if she wanted to say something, before she turned and walked away.

Ethan took a seat beside Mary and draped his arm casually around his wife.

Mary cleared her throat. "Ethan told me you almost married him, Rachel."

A loud choking noise erupted from Wade, as he'd chosen that moment to take a sip of coffee. Apparently, Mary's news startled him, and Rachel almost laughed. Served the man right.

"We were just kids. Too young to know what we wanted."

Ethan spoke up, "Papa Cooke was very protective of his daughters. He sent me packing."

Mary glanced at Rachel, "Why did your father object?"

"My mother had recently passed away and Papa was determined to take care of us. He didn't rate suitors too highly."

"Isn't it strange how life works? My father was not happy that I married Ethan, either. But he couldn't stop me."

Ethan squeezed Mary to him. "She loved me enough to leave her family behind."

Wade stood up and threw the rest of his coffee into the fire. The liquid made a hissing sound as it hit the flames. "I hate to leave such interesting company, but I have to go check on the stock."

His boots crunched on the dry earth as he walked away.

"It is getting late and we have to be up early," Ethan declared. Standing, he pulled Mary up beside him.

She laid her hand on Rachel's arm. "I'm so glad we joined up with this train and I met you. The trip has been lonely not having a woman friend. It's going to be nice to have someone to gossip with."

Rachel was surprised at her easy acceptance of Mary as Ethan's wife. But she genuinely liked the young woman, and was pleased Ethan was happy.

Ethan hugged Rachel. "We'll see you tomorrow."

He took Mary's arm, and they strolled toward their wagon. Rachel watched as they disappeared from sight.

Life was odd. As Rachel watched him go, she couldn't remember why she'd been so attracted to the preacher.

~

Shadowy with moonlight, Wade climbed inside the wagon, trying not to wake Rachel. She was close enough to touch, yet out of reach for a man like himself.

Quietly, Wade shucked his pants. He crawled into the pallet and pulled the quilt over his body. The night air was chilly. Chilly enough that he wanted someone to snuggle up against. Anything besides a damn board.

The thought of throwing the board out and curling up next to Rachel left him hotter than a warm summer day. He couldn't keep thinking of her this way. They lived in different worlds, traveled in different circles; and now her precious Ethan had returned, though he was married to another woman.

With a punch to his pillow, Wade rolled onto his side.

"Are you awake?" Rachel asked softly.

The sound of her voice, in the dark, sent shivers down Wade's spine.

"Yes," he replied through gritted teeth.

The bedclothes rustled from the movements of her body as she turned over, sending Wade's blood rushing. "What you did today, with the Bibles..."

"Yes?" he challenged, certain she was going to berate him.

"I'm grateful for what you did. This way they will all reach Oregon." Silence filled the wagon. "Thank you for not leaving them to rot," she whispered in the darkness.

"You're welcome. Does this mean you're not angry at me anymore?" Wade tried to tease, but his tone emerged serious.

"Let's just say you made the best of a bad situation."

Wade turned over, facing the board. On the other side of the wood lay the flesh-and-blood woman he found all too attractive. A woman he thought of all day long on the trail. And the nights...were worse.

"Wade?"

"Yes?"

"Do you like Ethan?"

"Quite frankly, no," Wade replied. "And you don't want to hear my reasons why."

Stillness filled the wagon. Rachel shifted and Wade wanted to moan. Every time she moved he imaged her nightgown inching up to reveal her hips, leaving her long legs exposed.

"Yes, I do, Wade. Tell me."

The assertion stunned him. "You won't like it."

"Probably not."

"There's something that's not completely honest about him. I think he's a man who uses his profession to get women."

Rachel laughed, her voice filling the small wagon. "You couldn't be further from the truth. Ethan is completely devoted to God and his word. The only reason women flocked to him was because he was single."

"That and his kissing, which I know you took part in," Wade growled.

"I was only eighteen," Rachel whispered in the darkness. "He left when Papa sent him away."

"Did he tell you that he loved you? Did he promise never to leave you?" Wade asked.

"Yes."

"Your father must have been intimidating as hell to scare him off, or he didn't love you enough to stay." Wade paused. "Which one was it, Rachel?"

"I don't know why you think this is any of your business."

"It's not. But you asked. And you moaned his name that night around the campfire. The night I almost made love to you."

A sharp intake of breath filled the wagon. "We did not almost make love. You tricked me."

Wade raised up and leaned over the bundling board. "I don't have to trick women into kissing me or making love to me."

"Well, I didn't do it voluntarily."

Something in Wade snapped. He knocked the board down. The hunger of the last few weeks, the yearning to taste her again, overwhelmed him and he rolled over the wall to slake his desire.

In the darkness, his lips searched hers. His arms clasped her to him, and he felt her breasts pressing into his chest through the cotton of her nightgown. His hands stroked her face, while his lips devoured hers like a man starved.

This was what he'd thought about all day. This was what he'd dreamed about at night.

She brought her hands between them and tried to push him away. He kept kissing her until her gentle shoves changed to a tentative embrace. She grasped his undershirt and pulled him closer, moaning deep in the back of her throat. Her tongue gently found its way into his mouth and teased him with a timid touch. Feeling the satin of her skin, he rubbed his hands up her arms, across her shoulders to the buttons on her lace trimmed nightgown. His fingers fumbled at the silk tie of her nightdress, while his lips never left hers.

Succeeding at last, he pushed her nightgown down past her shoulders, past her bosom. His mouth trailed the soft cloth, descending as he kissed his way down her throat, down her silky shoulders, to the sweet nubs of her breasts.

She sighed with pleasure as his lips found the soft tip of her nipple and he gently teased the nub until it firmed against his mouth. Unable to resist the promise of sweetness, his lips suckled her breast.

"Wade," she murmured, the sound intoxicating to his ears.

He was past the point of no return, past the point of apprehension or second thoughts. He wanted only to feel himself deep inside Rachel, filling her with his need.

For a moment, his brain failed to register the loud scream that tore through his passion. But suddenly he knew something was dreadfully wrong.

"Damn," he cursed as he jumped away from Rachel and tugged on his pants. Grabbing his gun, he crawled out of the wagon. The screams came from the tent where the children slept, rending the still night air.

Wade reached the tent and tore open the flap. A lantern illuminated the inside where Becky was ranting. Her eyes were wide with anger, her breathing shallow. She raised a hand to strike Grace.

"You brat! I'll teach you to put a frog in my blankets."

Wade reacted without thought. He grabbed a startled Becky, pulling her arm behind her. "Don't you dare hit that child," he said, his voice a menacing growl.

Becky's body shook with anger. "Just look at my pallet. That frog wet my blankets."

Four green frogs hopped over Becky's covers, anxious to escape the overcrowded tent. Toby held Daniel, who was crying with fright at the noise and commotion. Wade tried to suppress his smile as the toads sprang about the bedding.

Rachel jerked open the flap of the tent, her wrapper covering her nightgown, her face flushed from his kisses.

She glanced at Wade, then Becky. "What happened? Who's hurt?"

"Just a few startled frogs." Unable to contain his laugher any longer, Wade threw back his head and howled.

Rachel looked puzzled, her hazel eyes encountering his in a nervous glance. "Frogs?"

Becky jerked her arm free of Wade, and gave him a despicable glare. "Yes, that brat put them in my pallet. I refuse to let her sleep in here anymore."

Grace stood aside, her head bowed. "I didn't mean to. They crawled out of my pocket."

"This little minx has hated me from the day you made me sleep here," Becky said with a pout.

Squatting down next to Grace, Wade asked the child. "Are there any more frogs missing, Grace?"

"Nope. I only had four. I lost two others yesterday."

Rising, Wade ran a hand through his hair. Never before had his ardor been cooled by frogs on the loose. "It's late. Why don't you sleep with Rachel and me tonight, Grace?"

"Thank you!" she exclaimed. She grabbed her doll, hooked it under her arm and headed out the tent without a backward glance.

Wade gazed at Rachel. Grace's timing couldn't have been any worse. Then again, maybe it couldn't have been better. After all, he knew the natural conclusion to their kisses and caresses. But Rachel...

Suddenly her anxious expression was gone. "I'll go make space in the wagon."

"Okay, the excitement's over. Everyone back to bed," Wade declared.

"I don't think I'll ever be able to sleep in the dark again without feeling those things crawling on me," Becky raged.

"Help Toby get Daniel settled," Wade commanded. "That will make you forget."

While Wade collected Grace's escaped frogs, Rachel readied the wagon. He put the frogs in a bucket for safekeeping, then lifted Grace up in the wagon and crawled in after her.

For a moment, he was stunned. The bundling board had been tucked away. The pallet, still small, would barely encompass three people. They would be crowded, forced to sleep side by side, hip to hip, shoulder to shoulder, sandwiched together. Just what his overactive imagination needed, to be curled up to a woman who was untouchable, yet left him hotter than the longest day in the desert.

∼

The next morning, neither she nor Wade spoke of the ridiculous fact that four green frogs had saved her virginity. But the feelings Wade aroused had lingered long after they'd separated. Her breasts and mouth were tender from his kisses, her heart bruised with the realization that he'd proven his point. She'd enjoyed every minute.

When she awoke, only the indention of his body on the pallet reminded her that Wade had slept beside her. But Rachel knew he'd left an indention on her heart as well.

She craved his touch, relished his kisses, hungered for his smell. Shamefully, this morning her only regret was that their lovemaking had been interrupted by Becky's screams.

But then again, what was wrong with Wade? Besides the fact that he gambled, drank and swore on occasion, nothing. Quite frankly, he was a good man with a kind but stubborn heart. He was generous to a fault, and even though he professed to dislike children, he had more patience with them than most men.

Because she knew, when they reached Oregon, Wade would leave her behind, her heart wanted to stay on the trail forever. For when they arrived in The Dalles, she would find it hard, if not impossible, to forget Wade.

The bright afternoon sun shimmered on the trail ahead as Rachel slapped the reins to keep the oxen moving. A few more miles closer to Oregon, a few more miles closer to the Sweetwater River. A lone rider approached their wagon, atop a palomino pony with a white mane and tail. As the horseman came closer, Rachel was surprised to recognize Ethan.

He touched the tip of his hat. "Good afternoon, ladies." Ethan touched the tip of his hat.

"Ethan, where did you find such a beautiful horse?" Rachel asked.

"He belongs to my wife," Ethan replied. "How are you this afternoon, Miss Becky?"

Rachel turned to glance at her sister. She'd been unusually quiet the last couple of days, and Rachel didn't know if the heat was bothering her or if she was just in a nasty disposition.

"Perfect, Mr. Beauchamp," Becky replied, a smile she reserved for her best beaus upon her lips. "And how is your wife."

"She's well," Ethan replied, his deep voice smooth as honey.

"Does she like being a preacher's wife?" Becky asked.

Rachel watched Ethan smile at Becky, his expression sincere. "Certainly. That's one of the reasons she married me."

"It's obvious Mary adores you," Rachel replied.

"But she wasn't my first love, was she?" Ethan said softly.

A tug on the reins drew Rachel's attention back to the team of oxen. Out of the corner of her eye, she watched Becky shift positions on the hard seat.

"We were young, Ethan. You probably courted half a dozen women between the time you knew me and Mary," Rachel replied as she tried to make light of Ethan's words.

"But none as pretty as the Cooke sisters," he acknowledged.

"You're such a flirt. No wonder the ladies used to chase you," Rachel teased.

"I ran just fast enough so I could be caught, too," Ethan proudly proclaimed.

"Humph!" Becky said under her breath, just loud enough that Rachel heard. "You should have stayed and married one of us, Ethan."

"I should have, Becky, but I couldn't," Ethan replied, his voice quiet.

Becky coyly looked out from under her hat. "Your loss."

"Yes ma'am, it is." Ethan's face broke out in a smile, his eyes twinkled.

Rachel frowned. "Things turned out for the best for all of us."

Becky rolled her eyes. "She's been this way since she married that specimen of manhood she calls a husband."

Rachel frowned at her sister with annoyance. If Becky only knew the truth behind her marriage, she wouldn't say such ridiculous things. Rachel was certain she wasn't acting any different since the announcement of her marriage.

"Sounds like you have a real affliction, Mrs. Ketchum. Maybe I should have a talk with this husband of yours. Make him realize what a lucky man he is."

"Oh, no, please don't," Rachel flushed with embarrassment. She didn't need Wade to get any more ideas about how she felt about him. All he had to do was touch her, and her traitorous body responded in ways she'd never imagined.

Ethan looked at her oddly. "Why not, Rachel?"

"It's just that...he's so busy right now, watching over the livestock, scouting for Frank, and taking first shift each night."

They rode along in companionable silence for a few moments. Ethan handled the fine pony with the skill of an excellent horseman.

"When did you learn to ride so well?" Rachel asked. "Before you could barely sit a horse."

Rachel realized she knew less about Ethan than she did about Wade. Ethan had never volunteered information about his background. One day he'd appeared on their doorstep and started to preach in her father's church.

"Mary taught me," Ethan said as he glanced at Becky, a frown marring his face. "Miss Becky, why aren't you wearing gloves?"

Becky looked annoyed. "I'm not driving the team this afternoon, Rachel is."

"That sun will damage your lily white skin. Here..." Ethan slipped his hands from his gloves and handed them to Becky. "I insist you wear mine. You can bring them back tonight."

Becky looked at him with a strange expression and then graciously accepted his gloves.

"Put them on," Ethan commanded.

As she did so a puzzled expression crossed her face.

Rachel thought for just a moment that she'd seen a sliver of white paper inside the gloves, but when Becky didn't say anything, she thought she was imaging things.

"Thank you," Becky replied politely. "My hands do feel better."

~

Later that night, Rachel stepped out of the tent to see Wade sitting by the campfire, holding a drowsy Grace. From what she could hear, he was telling her a story. The picture sent a pang zinging through Rachel's chest, hard enough to make her step falter.

For a man who despised small children, he was unusually good with them. Last night, he'd brought Grace to their bed. He'd taught Toby how to shoot, and he played with Daniel, holding him most nights until she had supper ready.

Quite a contradiction for a man who disliked children. Could he have lost a child of his own? He'd never mentioned being married. Though she knew more about Wade than Ethan, she knew little about his background other than the fact that he'd grown up in a saloon and was searching for his brother. He'd said nothing about the other members of his family.

As Rachel strolled into the light of the campfire, Grace smiled sleepily at her. "Wade's telling me a story of a little girl traveling to Oregon."

"I think maybe it's time for a little girl to go to bed."

"After he finishes the story."

"Rachel is right. We'll finish the story another night," Wade said as he stood, holding Grace in his arms."

The other children were already tucked in bed and sound asleep as he made his to the tent. While he laid Grace on the pallet, Rachel glanced over at Becky's empty pallet and wondered where she was.

The little girl reached up and gave Wade a peck on the check. "Good night, Wade."

A look of utter misery crossed Wade's face. "Good night Grace." He turned and strode from the tent as if demons nipped at his heels.

Rachel bent down and gently tucked Grace in. "Sleep tight sweetheart," she whispered as she kissed the child on the cheek.

"Hmmm, don't let the bedbugs bite," Grace replied dreamily.

Stepping out of the tent into the light glow of the campfire, Rachel realized that something about Grace had touched Wade. "Why did you act like you hated children when we first met?"

Wade glanced at her across the fire, and she witnessed the pain reflected in his face. "Who says I don't hate them now?"

"If you hated children you wouldn't be so good with them."

Wade frowned. "There's a lot you don't know about me. Did you think just because I grew up in a tavern, I had no contact with children?"

"No. Some of your first words to me showed your concern about traveling with children, yet you're better with them than Becky is."

Wade put a cheroot between his lips and chewed on the end of it. "I came from a large family. My father owned the Captain's Tavern in Boston." He paused and stared at Rachel. "It was your typical barroom establishment."

"My mother was a saint to put up with my father. She was sickly, but she took care of us children the best she could. Since I was the oldest, I had to help out with the younger kids."

Wade stood and paced around the fire as if the memories made him restless, edgy. Memories shadowed his eyes, turning them a fierce green. Rachel felt a compelling need to ask further questions, but he put his fingertips to her lips.

"I have to go. I'm taking first watch tonight." He brushed a kiss on her forehead, spun around, leaving her without another word.

As Rachel watched him disappear into the night, she couldn't help but wonder about the hurt she'd seen in his eyes.

Chapter Eight

Dear Diary,

Today we reached Independence Rock and stopped to celebrate. This last week we've passed through the most grueling country yet. Everyone has suffered from lack of water, especially the cattle and oxen.

The children's faces have peeled from the dust, wind and sun, though I constantly apply salve. Everyone is tired, and today's arrival at Independence Rock couldn't have come at a better time.

Wade has been distant since the night Grace stayed with us. I feel as if he's avoiding me, afraid of me...

"Rachel," Becky called in the early evening air.

Rachel slipped her diary back in the trunk, then stuck her head out between the pucker ropes of the canvas. "What is it?"

"The women are setting up the tables."

"I'll be right there," Rachel said.

Frank had declared a day of rest and celebration for the weary travelers. For the first time in a week, Rachel had allowed herself the luxury of a sponge bath and the pleasure of washing her hair. With the scarcity of water, no one had been given the indulgence of a bath until today.

Though she tried to tell herself the party was the only reason she wanted to look her best, she knew Wade's presence spurred her efforts.

The brush slid through her hair until it glistened and shone, then Rachel looped it back loosely with a piece of ribbon, instead of securing it in the usual bun she wore every day. She dabbed just a drop of rosewater on her throat, then picked up Daniel, who sat on the floor of the wagon, watching her.

He giggled in delight and reached for her nose, just as she grabbed his hand. She cooed to the baby as she crawled out of the wagon, her long skirts a hindrance. When she turned around she came face to face with Wade.

Sweat glistened on his face. His shirt was damp with perspiration, his skin tanned from the long hours in the sun. She'd never realized before this moment how the smell of a man after a hard day's work could be so exhilarating.

His eyes leisurely traveled the length of her body, sending her blood racing to her cheeks. He stepped closer until only Daniel remained between them. "Mrs. Ketchum, you look stunning."

Rachel couldn't help but smile. His words, combined with his looks, left her almost breathless. "Thank you. I laid out clean clothes for you in the wagon. Change and then meet us at the Rock."

Wade's left brow rose. "You laid out my clothes?"

"I looked through your saddlebags and found fresh clothing for you. I thought you would want to clean up a bit."

He smiled. "Most definitely." He brushed his finger against her cheek, sending ripples of pleasure through her. "I'll see you in a few minutes."

Rachel's stomach fluttered with anticipation. "Yes." After a week of clipped sentences and seldom being seen by her, today he was back to acting like the charming rogue who tested her resistance. Somehow, it was a welcome change.

She quickly stepped away, picking up her dried apple pie and chicken dumplings, though the dish was more dumplings than bird.

When she reached the tables the women were busily laying out the food.

Mary greeted her. "I've been looking for you and that sweet baby. May I hold him?" she stretched out her arms and Daniel gladly went into them.

"I'm surprised at how he's taken to you. He fusses with Becky," Rachel replied as she set about putting out her chicken and pie. The table was overladen with food, and while it wasn't the quality of back-home cooking, the women had done their best with their meager supplies.

"Where is Ethan?" Rachel asked. "I haven't seen him today."

"He went hunting with several of the other men," Mary replied. "How about Wade, where is he?"

"He's cleaning up now. Funny, he didn't say anything about hunting."

Mary shrugged her shoulders. "Ethan left earlier this afternoon. Maybe Wade had something else to do."

They busied themselves, helping set up the tables of food, arranging stools and benches around the area so people might sit and enjoy themselves.

Soon the line around the food table began moving, and Rachel spotted Wade ahead of her. She helped Grace choose her food, balancing her plate very carefully. When she'd taken care of the girl, she turned to find Wade in front of her with not one plate, but two.

"I knew you would take care of everyone else but yourself, so I brought food for us both," he said sheepishly.

A spurt of giddiness rushed through her. He'd actually thought of her. "Thank you."

"You can sit by me, Wade." Grace patted a spot on the quilt beside her. Rachel sank down, cautiously balancing her plate and leaving room for Wade.

"I'd love to sit with my two favorite girls," Wade said sitting between Rachel and Grace. "Where's Toby and Becky?"

"Toby's off playing with the Simpsons' boy," Rachel replied as she spooned a bite of beans into her mouth. "And Becky was around here earlier. I don't see her now."

"I saw her and Ethan leave earlier," Grace replied.

Rachel glanced down at Grace in surprise. "Ethan's out hunting, sweetheart. Eat your dinner."

Wade raised his brows.

By the time dinner was finished, the stars were out in abundance, and while the women cleared the dishes away, several men warmed up their fiddles. After helping with the dishes, Wade disappeared. Rachel and Mary sat watching the younger couples dance.

"I'm beginning to worry about Ethan," Mary declared a frown on her face. "I thought he would have returned by now."

"Don't fret, Mary. He'll be back soon," Rachel replied.

"You're right," Mary said, her blue eyes dark with concern.

Rachel glanced around the campground, "Now I've lost Wade."

The two women laughed simultaneously. "We can't seem to keep them in line, can we, Mary?" Rachel said as she realized a steady stream of men seemed headed toward the back of one of the wagons. She frowned as she watched them disappear.

Leaning back in her chair, Rachel closed her eyes, gently rocking Daniel in her arms. She pushed all thoughts from her mind and let the music flow over her, easing her tired soul and weary body.

Footsteps crunched the soft earth and stopped before her. She became aware of a strong presence and looked up to see Wade standing before her. Her heart skipped a beat at the sight of his handsome face.

He stretched out his hand, "Dance with me, Rachel?"

She glanced at the couples moving gracefully in time with the music. Her palms dampened and she swallowed, trying to hide her nervousness. Though it looked like fun, Papa had never taught her to dance.

"I can't."

"Why not?"

"I have Daniel," she replied.

Mary reached out her arms. "I'll watch him. You go dance."

"No." Rachel held on to the baby tighter. "I can't."

Mary looked perplexed, and Wade frowned at Rachel. "Do you know how to dance, Rachel?"

Rachel glanced up at Wade sheepishly. "Uh – No."

"Then it's time you learned." Before she could protest, Wade plucked Daniel out of Rachel's arms. He handed the baby to a smiling Mary and pulled on Rachel's hand, tugging her up from her chair. "I'm going to teach the waltz. Once you learn the steps, we'll join the others."

Rachel's concentration fled the moment he drew her into the safety of his arms. As they moved to the music, he showed her the pattern. Somehow her feet managed to grasp the rhythm.

She shook back her hair and laughed, her gaze connecting with the warmth reflected from his emerald eyes. Heat shimmered from their depths, touching her everywhere as she felt her breathing quicken, her pulse pound.

"I think you've got the steps down," he told her. "Let's join the other dancers."

"Are you sure?" Rachel asked hesitant.

"You're ready," he announced.

Rachel didn't know if he was talking about her dancing or this connection between them, that seemed to leave her heated and radiating with color. She only knew that when Wade touched her, her body responded in ways she'd never dreamed possible.

They joined the other dancers, and soon Rachel was laughing, having more fun than she could remember. She swooped and twirled until finally the music ended and she pleaded for a break.

Breathless, she returned to Mary's side while Wade sauntered off with the men. "I'm sorry, Mary. I didn't mean to stick you with Daniel all evening."

"Nonsense. I love holding him, and I must say, you caught on quickly. Your husband is a wonderful teacher."

"Oh yes, my husband," Rachel said breathlessly. "I still forget sometimes that we're married."

"The way that handsome man looks at you?" Mary scoffed.

Rachel looked back at Mary, a blush staining her cheeks. Was it that obvious to other people, this awareness, between herself and Wade? These feelings were so new, they left her confused and daze.

She spotted Wade strolling toward her from the wagon behind which all the men had disappeared. His stride was confident and sure. Halfway to her, Sam Perkins stopped him and spoke. Wade pointed to the Simon's wagon and with sudden insight; Rachel realized what was going on behind it. Fury shook her.

In plain sight, a jug or a bottle of some kind of spirits was being passed around, each man taking a sip. Tomorrow morning would find many of the men suffering the effects of their drinking. She watched as Wade strode towards her, his long, lean legs moving with the grace of a panther.

For an instant she felt like his prey. Stalked, and pursued, she was the booty at the end of the hunt. He appeared to be courting her, though she couldn't imagine why.

Wade stopped before her, a smile gracing his face, "Ready for another dance?"

"Ask Mary to dance. I have to watch Daniel," Rachel replied knowing it was an excuse, wanting to be in his arms, but resisting, afraid of the emotions he provoked.

"Go on, Rachel," said Mary. "There's no sense in both of us being denied a good time. I don't want to dance without Ethan, so you might as well. I'll watch Daniel and Grace."

She wanted to dance with Wade again, but he had the smell of the devil's brew on him and the smile of Satan, too. Still, she yearned to dance with him again.

"Thanks Mary," Rachel took Wade's outstretched hand and followed him, to join the other dancers close to the fire. As the dance started, she whirled past him, the smell of whiskey wafting to her nose.

"Partaking of the devil's brew again, Mr. Ketchum?" Rachel asked, needing to challenge him rather than succumb.

"Just a wee nip to celebrate the fourth, Mrs. Ketchum."

"Haven't you heard a wee nip can send you to the gates of hell," Rachel replied, her voice serious.

Wade laughed, his voice vibrant and deep. "I've already been there and back. It's not too bad once you get used to the heat."

"It's dangerous to be talking this way, Mr. Ketchum."

"I hardly think a thimbleful of whiskey will send me to hell." His voice rang with amusement as he spun her around, just as the dance ended.

"Humph! The sinful never think they've done wrong."

Wade pulled her in close. "It's time someone showed you how to relax and have a good time. I wish I could be that man."

Rachel pushed herself off the muscular wall of Wade's chest. "I don't need you to teach me anything. I already know how to have fun."

They walked in silence back to Mary, and Rachel couldn't help but feel relieved that Ethan stood before his wife, Becky by his side.

Rachel smiled at Ethan. "I told Mary you would return."

"I was out hunting," Ethan said tiredly.

"Did you hit anything?" Wade asked, his voice cool.

"Didn't even unstrap my rifle from the saddle. But I enjoyed the day," Ethan said, his voice strong and sure.

"Your wife has been gracious to watch the children while Wade and I danced. Now it's her turn," Rachel insisted. "Dance with your wife, Ethan."

Mary looked up at Ethan in expectation. Ethan offered her his hand. "May I have this dance?"

With a smile, Mary handed the baby to Rachel and accepted Ethan's offer. Becky took Mary's chair until one of the young men approached her for a dance and she accepted.

Wade watched Mary and Ethan on the dance floor. Shortly, he turned to Rachel. "You know they just don't seem like they belong together."

"What are you talking about? They're perfect for one another," Rachel declared.

"That sounds strange coming from a woman who still cares for him."

Rachel jerked around to face Wade, all her attention focused on him. "Whatever are you talking about?"

"You moaned his name, Rachel," Wade growled, his voice low and hard.

Rachel glared at Wade as she tried to control her temper. "He's married, for heaven's sake."

"That doesn't seem to bother your sister."

"What are you blathering about now?"

"Watch Becky. Her eyes follow Ethan. She searches him out, and when he thinks no one is looking, he gazes back at her. If he wasn't married, I'd think they were in love," Wade said bluntly.

Rachel couldn't contain her frustration any longer.

"That is the most ridiculous thing you've said tonight. Becky has always cared for Ethan as a brother. Your thimbleful of alcohol has affected your thinking. Did you go behind that wagon again?

Wade smiled. "Are you counting?"

"Of course not. It's none of my business how you choose to live your life." Her finger came up and poked him in the chest. "But your drunkenness is starting to show."

"I may have had a wee nip as my father used to say, but I'm nowhere close to being drunk," Wade shrugged. "I've not had as much to drink as you and I shared one night."

Rachel drew in a quick breath. How dare he refer to that night!"

"Mr. Ketchum, may I remind you that we are in a public place. One more remark regarding that night and I will feel pleasure in releasing my anger on the side of your face."

Wade threw back his head and laughed. "You know, Rachel, I don't believe you could actually do it. Not my sweet angel."

"Don't count on it, Wade. I'm not anyone's 'sweet angel'!"

Suddenly the joy of dancing in his arms didn't seem quite so delightful. She gathered up Daniel and Grace and returned to the wagon. For her, the party was over.

～

The children were tired and weary and quickly dropped off to sleep, leaving Rachel alone. She prepared for bed, and then lay in the stifling wagon, listening to the music, remembering the dancing, angry at Wade and unable to sleep.

For several hours, she tossed and turned, waiting for sleep to overcome her, waiting for Wade to return to their wagon. Finally, after midnight, the fiddlers packed away their instruments and the revelers quieted for the night.

Still Wade did not return. He really wasn't drunk when she left him; he'd only had a few sips of the devil's drink or so he said.

Punching the pillow, Rachel turned over, wishing sleep would overcome her. The man was quite capable of taking care of himself.

Crickets chirped, owls hooted and nocturnal voices cried to one another in the still night air. The crickets quieted as another voice joined in their nightly song. Wade's deep, baritone voice, filled the air as he sang at the top of his lungs.

"Rachel Cooke, won't you come out tonight? Come out, tonight. Come out tonight. Rachel Cooke, won't you come out tonight and dance by the light of the moon?"

She fought a sudden urge to giggle. It really wasn't funny. The man was singing loud enough to wake the entire camp and the dead, too, and using her maiden name to boot.

She scrambled to the back of the wagon and yanked open the canvas. "Shh! People are trying to sleep!"

"Honey, I really don't give a damn! I want to dance and you left me without a partner," he replied in a drunken slur. "So I had me another little nip."

"From the way you're acting, I'd say you had more than a nip. How much whiskey did you drink?"

"Not nearly enough," he replied.

"Mr. Ketchum! It's time for bed. You're not going to remember any of this in the morning," she announced, her voice stilted, her emotions raw.

Wade shook his head drunkenly. "Not until I get to dance with you again."

"Another night, Wade. Come to bed."

"Okay. I warned you." He took a deep breath and broke the silence again. "Rachel Cooke, won't you come out tonight? Come out tonight. Come out tonight. Rachel

Cooke, won't you come out tonight and dance by the light of the moon?"

"Would you please be quiet!" she said, her voice harsh.

"Are you going to dance with me?" he asked.

"No!"

He inhaled a robust breath. "Rachel Cooke...

"Very well! Just quiet down before you wake the children and the entire camp," Rachel grabbed her wrapper, covering her nightgown. She couldn't believe she was actually going to dance with this drunken fool in the middle of the night. Come morning he'd pay dearly for what he'd drunk tonight.

She climbed out of the wagon and turned to face him.

He stepped toward her until he was so close she felt almost overpowered by him.

"God, you looked beautiful tonight, Rachel." He brushed her hair back away from her face. "Wear your hair down more often."

Rachel grabbed his hand. "The dance, remember?"

Wade shook his head. "Oh, right. We were going to dance." He took her in his arms, then stopped. "But there's no music." He paused and said, "I'll sing."

"No! Wade, it's late. Just pretend we hear music."

He frowned down at her, then his feet began to move, but it wasn't in the rhythm of the Waltz he'd taught her earlier in the evening. This time the dance was much slower, much closer. Rachel had never seen anyone dance this way before, bodies brushing, breaths mingling.

He moved her arms up around his neck and pulled her body tight against his. A cool breeze alerted her, he'd undone the ties to her wrapper and slipped his hands inside to her thin cotton gown.

A searing kiss that tasted of whiskey left her knees weak. A swirling curl of desire began in the pit of her stomach. Then the overpowering stench of liquor rocked her senses back to reality.

She brought both hands up between them and pushed with all her strength, sending him flying into the dirt, where he landed with a plop on his backside.

He glared up at her in stunned surprise. "Why in the hell did you do that, woman?"

"You're stinking drunk!"

"Damn it, I had to do something to get my mind off you. Otherwise, I was going to crawl over that damn board and take you like a real husband would," he said with a low moan and laid his head back on the soft earth.

His admission stunned her. Part of her secretly wanted him to crawl over that board and take her. She wanted to completely experience the feelings Wade aroused in her, but left unfulfilled. Then her sensible voice whispered that she'd regret her actions later. The liquor was talking, not Wade.

"There's no excuse for becoming drunk, Mr. Ketchum."

He grabbed her wrapper and tugged just hard enough to pull her down. She landed with a thud on top of him. Through the thin cotton the hard muscles of his chest pressed against her breasts. With stunning clarity, she felt every muscle, including the one between his legs, which was hard.

His lips touched hers and an instant sizzle burned from her mind all thought of anything other than Wade. His arms molded her tightly against him as desire slammed through Rachel, igniting every nerve ending.

"Mrs. Ketchum, it's obvious you know nothing about men. I suggest you get your pretty little bustle back inside that wagon and keep it there. Or else you're not going to be a virgin when you reach Oregon."

Shame and embarrassment replaced the desire that had filled her. Without thinking she broke free and slapped him

as hard as she could. She gasped, shocked at this act.
Quickly, she jumped up and fled into the wagon.

Chapter Nine

"What in the hell?" Wade sat straight up, ice water cascading from his face. The predawn light shimmered around Rachel as she stood before him, her face set in angry lines, an empty bucket in her hand.

"Get up from there, Mr. Ketchum!" Rachel commanded. "I'll not have you embarrassing me or the children by having the whole train awakening to find you sprawled on the ground, snoring drunkenly."

Wade shook his head, trying to clear the cobwebs from his muddled brain. When he moved, his head pounded like a steam locomotive.

The last he remembered of the night before he was dancing with Rachel, her sweet fragrance, gentle curves and pleasant smile driving him crazy with desire.

With startling clarity, he remembered consuming enough whiskey to dull the fire in his loins and any intelligent thought in his head.

"Get up, Wade," she demanded, her face tight with barely restrained control.

Wade eased himself up from the ground, his head throbbing from the movement. His stomach reeled from the whiskey. He looked at Rachel and knew he was in hot water with the righteous Miss Cooke.

"Couldn't you have awakened me with a gentle kiss sweet Rachel?" he asked, goading her anger even further.

Her face turned scarlet, and he watched as she clenched her fists. "Get yourself cleaned up and take care of the animals."

He looked down at his dripping clothes. "I think you've already bathed me for the day."

"I had to do something to get the stench of whiskey off you," Rachel spat out before she stalked off and proceeded to stir up their small fire.

"Just what exactly did I do to put such a bee in your bonnet this early in the morning?" he asked.

His words seemed to light a fire beneath her as she approached him, her chest heaving. "Oh! You don't remember, do you? What part shall I tell you first? That you accused me of still loving Ethan? Or that you slipped behind a wagon and drank to excess. Or how you came back drunk and singing tawdry saloon songs at the top of your lungs? Shall I continue?"

"Please continue, it sounds like I had a fine time."

"You also said I didn't know anything about men. Then you kissed me until…" She drew in a sharp breath. "Well, you kissed me."

"My behavior sounds absolutely deplorable, Mrs. Ketchum," he said in tight-lipped mirth. "But I have kissed you before, and if I get the chance, I will do so again."

"I don't know why you persist." Rachel said perplexed. "We both know eventually we'll go our separate ways."

Wade closed the distance between them. "That's true. But you can't deny there is something between us."

"I don't know what you're talking about," Rachel murmured.

"You're naïve, Rachel, but you're not stupid. Even you have to recognize that we're drawn to one another," he said as he brushed a stray lock of hair away from her face.

"Leave it be, Wade. You drink, you cuss, you're not a Godly man. I hired you to take us to Oregon, not become my husband in the flesh," she whispered.

"Maybe it's time someone showed you what being with a man is all about," he said as he moved swiftly to take her in his arms.

She took a step back away from him. "See that's just the kind of response I should expect from a man like you."

"Rachel you can expect that kind of response from any man when there's a beautiful woman like yourself tempting him."

"Not the men in my Papa's church," Rachel argued.

Wade resisted the urge to grab her by the shoulders and shake her until she listened. "Are you certain about that? My daddy's business was full of good men who attended church on Sunday morning after being in his saloon Saturday night."

Rachel gasped. "I don't believe you."

"I don't give a fig if you do. But they were the same men I saw in church the next morning."

"You were in church?" she asked incredulously.

"I know you may find it hard to believe, but there was a time in my life when I attended."

"Why didn't you tell me?"

"Why didn't you ask?"

"I don't know," she replied meekly. "I just assumed..."

"You assumed I've never been to church. You're as big a hypocrite as the rest of 'em," he said, annoyed at her response.

Rachel became indignant. "I am not."

She turned away, disillusionment on her face. Her voice became low, almost sorrowful. "I don't like lying to everyone I meet. I don't like pretending to be something I'm not. But I had no choice! I'm lying because I have to."

Wade felt bad for calling her a hypocrite, but damn, the woman was trying his patience. And it infuriated him that she always assumed the worst about him.

"When my mother was alive we attended church every Sunday, though we were shunned by the parishioners because of my father's saloon. I've had a lot of experience with hypocrites."

Rachel turned around to face him, the shock apparent on her face, and in her hazel eyes. "I thought..."

Wade took two steps toward her. He was inches from her. His hands were clinched, his breathing ragged, his head vibrating at the sudden memories. The memories of a small boy shunned by the other kids every Sunday because his father owned a saloon.

"You thought I was a lying, womanizing, card-playing drunk. You assumed the worst about me. And just maybe your assumptions are correct, because I can't say I want to be the bloodless imitation of a man you think you want. Someone like Ethan."

Rachel whirled around and almost ran inside the wagon.

~

That night after the children had been put to bed, Rachel went to Ethan and Mary's camp, hoping Mary would talk her out of this slump. Wade had disappeared after their confrontation in the morning and had yet to return. Rachel had spent the evening wondering how she could go on pretending with Wade, yet fearful he would never return.

Strolling into the Beauchamp's camp, she realized Mary was nowhere in sight. Ethan sat by the fire, relaxing.

Rachel said, "good evening. Where's Mary?"

"She went down to visit Emily for a spell," Ethan replied. "You look tired tonight. Are you feeling all right?"

Rachel wanted to open up her heart, but part of her resisted. "I'm fine. It's just that sometimes I miss Papa more than I let on."

"He's not been gone that long, Rachel. Grief takes a while to get over."

"I know. It's just that I miss going to him whenever there was a problem with one of the children. At night we used to sit around the fire and talk about them."

Rachel pulled her shawl tighter around her trembling shoulders. The night air was crisp, the stars were bright.

Ethan glanced up at the stars. "It's too pretty a night for us to be sitting around having a spell of the doldrums. Why don't we go for a walk?"

"Mary wouldn't mind?"

"Mary knows you're an old friend. But how about Wade?"

A tiny laugh escaped her lips. "He doesn't care."

Rachel twisted the edge of her shawl in her tightly closed fist. She swallowed, holding back the flood of tears that threatened to spill.

Ethan placed her arm in the crook of his elbow. "I'm a good listener, if you want to tell me what's troubling you."

"Please don't ask, Ethan. I can't tell you," Rachel implored.

"My dear, I'm a minister. You can tell me anything. Your secrets are safe with me."

The need to talk about her burdens to someone was more than she could bear.

"When Papa died, Becky and the children were depending on me to get us to safety. We had no one." Rachel paused, unsure if she should continue. "Wade guided us to Fort Laramie, but Frank Jordan wouldn't let us join up with the wagon train, because I didn't have a husband. So I found Wade in the saloon and asked him to marry me."

"Rachel, a lot of marriages began on less," Ethan said with a dismissive wave.

"It's not that." Rachel twisted her hands around her shawl. Finally she blurted out, "Wade didn't want to get married."

Ethan paused in the dark, his hand gripping her arm as if she would run away.

"Rachel, what are you saying?"

She drew in a deep breath. "We agreed to pretend we were married until we reached Oregon."

"You're not really married?" There was surprise in his voice.

"No."

"I don't know what to say, except I'm shocked."

Even in the darkness she could see his eyes searching her, could feel them probing her almost as if he wanted to touch her. The sensation made her uncomfortable.

"We're not sleeping as man and wife. We've never...." She couldn't continue.

The hand that rested on Ethan's arm was suddenly covered by his other hand. "You've never consummated."

"No," Rachel whispered in the darkness, mortified they were discussing her virginity.

He squeezed her hand, drawing her in closer.

"It was the only way to continue on to Oregon."

"You took a mighty big chance with your reputation," Ethan responded, with a sigh.

"I didn't have a choice. We could have been stuck in Fort Laramie the rest of our lives. I would never return to Tennessee," Rachel explained, and a brief flash of anger struck her as she realized Ethan didn't understand her lack of choices.

Crickets twittered in the night air before he finally said, "What's wrong, Rachel? You've explained how you got to be in this situation, but you haven't told me what's really wrong. Are you starting to have feelings for Wade?"

Rachel had avoided this for fear the answer would be unacceptable. "I don't know. He's not the kind of man you are, yet he's kind and gentle. He drinks and gambles, but I can't wait to see him in the evening. I watch for him all the time, and I feel different when he's around. I'm so confused.

Ethan patted her on the back.

"He accused me of being self-righteous. He says I always assume the worst about him, and he's right." She paused to wipe her tears with the end of her shawl. "I don't know what to do, Ethan? How can we continue on to travel this way?"

Rachel watched as Ethan ran a hand through his hair. "You're a good woman, Rachel, in a terrible mess."

"I don't think straight when he's around."

Ethan shook his head. "I respect your desire to reach Oregon, but you're paying a price for your lying and deceit." He paused. "Would you like me to talk to Wade?"

"Oh, no, Ethan. If he knew I'd spoken with you, he'd be upset. It would only make the situation worse."

"Then the only thing I can suggest is prayer, dear Rachel. Lots and lots of prayer."

"I know, Ethan. But I needed to talk to someone. And since Papa is...."

Ethan pulled her into his arms, holding her close enough Rachel could feel her breasts smashed against his chest. The top of her head fit up under his chin and he kissed her forehead. The touch of his lips, the feel of his body against hers, didn't seem right.

"If you need comforting, you know where I am," Ethan replied, his voice earnest.

Rachel pulled out of his embrace. "Thank you. Just telling someone has relieved my burden. I better get you back to Mary."

Ethan took Rachel's hand and put it back in the crook of his elbow. "Don't worry about my Mary. She's very understanding."

Rachel and Ethan strolled back toward camp. When they reached the edge of the clearing, a lighted cheroot flared in the shadows. Startled, Rachel halted.

"Nice evenin' for a stroll, isn't it, Ethan?" Wade said, his deep voice cutting through the darkness. "Especially with another man's wife."

Rachel felt Ethan tense. "I think I better get back to Mary. Thanks for the walk, Rachel."

Ethan dropped her arm and hurried away.

"Was that necessary, Wade?" Rachel asked.

Wade grabbed her by the arm. "We may have a mockery of marriage, but you're still mine until we get to Oregon. And I don't intend on sharing you with any man. Understand?"

"You're being vulgar. Ethan is married."

"To most men that means nothing. Go to bed, Rachel. We've said enough hurtful things to one another for one day."

~

The high-pitched scream woke Rachel with a start. The noise was eerie, frightening with its intensity. Wade was already up, pulling on his pants.

"What is it?" Rachel asked fearfully.

"Probably a mountain lion or panther," Wade replied as he stepped into his boots.

Rachel jumped out of bed, pulling on her wrapper.

"Just where do you think you're going?" Wade asked.

"The children will be frightened. I'll stay with them."

"I have enough to worry about right now. I don't want you out of this wagon running around. I'll check on the children and tell them to stay put. You stay in the wagon."

Rachel knew from the tone of his voice it would do no good to argue.

"He's probably trying to kill one of the oxen or horses."

Suddenly, she realized the danger he was going out to face, and she didn't want him to leave her side. "Please don't go, Wade."

In the darkness, his hurried movements ceased.

"Afraid you're going to lose your man, Rachel?" he mocked. "I'm sure Ethan would be happy to take over."

His words pierced her with their cruelty. "Don't, Wade. You know that's not true."

"I don't know anything of the sort. Ethan returns, and he's either at your side or Becky's. And then, tonight I find you two out for a stroll, without his wife. What am I supposed to think?"

Guilt covered her like a cloak until she quickly reminded herself there was no reason for her to feel ashamed. She'd done nothing wrong. "Ethan is my friend."

"Just like me, Rachel?" Wade asked as he crawled out of the wagon, leaving her bewildered.

"Be careful," she called into the darkness.

When the cry came again, she felt as if her spirit was in tune with the animals. Frightened and forlorn, she lay listening in the darkness, worrying about Wade.

Chapter Ten

Wade saw Rachel's wagon off in the distance and pulled his big roan in her direction. Since the night of the dance, they'd been snapping and growling at each other worse than the panther of several nights before.

But seeing Rachel and Ethan together had ignited a fierce anger within him that seemed to build with each passing day, surprising him with its intensity. Was she blind? He wanted to rant at her for not recognizing the swindler in Ethan. Then again, if her heart pined for Ethan the way he thought it did, even eyeglasses wouldn't help her see the man's faults.

The afternoon heat was oppressive as he made his way to her. Alone, she guided the oxen along the barren trail.

He pulled Sadie alongside the wagon. The horse shook her head, snorting at the dust the oxen kicked up in the air. Rachel pointedly ignored him, her gloved hands working to guide the oxen up the trail, her bonnet shading her face from the afternoon sun.

"Hi," he said, breathing heavily from the exertion of the ride. "Where are Becky and the children?"

"Daniel, Grace and Toby are spending the afternoon in Mary's wagon," Rachel replied, never glancing in his direction. She sat like a statue, with only her hands moving.

Wade wiped the back of his shirtsleeve against his sweat-laden brow. "What about Becky?"

"She's riding with Mrs. Simpson," Rachel said, her voice clipped and short.

"Pull over. I'll drive the wagon for awhile."

"That's not necessary."

Wade shook his head. The woman was bound and determined to try his patience. "I don't like you driving alone."

Rachel threw him a nasty look, her mouth pinched with disapproval. "I've driven this wagon the last two hundred miles without you. What makes me so incapable today?"

"You handle a team of oxen better than most men, but the closest wagon is a quarter of a mile back."

"And the children would make a difference?" she retorted.

"No, but at least they could holler for help."

"I know how to scream."

"Just stop the wagon and let me drive," Wade demanded as he leaned over his saddle, trying to reach the reins.

Rachel moved them out of his reach. "Just a moment," she said, reluctantly pulling the team to a halt. "I was enjoying my solitude this afternoon. It's not often I have time alone."

"It's not often we have time alone," Wade replied.

Rachel's glanced at him, a stunned expression on her face.

The wagon came to a halt, and Wade tied his horse to the back. He walked to the front and climbed up onto the seat beside Rachel. Taking the reins from her hands, he called to the oxen. When they were moving at a maximum trudge, Wade turned to Rachel.

His gaze skimmed her. "You're mighty quiet today."

"I'm hoping you'll go away if I ignore you," Rachel said, staring at the countryside.

"Are you going to ignore me the rest of the way to Oregon?" he asked.

"If that were possible, I just might consider it. Especially after you left me alone to worry about you the other night."

Wade couldn't help but smile. Though she'd said it in irritation, it felt good to hear her concern. "I thought you'd be happy to hear that the panther had me for breakfast."

"You'd have given the poor animal indigestion."

"Maybe so. But I'm sure Ethan would be happy to take my place by your side. He could have you and Mary, both" As soon as he said the ugly words, he wanted to take them back.

Rachel turned and gazed at him like she'd smelled a skunk.

"What are you talking about?" she asked.

"Oh come on, Rachel. You were out strolling around in the dark with the man. Married women don't stroll with other women's husbands. Especially men who used to court them."

"You're being ridiculous. Mary knows it was innocent."

"You told me at the dance that you didn't love him anymore, but then I find you out sauntering in the woods with him, your arm entwined with his. You moaned his name when I kissed you that first time. What do I believe, Rachel?"

"You don't know me very well if you think I would sin with another man's husband," she replied, her chest heaving with indignation. "How could you even question what I would do with Ethan? He's married to my friend."

"Because it doesn't matter to men like Ethan if they're married or not. They'll drop their pants for just about any woman who is willing."

"Wade! That's despicable! You obviously don't know Ethan."

"I see him with you. I see him with Becky. He's a blatant skirt chaser, Rachel. Or in your starry-eyed puppy love, have you failed to notice?"

"Puppy love! I love Ethan as a brother. Nothing more!"

"Open your eyes, Rachel. The man likes women. He undresses them with his eyes. He stands so close he's almost touching them," Wade said as he pushed his hat back off his face.

"You're being ridiculous. Ethan's no different from any other man. You're assuming he thinks like you."

"Honey, I don't just look. If I see something I want, I go after it. But I'm not married."

"Thank God."

"What does that make you?"

Rachel glared at him. "Our marriage is only pretend!"

"If Ethan is so wonderful, why didn't you marry him when you had the chance?" Wade asked.

"I told you, my father sent him away. My mother had just died, and he needed me to help him run his church and orphanage."

"If you'd loved Ethan, it wouldn't have mattered. You'd have married him anyway."

"I was young. Papa needed me."

Wade took a deep breath and clicked to the oxen. "But those feelings are still there, aren't they, Rachel?"

Rachel clenched her fists. "You stubborn man, I told you the other night I didn't love him. Nothing has changed today!"

"But that was before I caught you stargazing with him."

She took a steadying breath before she replied, "I don't love him, Wade. We were talking about my father."

The wagon rumbled along in silence. He'd believed her the night of the dance when she said she didn't love Ethan anymore. Maybe stars had gotten into his own eyes that night, blinding him to her infatuation with the other man. Still, seeing her with Ethan had made the pointed toes of his boots curl and his fists clench.

"You know, if it'd been Becky out strolling in the dark with that rascal, I wouldn't have been surprised. But when I saw the two of you – Hell, Rachel, I know we're not really married, but you've got to at least act like my wife."

Rachel started to laugh. "When have you ever been concerned about how things looked to other people, Wade Ketchum? You come home drunk and singing at the top of your lungs in the wee hours of the morning and expect me to believe you're concerned about appearances?"

"Well, you're supposed to be my wife. Decent women don't go walking with men who aren't their husbands after dark."

Rachel's chuckles filled the air. "For once in your life, be honest. Tell me what's really bothering you. Admit that you're jealous of Ethan and the attention he receives."

"Is that what you think?" Wade demanded, yet he inwardly cringed. He wasn't jealous, but damn, the sight of Ethan and Rachel strolling alone in the moonlight had twisted his insides into one big knot.

Rachel chuckled. "Well, you're certainly acting jealous."

Wade pulled on the reins. The oxen bellowed at the abrupt tightening of the harness around them. The wagon creaked and groaned until it came to a stop.

Reaching down, he set the brake, and then tied the reins around the handle. He glanced into Rachel's challenging eyes and felt himself drawn into their depths. With lightning speed, he hauled her into his arms, and onto his lap.

"Why in the hell would I be jealous of a scrawny preacher man?" he asked in a deep, gruff voice.

"I don't know. Why don't you tell me?" she said, flustered, her tone taunting.

With a muffled curse, he crushed her lips with a punishing kiss. Instantly, a sizzle of heat spread throughout his body, replacing the urge to hurt with a burning inferno designed to give pleasure.

She tasted of honeyed sweetness and innocence, and he knew one quick taste would not be enough. He wanted to pull her into the back of the wagon and show her how a man could make a woman feel. He wanted to be the man she dreamed about. He wanted to hear her whisper his name.

With a flourish he pushed back her bonnet until he found the pins that held her finely-textured tresses. With practiced ease, he undid the topknot, releasing her hair in glorious waves. With a whisper, the pins fell to the floor of the wagon.

Reluctantly, he released her lips and slowly raised his head, his fingers still threaded through her hair. Their eyes met and clashed.

Her breathing was fast and shallow, her pupils dilated with passion. "Are you trying to brand me with your kiss, so everyone will believe I'm your wife?" she whispered.

Wade felt a clutch at his heart. Why? This woman was strictly off limits. If he wasn't careful she was going to tie a permanent marriage knot around him.

"You're not, my wife."

The flames of desire burning from her eyes quenched. She pushed at his chest until he released her. Plucking the pins from the floor, she had her hair back in place with two quick twists.

Finally she turned to look at him. "You're right. I'm not your wife. Don't forget it again, Mr. Ketchum."

With an irritated growl, Wade untied the reins and released the brake. He didn't know what he wanted anymore. Part of him wanted Rachel, part of him said he was a fool. He called to the oxen, and with a gentle lurch the wagon took off.

~

The last week had been torture. They had made it beyond Devil's Gate, Split Rock, the Ice Slough, and they had crossed the South Pass over the Continental Divide.

Wade had dreaded the crossing, expecting a narrow gorge at a high, mountainous crest, but the pass had turned out to be a grassy valley. The emigrants had never known when they'd passed from the east to the west of the Divide, the crossing unspectacular with its flat meadows. Tonight, for the first time, they camped on the west side, closer than ever to Oregon.

Wade rode around the livestock and horses, checking on them before settling down for the night. He'd spent as little time as possible in his own camp in the last week. Rachel had been polite yet distant when they saw one another.

Maybe it was best this way. He could only be who he was, and that would never be good enough for Rachel.

Now, if only he could convince his body this attraction was impossible, he would be okay.

Deep inside, Rachel hid her desire from the rest of the world. Just once he wanted to unlock that desire, revel in its intensity. Then this temptation he thought of night and day would be satisfied, and he could go on his way.

Riding into camp, Wade watched Toby chase baby Daniel back to his pallet. Rachel was busy tending the fire, cooking the evening meal. Grace played with her dolls.

Frowning, Wade halted Sadie in front of Toby and swung his leg over the saddle, sliding down to the ground.

"Where's Becky?" Wade asked.

"Uh...I don't know," Toby stammered.

Something in Toby's voice drew Wade's attention.

"Isn't she supposed to be watching the younger kids, not you?" Waded asked.

"Yes, sir."

"Did she say where she was going?" Wade questioned, unsure if he really wanted to know where the silly girl was.

"No, sir." Toby ducked his head.

Wade glanced around the camp. Other families were bustling about their own campsites, busily preparing their meals. He saw no sign of Becky.

Toby shuffled his feet in the dust, obviously uneasy.

"I'm going to look for her," Wade said, annoyed. "If you see her, tell her to stay put until I get back."

As he walked through the camp, his feet automatically carried him toward Ethan and Mary's site. Three wagons down, he found Mary sitting alone by the fire. "Good evening."

"Hello, Wade. You haven't seen that husband of mine, have you?"

A trickle of unease scurried down Wade's spine.

"No, ma'am. I'm sure he's around. If I see him, I'll tell him you're looking for him," he said, feeling a new sense of urgency. If he found Ethan, he would remind the man of his wife.

"Thank you, Wade. Supper is ready, and I hate to eat without him. He comes in later each day," Mary said as she stirred a pot of stew over the fire, her face shadowed with anguish.

"He probably rode out farther than he intended. It seems the game has been further off the trail in the last few days." Wade tried to reassure her, though his disturbing suspicions appeared more accurate all the time.

"Yes. That's what Ethan said. If you find him, I'll be down at your camp, visiting Rachel," Mary said.

"Don't worry, I'm sure he'll be here soon."

Wade's treacherous thoughts spurred him on. With the entire camp area examined, he stalked off into the early twilight. Except for a small knoll in the distance, the prairie was flat and open, with no place to hide. Long shadows fell across the land as the sun slowly disappeared.

Wearily, Wade strolled toward the hill, his boots sinking in the sandy soil. When he reached the mound, he climbed to the top to gaze across the prairie in the dusk, hoping to spot one lone rider and not two.

Instead, he found Ethan and Becky tucked in a cleft on the side of the hill a blanket spread beneath them. They lay entwined in one another's arms, their clothes in total disarray.

The sight burned into his vision, all but blinding him with fury.

Wade cursed and, in two long strides, attained their sides. Before either one could react, he reached down and yanked Ethan off of Becky.

"Well, if isn't Preacher Beauchamp and Miss Cooke," he said as he released Ethan with a shove, sending the minister sprawling onto the rocky hillside on his bare buttocks, his pants hanging around his ankles.

Becky pulled her clothing over her nakedness, her cornflower blue eyes wide with fright.

"Ketchum!" Ethan gasped as he gingerly picked himself up, pulling up his trousers. "What – are you doing here?"

"Looking for Miss Cooke," Wade replied. "And searching for Mr. Beauchamp. Whose wife is waiting."

"Well, you found both of us," Ethan said, obviously annoyed.

"So, I did."

Wade dismissed Ethan. The man was not worth his time. He would like to turn a blind eye with Becky, but she was Rachel's sister. "You're supposed to be watching the children."

"I'm an adult. I don't have to answer to you," Becky snapped. Her dress was re-buttoned, her skirts back in place.

"You call this acting like an adult? Sneaking off, sleeping with another woman's husband. What about

Rachel? I'm sure you've managed to keep this little secret from her," he growled.

Becky glanced at Ethan for support, but he was busy saddling his horse.

"Of course she doesn't know," Becky replied defensively. "And I don't need you to run back and tell her."

"Why shouldn't I? Why shouldn't I tell Mary?" Wade asked.

"No one would believe you, including my wife," Ethan challenged.

Becky smiled wickedly. "It will be your word against ours. And who's going to believe a two-bit gambler."

"Leave it be, Becky. I'll take care of this," Ethan called from the shadows.

He tightened the cinch on his horse and finished loading the blanket. Wade watched as he walked over to Becky. In the last five minutes, he'd undergone a subtle change from annoyance to self-confidence.

"Go back to camp, Becky. I'll handle this situation with Wade," he said, dismissing Becky with a frown.

The look she gave Ethan before she finally stalked away, leaving the two men alone, should have singed his blonde curls.

The grin on Ethan's face left an evil twist around his lips. "Before you decide to tell my wife about me and Becky, I think there's something you should know." He paused, his eyes twinkling wickedly in the twilight. "I know about you and Rachel."

Wade kept his face expressionless while inside he burned. Rachel must have confided in this sermonizer who spouted religion and brandished deceit. "What about us?"

"Rachel told me about your marriage," he grinned, "or rather your pretend marriage."

Trying to remain indifferent, but itching to put his fist through Ethan's face, Wade shrugged his shoulders. "So?"

"Frank would find this tidbit of gossip rather interesting."

"Tell him," Wade said nonchalantly.

"He could force you to marry Rachel, leave you along the trail or let you continue as you are – but shunned by everyone." Ethan paused, obviously delighted with his information. "Everyone would assume the worst regarding dearest Rachel. She would be the one hurt by the ugly gossip. Not you."

Wade smiled menacingly. "My guess is you're going to tell me that if I don't keep my mouth shut about you and Becky, you'll tell everyone about Rachel and me?"

"That about sums it up," Ethan declared triumphantly. "It would cause quite a stir."

Wade spit on the ground. What a choice! Let Rachel suffer the embarrassment of a ruined reputation, or keep quiet about Becky and Ethan. The options rankled him.

He wasn't afraid of Ethan threats, but Rachel's reputation would be in shambles. No one would believe they'd never known each other intimately.

"I'm not going to say anything. Not to protect either one of you and not because of your threat. But if you hurt Rachel..." Wade glared at Ethan. "You won't have to worry about cheating on Mary anymore. I'll sharpen my knife on your face; then I'll pretend it's springtime and we're castrating the bulls. You get my drift?"

~

How could life get so complicated, Wade wondered.

When he arrived back at camp, he discovered Rachel and Mary sitting around the fire in the evening twilight, sewing. Rachel was working on a sampler, while Mary sat beside her, putting the finishing touches to a shirt for Ethan.

He watched from the shadows as they talked, their heads bent low over their needlework, laughing at something Mary said. How would the news of Ethan's affair affect their friendship?

"Good evening, ladies," he said, startling them from their sewing.

"Good evening," they murmured.

"Did you find that misplaced husband of mine?" Mary asked.

"No," Wade lied. "But I bet he'll be along shortly."

Mary sighed. "Lately, he's gone more and more. I'll be glad when we reach Oregon City and settle down to a normal life."

"I'll be glad when we can get back to normal meals," Rachel groaned. "I'm tired of beans and bacon. Speaking of which, I left some beans on the fire for you, Wade."

Mary turned and asked, "You look tired, Wade. Are you as tired of the trail and ready to reach our destination as we are?"

How could he respond? Yes, he was ready to reach Oregon, to leave behind the problems of Becky and Ethan, the sight of Mary's anxious face. But part of him didn't want to reach their destination. Part of him didn't want to leave Rachel. The realization rocked him back on his heels.

He took a seat before he answered, "Yes, I'll be glad."

"I wish you all were going to Oregon City with Ethan and me. It would be wonderful to start our new life together."

Wade sat silently, eating from his plate. He couldn't help but think, when hell freezes over.

"Do you and Ethan have to go Oregon City?" Rachel asked. "Why couldn't he teach in The Dalles?"

"He has a job waiting for him," Mary replied, her disappointment visible in the firelight.

"He might find a teaching or preaching position in The Dalles," Rachel said wistfully. "The position my father was going to take is now available."

"When he comes in tonight, I'll talk to him," Mary said, her voice full of hopes and dreams.

Becky walked into the circle of firelight, her face cold and sullen. Rachel glanced up, "Where have you been? I've been worried about you."

"Mrs. Simpson's baby is due any day now, so I helped them set up their tent," Becky replied, her eyes searching Wade's.

With a disgusted snort, Wade threw his half-eaten food into the fire. "I'm sure Mrs. Simpson appreciated your help," he said, sarcasm dripping from his voice.

Becky shot Wade a smirk. "Yes, she did."

Ethan strolled into camp, a confident bounce in his step. Mary jumped up from her chair, throwing aside the shirt she was hemming the worry lines around her face easing. "You're back. I was getting anxious."

Wrapping his arms around his wife, Ethan glanced at Wade, his eyes gloating. It was all Wade could do to keep from jumping up and throttling the man.

"I didn't mean to be gone so long, but I'm home now," Ethan said, enveloping his wife in a reassuring hug.

Becky watched the couple a scowl on her beautiful face. As Mary stroked her husband's cheek, Becky's expression turned icy, hatred shimmering in the sapphire depths of her eyes.

"Where were you, Ethan?" Rachel asked, her eyes questioning.

"Trying to locate some stray cattle." He sighed and sent Wade a measuring glance. "Maybe I'll have better luck tomorrow."

Wade couldn't help but wonder how Becky liked being referred to as a stray cow, and couldn't resist saying, "I didn't know we were missing any cattle?"

"Frank lost ten head yesterday. I volunteered to help him find them," Ethan replied.

If Frank had indeed lost cattle, Wade hoped he'd found them, but if this was a lie, he wished it would blow up in Ethan's face.

Apparently unaware of the challenge flowing between the two men, Rachel said, "Ethan, we were just talking about how nice it would be if we were all together in one city. You could replace my father at the church in The Dalles."

"I may consider that proposal," Ethan said as he glanced toward Wade, with a smirk on his face. "Right now, all I want to think about is a nice warm bed. Come on Mary. Let's go home."

Mary picked up her sewing. "See you tomorrow."

"Good night," Rachel replied.

Wade felt the urge to reprimand Rachel. How could she consider inviting the man without first consulting him? Then again, he would no longer be her husband in The Dalles. She would no longer be his concern.

He would disappear, Rachel would tell everyone he'd been killed in a mining accident and Ethan's threats would no longer apply. Or would they?

God, what had they done? What a web of lies they'd devised, ensnaring themselves without realizing the consequences to their lives. What should he do now?

～

Thunder echoed through the mountains, its rumble fading in the distance. Lightning traced wicked paths to the ground, and the air smelled of rain. The animals moved restlessly, stomping on the earth and snorting.

Unable to sleep, Wade watched the storm move across the western sky. The animals were secure, or at least as protected as possible, and the tent was tied down tightly, the children asleep.

He struck a match to light the last of his cheroot. For the second time in a week, he savored several puffs off his last cigar. It was going to be a long, wet night, so he might as well enjoy himself before the storm began.

"Wade, something's on fire," Rachel said as she hurried around the wagon, her wrapper, tied securely around her waist.

Leaning back against the wagon, Wade looked down at her. He drew a deeply on his cigar and blew the smoke away from her.

"Oh, you're smoking that..."

"Cigar, cheroot or cigarette," he supplied coolly. The breeze lifted a corner of her wrapper exposing her night rail beneath, twisting tendrils of silky brown hair around her face.

"Whatever. It smells disgusting," Rachel announced.

"I really don't care. It's about to rain, and I'm not going to let a good cigar go to waste, so I'm finishing it off."

Rachel glanced up at the sky. Her manner changed abruptly to one of concern. "Are the children going to be okay, sleeping in the tent?"

"I've already checked. The ties are secure. Unless we have a real blower, they should be fine."

With a worried frown, she strode over to the tent to listen for the children. "They're asleep."

Wade took a deep drag on the cigar and almost choked when she turned around to face him. The glow of the fire shone through her wrapper, hiding nothing from his overactive imagination as she walked toward him.

He nodded, trying to still his rapidly beating heart and the throb between his legs. "So why are you still awake?"

"I couldn't sleep. The wagon seemed stuffy," she admitted. A big clap of thunder sent her flying to Wade's side. He tossed his cigar into the fire and opened his arms automatically, enfolding her in his embrace.

She glanced up at him, her hazel eyes pleading. "I'm sorry. I've never liked thunderstorms. They frighten me."

"Storms aren't so bad once you understand them," he said, holding her shivering body against his. "My sister, Sarah, used to scream and cry during storms until I explained to her that God was watering his garden, and every time it thundered, he'd turned over his potato wagon."

Rachel smiled. "How did you explain the lightening?"

"I told her he needed the lightening to see the earth."

"What a silly tale to tell a child," Rachel admonished, but she didn't move from his arms.

He hadn't meant to tell her, but whenever he was with Rachel, his guard crumbled. Wade shrugged. "Well, at least while I was telling her a story, she wasn't crying."

"I'd like to meet your sister some time," she said.

Wade sighed. "I'd like for you to meet her to, but that's not possible."

Rachel looked puzzled. "Why?"

Wade couldn't say the words. Even after all these years it was much too complicated, and he didn't want to explain to Rachel what had happened to Sarah.

Instead, he placed his hands on her shoulders. His gaze grazed her breasts, sending a shiver of desire through him. "I think it's time you crawled back inside that wagon. It's going to start pouring any moment now."

Rachel looked perplexed. "What are you going to do?"

He could see the confusion in her eyes and knew she was wondering why he hadn't answered her question. But for now, the bewilderment would have to remain. Talking about Sarah and Michael would bring up more questions, more speculation about his family life, and he didn't need that tonight. He didn't want to tell her things he'd kept sheltered from himself and others too long.

"I'll stay out here and try to keep the horses calm. Hopefully, I'll manage to keep dry under the wagon," he said, watching her lower lip, wanting to run his tongue across the smooth texture.

She tilted her head to the side as she glanced up at him. "Wade Ketchum, if that storm comes like I think it's going to, there won't be a dry spot left under this wagon. You'll catch your death of a cold if you stay outside tonight."

Wade grinned. How would she react if he told her there would be no sleep if he stayed beside her in the wagon tonight? How would the proper miss respond when he told her he was hard enough to split his pants?

"That's twice you've expressed concern about my well-being. If I didn't know better, I'd think you were beginning to like me."

She stiffened in his arms, and instinctively Wade knew if there was enough light, he would see a blush staining her cheeks.

"Of course I like you, Wade. I just don't always agree with what you do," Rachel said, annoyance filling her voice. "Like drinking, cursing—"

Wade put his mouth to hers, effectively shutting her up. But the trick backfired on him when she wrapped her arms around him and pulled him deeper into the kiss.

For a moment, he was stunned at her response. But then he eagerly deepened the kiss, pulling her against his rigid manhood. She moaned, and he traced the edge of her lips with his tongue as he suckled her mouth in a craving gesture, wanting to absorb her into his body like a man dying of thirst.

And surely he was dying as she returned his kiss, shocking him as he consumed her lips, not wanting to think about the consequences of his actions or what tomorrow would bring.

Her skin felt like silk as he held her face, refusing to let her go. Lightning flashed around them. Thunder rumbled closer. The wind whipped Rachel's wrapper around their legs, entwining it about him like a lover.

Sprinkles of rain began to pelt them softly. Wade moved his hands down her back and across her buttocks, pressing her ever closer, wanting to rip away the nightgown that acted as a barrier to his touch. He wanted to feel every naked inch of her. He wanted to gaze upon her flesh.

They kissed for minutes, but it seemed like hours, trying to express with their bodies what neither could say with words. With a thundering roar, the rain came pounding its vengeance, cooling their embrace, but not his desire. It was a wonder the raindrops didn't sizzle off his skin.

Reluctantly, Wade let Rachel go. When he opened his eyes to gaze into hers, he saw fear and bewilderment and didn't know if the thunderstorm or his kiss had caused her apprehension.

With a tug, he pulled her toward the back of the wagon. "Come on. You're getting soaked."

Water ran down her face, her neck, and when his eyes wandered lower, he gasped. The wrapper clung to Rachel's body like a wet sheet, showing off each tempting curve she tried so hard to hide. The sight was like a blow to his midsection, leaving him aching.

At the back of the wagon, he turned her to face him. His gaze took in her full breasts and small waist. Her nipples stood out against the soaked fabric, taunting him.

"Get in out of the rain," he commanded.

She frowned. "What about you?"

"I'll be okay. You're soaked. Get in."

Her hazel eyes were dark with worry, and she raised her mouth to his. He moaned like a man drowning and tasted her wet lips, licking away the rainwater that streamed over both of them. He knew without a doubt that if he didn't break off the kiss now, he never would.

Reluctantly, he broke away. He reached down and in one motion, lifted Rachel into the wagon. Then he turned and walked away, knowing if he looked back and saw her face, there would be no turning back.

Chapter Eleven

The noise of people stirring outside woke Rachel, though the inside of the wagon remained dark. She stretched and yawned, the chill of the morning air caressing her arms, sending her scurrying back under the covers. The mountain nights were cold, and she wondered how Wade had faired beneath the wagon in last night's storm.

Memories of the previous evening assailed her, leaving her shaken. She'd kissed him. Reached up and planted her lips on his like some wanton hussy clamoring for his attention. But she had no feelings of shame this morning, only a sweet yearning.

When he'd kissed her back, she'd wrapped her arms around him, hungrily accepting his embrace. Although the rain had dampened their ardor, the longing had persisted, leaving her wanting and reeling with passionate intensity. How much longer could she fight this temptation? How much longer could she pretend to be his wife and not allow herself the intimacies of marriage?

The mention of Wade's name made her skin tingle with anticipation, with reckless abandon. She wanted Wade to do more than kiss her, to do more than touch her. She wanted him the way Eve had wanted Adam, the way Rebecca had wanted Isaac.

Yet fear held her back. Just as Wade was holding back. She could feel it, could see it in his eyes. He was afraid of any lasting commitment and the apprehension had something to do with his childhood.

But what could have happened to cause him to dam up his emotions behind a barrier?

For her to understand Wade, she had to know all of him. Because, when he left, she wanted no regrets, no doubts about the kind of man who had broken her heart. And he would leave her. Her time with Wade was but a brief trip across the country, just long enough to find out he filled some need she hadn't even known existed. Just long enough to fill her hollows and make her realize what she was missing.

Rachel sighed. She'd left Tennessee believing she was a self-sufficient woman. With the subsequent death of her father, every day on the trail made her realize how dependent she really was on her fellow travelers. How much she needed a strong man beside her. How much she wanted that man to be Wade.

The girl who'd left Tennessee had been filled with dreams of a different life. The woman who traveled the trail had endured great hardships and losses, and now prayed she'd reach its conclusion without further heartache.

But she would have to be on guard against falling in love with Wade because he would break her heart into little pieces and leave her behind to put it back together without him.

The thought chilled her deeper than the early morning cold.

Though the sun was only a thought in the eastern sky, she jumped out of bed and hurriedly dressed.

As Rachel crawled out of the wagon, the sight that met her eyes left her gasping. Wade stood before a mirror hung on the side of their wagon, wearing nothing but his pants in the cool morning air. With long slow strokes, he scrapped the whiskers from his soap-lathered face. The muscles in his back flexed with each movement of his hand, creating a ripple of his naked, bronze flesh.

Her breathing quickened, and her knees turned to mush as she gazed with longing at his muscular profile. The smooth texture of his skin made her want to trace each muscle with the tip of her finger, to touch her lips to the back of his neck. Rachel shook her head, trying to clear her wicked thoughts. Why did he always affect her this way?

Hurriedly, she brushed past him, picking up her milking stool and pail as she scurried off to the livestock.

"Good morning, Rachel." he called. "Sleep well?"

"Like a lamb," she said as she walked away quickly, afraid her face would reveal the dreams that had plagued her all night long, dreams of Wade naked in her arms.

The cow they'd picked up along the way greeted her with a long moo of welcome. The poor animal was thin from the weary days on the trail. Rachel quickly milked her, relieving her swollen udder. Steam rose from the warm milk, tantalizing Rachel with its smell.

Finished with her task, she hastened back to the wagon to begin breakfast, the dew-dampened grass moistening the hem of her dress. As she stepped around the side of the wagon, Wade's arms reached out to encircle her, surprising her so she almost dropped the pail of milk.

"Is this how a milkmaid looks early in the morning?" he asked, teasing, as he planted kisses along the nape of her neck, sending delicious tingles down her spine. God, in her dreams his lips had followed the same path. And her body had responded in much the same way, as if aching to get closer to him.

Pushing back with her free hand, Rachel glanced up at the forest green eyes dancing with merriment. She felt awkward in his arms, frightened not of Wade, but of herself.

"Wade, someone might see," she protested.

"What will they see?" he questioned, his voice low and seductive. "My arms around my wife? Me kissing her good morning?" he added as his lips lowered onto hers.

Rachel felt the familiar curl of some unknown feeling in the pit of her stomach. Her stiff body relaxed and softened in his arms. His lips gently coaxed hers until she longed for this feeling to last forever. She yearned to forget about the dangers of the trail ahead, to forget about the children. To allow her desire to take root and grow within her until she reached some unknown destination yet to be explored.

Wade ended the kiss and gazed down at Rachel, his eyes smoldering in the morning light. She didn't know what to do. In the moonlight, and even last night in the rain when he'd kissed her, she hadn't felt clumsy, unsure.

But now, in the dawning sunlight, she felt awkward, uncertain how to face Wade and accept the fact that no matter how much she fought him, being in his arms felt right. No matter what happened, she wanted him to kiss her.

The feelings were too new to be shared with anyone, particularly Wade, and Rachel did the only thing she knew how to do. She pulled away and fled. "Excuse me. I must get breakfast started."

~

The small group of people gathered in a semicircle while Ethan read a verse from the Bible and said a quick prayer over the grave of Mrs. Perkins. An ordinary cold that would normally have ended with a week of bed rest had lingered on, draining her strength until, sometime during the night she had succumbed to the Grim Reaper.

Rachel couldn't help but think of her father. The woman's death was the first since she and Wade had joined this wagon train, and it cast a pall of fear and depression over the group.

As soon as the last spade of dirt was turned, the wagons began to roll over the grave hoping to erase its presence from Indians and animals. Rachel urged the oxen over the mound of dirt, helping to pack the earth down, yet feeling disrespectful for driving over the poor woman's grave, even knowing it was for the best.

Toby and Grace skipped beside the wagon. Becky walked with Emily, her friend. The young woman was a pleasure to be with and Rachel could only hope her presence would somehow influence Becky. Mary rode beside Rachel, watching Daniel as he slept on a quilt.

"How can he sleep with this wagon jostling so much?" Mary asked as she grabbed the side of the wagon to keep from being pitched out. "I'd give my right arm to sleep through the night like that."

Rachel glanced at Mary. Dark shadows circled her cornflower-hued eyes, giving her the appearance of a blue-eyed owl. "You're not sleeping through the night?"

Mary looked away and shrugged. "No. After all the work I do around camp every night, plus driving the team most days, you'd think I'd sleep like a bear in winter. But I keep waking up in the middle of the night, anxious and worried."

"About what?"

"I don't know. Sometimes I think my fears are silly. But then the doubts start in and..." Mary bit the inside of her lip, then whispered. "Ethan comes back to camp late each night, and sometimes disappears in the middle of the night."

"What for?" Rachel asked. "Is he checking on the livestock or taking the late watch?"

"I don't know," Mary replied.

Rachel glanced at her friend and for the first time noticed the lines of strain and worry evident around her eyes and lips.

"Have you asked him what he's doing?" Rachel queried.

"He shrugs his shoulders and tells me not to worry. Which, of course, makes me worry more."

"Oh dear. No wonder you look exhausted."

Mary turned to face Rachel. "It's more than just his disappearing at night. Marriage is so...difficult. Ethan is not the man I thought he was."

Rachel stared out at the rolling prairie before them. Ethan had not turned out to be the man she'd thought him, either.

"I'm sure he loves you. He's probably taking over watch for one of the other men and doesn't want anyone to know."

"No. It's more than that. I don't think my husband loves me. I've watched you and Wade. Ethan and I never cared for each other that way. He never looked at me the way Wade looks at you."

Rachel glanced at Mary to see if she had stars in her eyes. What was the woman referring to? Had she and Wade played at being married so long that not only had they convinced everyone they met, but they were beginning to convince one another?

"Mary, sometimes things are not as they appear."

"Huh! Your husband gazes at you constantly as if he'd like to carry you off to your wagon, away from prying eyes."

Blood rushed to Rachel's face. "That's ridiculous." But Rachel couldn't help but wonder if Wade really looked at her like that.

"How do you keep the fire in that man's eyes?" Mary asked; then she quickly said, "Of course, you've only been married a short time."

"Ethan looks at you the same way," Rachel replied, anxious to get off the subject of herself and Wade.

Mary laughed, the high sound almost hysterical. The noise died away and a sob escaped her.

Rachel reached out and touched the sleeve of Mary's dress. "Are you all right?"

The woman's eyes filled with tears, though she tried valiantly to restrain them. "I don't know. You say that Ethan looks at me with love in his eyes, and he tells me he loves me, yet something is wrong." Mary ducked her head, wringing her hands in her lap. "I think there's another woman."

"Mary!" Rachel gasped. Wade's voice haunted her memory, reminding her of their conversation regarding Becky.

Becky, wouldn't would she?

"I'm sorry, I must be exhausted to say such a thing," Mary said, wiping away her tears. "The heat and the dust are wearing me down, for me to have such awful thoughts. Please forgive me, Rachel, for saying anything. I should have kept my crazy illusions to myself."

Rachel reached out and squeezed Mary's hand. "There's nothing to forgive. You're my friend. The men are just as worn out as we are. Things will be better once we arrive in Oregon." Fear gripped her tighter than her hands clenched the reins.

Becky wouldn't sleep with a married man. Would she?

~

A thousand stars lit the evening sky, their brightness shining across the darkness. Most people had already bedded down for the night, but Rachel was anxious. The conversation with Mary earlier in the day stayed fresh in her mind.

Everyone was safely accounted for. Everyone but Becky.

Wade took the first watch. Grace and Toby were already in bed, worn out from the long day.

Mary had taken Daniel into her wagon for the night. Taking care of a baby would keep her mind occupied.

A coyote howled in the darkness, the sound frighteningly lonely.

Since the wagon trail had stopped for the evening, Becky hadn't returned. She'd spent the afternoon walking with some of the other women, but tonight Rachel had searched the camp, unable to locate her sister.

Her mind refused to contemplate where Becky might be – and with whom. Finally, as the moon climbed toward its highest point, Becky came strolling into camp as if she were returning from a social. She hummed a perky tune under her breath as she skipped along, unaware that Rachel sat there, waiting.

When she saw her sister, the song on her lips suddenly died, the skip in her step slowed.

"Why are you still up?" she asked cautiously.

Rachel said calmly, "I was worried about you."

Becky laughed. "Didn't I tell you? The Simpsons wanted me to have supper with them tonight?"

The lie slipped so easily off Becky's tongue that, for a moment, Rachel was stunned. "No. You didn't."

Shrugging, her sister said, "I told Toby. He was supposed to tell you. That boy never can remember anything."

Rachel couldn't help but test to see just how far the girl would go. "It's kind of late for you to have stayed at their wagon."

She'd passed the Simpsons' wagon several times during the evening with no sign of Becky. Her sister was lying and Rachel knew it.

"Afterwards, we sat and talked around the fire. They really are a very friendly couple. When they reach Oregon, they're going to start a farm."

"How nice," Rachel said dryly. "You seem to be out quite a bit lately. I'm glad to see you're making friends."

"It's still not like back home. But a girl has to do something for entertainment."

"I hope your entertainment would not cause anyone harm, Becky."

"I don't know what you're talking about." Becky sounded defensive.

"I know you weren't with the Simpsons tonight. I went to their wagon. You weren't there."

Becky rolled her eyes at her sister. "You worry about every little thing, Rachel," she replied nervously. "You can put your suspicions to rest. Emily and I went for a walk."

Rachel enjoyed a sense of relief before the doubts begin to set in. The answer was much too simple. Still, it was possible the girls had gone for a stroll. And at least by being with Emily, she hadn't been with Ethan. She had to believe Becky.

"I knew you had a sensible answer. Just be careful. I worry about you."

"Don't. I can take care of myself," Becky replied and turned her back on Rachel and sashayed to the tent.

～

Several busy days passed and Rachel saw very little of Mary. The trail had once again become extremely difficult, the roads mountainous and rocky as they crossed through an area known as Idaho. Rachel had taken over driving the wagon full-time wary of Becky's driving abilities on this tumultuous section of the trail.

Wade had offered to drive, but she'd refused, knowing he was busy scouting ahead with Frank and checking on the stock. Toby and Grace walked beside the wagon, while Becky watched over them.

And Rachel watched over Becky.

The last two nights had found Becky sitting around the fire with Rachel and the children. Rachel hoped her talk with Becky had put an end to her sister's suspicious activities.

A cool breeze ruffled Rachel's bonnet as she headed the oxen in a northwesterly direction. As August rolled into September, the mountain air was beginning to get cooler, the nights colder.

Wade came galloping up on Sadie, dust flying from the horse's hooves. The man made riding a horse look like a work of art. Something about his graceful movements that set Rachel's blood afire, her pulse pounding and her heart skipping into next week.

"We're about to climb a pretty good incline. Why don't you let me drive?"

Rachel turned to Wade. "Is it steeper than we've gone up before?

"No, but the trail is rocky with worn wagon tracks going up the side of the mountain. I think it would be safer if I drove," he replied.

With a stubborn shake of her head, Rachel replied, "Take care of the stock. I'm just fine."

Frank whistled at Wade, motioning he needed help. "You're sure you'll be all right?"

"I'm quite capable of driving this wagon. Now go away. If I need you, I'll call."

"All right, but I'll be back to help you up the steepest part of the mountain."

She turned her attention back to the trail and noticed for the first time just how steep the trail was becoming. For a moment, a shot of fear ran through her, and she doubted her ability. But there was no turning back, no quitting now. If she stopped to find Wade, the whole train would bog down, and she could already hear his I told you so.

Still, the wagon in front of her had slowed to almost a crawl, its body shaking as it proceeded up the side of the mountain.

As the incline increased, the speed of the oxen decreased, their necks bulging under the strain of the heavy load. Grace and Toby walked along either side of the wagon, pointing out the best way up the mountain.

With a creak and an occasional sliding sound, the pull of gravity shifted the packed boxes inside the wagon. No matter how many times she checked their cargo, something always seemed to come loose during the day.

Toby called out to her, "Rachel, watch out! There's a boulder two feet to your left."

Rachel pulled hard on the reins trying to make the sluggish oxen turn to the right. They moved with the speed of a tortoise and turning them was like changing the direction of mud. Her timing was off a bit and the front left wheel scraped the side of the huge rock, causing the wagon to shudder.

Her heart pounded. That had been a close call; the rock might have tipped them over. She slapped the reins across the oxen's back, trying to urge them on as they slowed even further. It seemed cruel to use the whip on them, but she couldn't allow them to stop. Stopping on an incline was much too dangerous.

For just a brief second, she wished she had let Wade drive. Glancing back, she spotted him down at the bottom of the sloop, talking to Mary. At that precise moment, she heard the loud snap of the rope.

She jerked around in her seat and saw the organ tied to the inside corner of the wagon, sway. One of the two ropes lay loose, hanging. Only the second rope kept the heavy instrument from falling out the back.

Without thinking, Rachel pulled on the reins, stopping the oxen. Her mother's organ was at stake.

Toby called out, "Rachel, keep going. You can't stop."

She pulled on the brake and wrapped the reins around the handle, preparing to alight.

"The organ is about to fall out. I have to fix it," she called.

With a groan, the brakes started to give way and the wagon started to slide backward. The oxen grumbled in fear, straining on their yoke.

Rachel grabbed the reins. Her heart pounded fiercely in her chest. She wanted to jump out of the wagon and tie the organ back up, but was afraid to move for fear the wagon would roll again. And once it started its backward flight, it would never stop.

Wade's frantic yell broke through her panicked thoughts.

"Rachel, get those oxen moving."

His horse came galloping up beside them. She glanced at him with indecision. If she moved, the organ would surely fall. If she didn't move, the wagon would slide back down the mountain.

Wade made her decision. He reached over and whacked the backs of the oxen. "Get a move on!"

Rachel released the brake and popped the reins at the oxen, praying the rope would hold. The wagon slowly started forward.

The second snap sent chills through her. She glanced quickly behind her. The organ swayed and rocked at the back of the wagon like an old man. At this angle, it wouldn't be long before the beautifully polished instrument toppled out.

"Dammit, Rachel, keep your eyes on the trail!" Wade yelled, his voice harsh and stern.

"My mother's organ!" she cried.

He glanced behind her. "Keep moving. Don't stop. Don't look back."

"But the organ is going to fall out."

"Keep moving!"

"But—"

The wagon gave a sudden lurch, as if belching. Rachel jerked her head around.

The organ crashed to the hard dirt falling end over end as the thud of splintering wood wrenched her heart. The pipes reverberated with a painful clang that seemed to echo in the still mountain air. The organ splintered, shredding into a thousand pieces, as it came to rest against a rock.

As the dust settled, Rachel could see that nothing remained but kindling. The ground was littered with splintered wood and ivory. Her heart felt as shattered as the once beautiful organ. Rivulets of tears ran down her face while the oxen suddenly picked up speed, plodding upward.

Reaching the top of the mountain, Rachel pulled the wagon to a halt. She put her face in her hands and sobbed. Why had this journey cost her everything? Her father, his Bibles, and now her dearest possession, her mother's organ. A few doilies and linens were the only other things left of her mother.

Wade rode up and jumped off his horse. "What in the hell were you thinking about, stopping this wagon halfway up that mountain? Were you trying to kill yourself?"

Rachel raised tear-dampened lashes. She wanted to slap him, to inflict some of the pain she was feeling onto his cold heartlessness. She wanted to make him hurt like she was hurting. Instead, she crawled down from the wagon and stood before him.

"My mother's last remaining possession, was about to fall out of the wagon," she replied, her voice tightly controlled.

"Did you think saving it was worth risking your life?"

"Of course. Why else would I have stopped?"

"You damn pigheaded fool. That could be you down there right now, instead of that blasted organ."

"You'll never understand how I feel. What if it had been your mother's, Wade?"

"My mother never would have owned the instrument. And even if she had, she would have been smarter, than to have risked bringing the thing along."

Rachel clinched her fists, not caring who heard her. "I suggest you get back to my wagon Wade and do what you were hired to do. I'm going to ride with Mary."

~

It was early evening, before Wade had the courage to come into camp. It wasn't his fault the organ had fallen from the wagon, but she obviously blamed him for the loss, since he'd refused to let her stop the wagon and be dragged to her death.

He shook his head. The need to see her, check on her one more time to make sure she wasn't hurt, was overwhelming. But he dreaded facing her wrath once again. He'd already forgiven her remark about his job this afternoon. She was grieving and had wanted to hurt him.

But his heart still hadn't recovered from seeing the wagon and her perched perilously on that hill. He'd been so afraid, and yet by some miracle, she'd kept the wagon from rolling back down that mountain.

The depth of his fear for her had stunned him. What if something happened to her? What if she'd been killed? The situation brought back painful memories and the gravity of his feelings shocked him.

He refused to fall in love with Rachel. He refused to care for her. They could never be together, but that determination hadn't helped him today when he'd watched her on that slope. Nothing had stopped the panic that gripped him when the oxen stumbled backward.

Wade tried to shake off the feelings. She was safe, the children were safe, and yet he felt as if a war raged inside him. He'd tried to detach himself from Rachel, but part of him was somehow connected to her heart and refused to let go. And that scared him, for it left him vulnerable to a hurt bigger than these mountains.

He stalked into camp, his emotions raw, his need to see Rachel intense. She was bent over the fire, stirring something in a large pot. The fire reflected the soft planes of her face. She looked tired and withdrawn. The day had been tough on her.

When he spoke, she jumped with fright. "Can I help?"

"No, thank you," she replied, her voice cold as she continued to stir the pot without sparing him a glance.

Frostbite would have been warmer than the reception he received. "Are you all right?"

"I'm fine."

"Do you want me to call the children for supper?"

"No."

Wade sighed. He was getting nowhere. He watched as she started to lift the pot from the fire.

"Let me," he volunteered.

"No!"

He tried to warn her. "Rachel—"

The pot started to slip from the hand that held it with a cloth. She automatically reached out and grabbed it with her free hand before Wade could stop her. She screamed, and the pan dropped with a clank to the ground, spilling the hot stew.

Rachel cried out, cradling the burned hand to her chest.

"Let me see," Wade said as he reached for it.

At first, she resisted, her arm and hand stiff. But Wade refused to be put off and pulled until her hand was in front of him. The burn appeared red and angry. He led her over, to the water barrel and filled a bowl full of cool water. Gently, he placed her hand in the water, leaving her to soak it while he found the box of emergency supplies Rachel kept stored away.

When he came back, he took her hand and carefully patted it dry. Her eyes scorched him as he dipped his fingers into the salve and, with tender strokes, rubbed the medicine onto her wound.

He glanced up to see tears pooled in her fawn-colored eyes.

"Does it hurt bad?"

She sniffed. "No."

"Then why are you crying?"

Her bottom lip trembled as the tears flowed in earnest down her cheeks.

Wade took a clean cloth and wrapped it around her hand, covering the burns. Tying the ends of the bandage, he pulled her onto his lap and kissed away her tears.

His gentleness turned her tears into sobs, and Wade held her in his arms until her weeping changed to little hiccupping sounds.

When the storm subsided, he said, "I'm sorry about your mother's organ. I didn't want it to end up at the bottom of a mountain, smashed to pieces." He paused, his voice intense as he held her closer. "But I was so afraid when I saw you stopped on the side of that hill. I was afraid you would end up where the organ eventually landed."

Rachel sniffled. "You've always wanted to get rid of the organ."

"But not this way."

"It's just...it was my mother's most cherished possession."

"I know how much it meant to you, and I'm sorry to see it's gone. But hasn't this trip taught you that possessions are not important? What's important are the memories you have here." He pointed to her head. "And the feelings you have here." He pointed to her heart.

"I know you're right, but I didn't want to give up the organ. Sometimes it seems I've lost everything precious to me on this trip. Almost as if God is testing me?"

Wade hugged her tighter to him. If anyone was being tested, it was him. So far, he'd had the strength of a saint, but many more days like today, he'd fail this test.

"Actually, we've been pretty lucky. We're all healthy." He paused, gazing into her hazel eyes. "I know that doesn't make the loss of your father any smaller, or even the loss of the organ any easier, but every day we're getting closer."

And closer meant one less day to spend with Rachel. The thought shook Wade. Did he really want to reach Oregon and give her up?

Chapter Twelve

Dear Diary,

The last two weeks have seemed longer than the entire trip. For four nights we traveled through the desert, bypassing Fort Bridger, to save almost a week's worth of travel time. When we reached the Bear River, we stopped to rest for a day before continuing to Soda Springs.

Wade continues to haunt my dreams at night. He has all but discontinued sleeping in the wagon with me. In some ways, I'm grateful, yet I miss him. He comes to camp for his meals and even spends time with the children around the fire.

I know he watches me, for I have caught him staring, with a strange look in his eyes that leaves me flushed. I must not fall in love with this man.

The stars were shining bright when the smell of cooking drew Wade into camp.

At The sound of his boots against the packed earth, she glanced up from dishing plates of stew for the children. Glistening eyes, the color of sweet honey, welcomed him, sending his pulse racing, making his breathing uneven. How could she look so beautiful after a long dusty day on the trail?

Rachel smiled a warm greeting. "Are you hungry?"

"Yes," he said, barely able to get the words out.

"Join us," she said, dishing him up a plate.

He knew he shouldn't spend time with her, but the longing to sit beside her was more than he could endure. Soft curls escaped her chignon, falling with abandon around her face. Streaks of amber glistened in her tresses, reflecting the firelight. He clenched his fists to keep from stroking the tempting curls.

She handed him a plate and went back to the task of feeding Daniel, who didn't seem to appreciate the stew as much as the other children.

"There's corn bread on the back of the wagon. You can sit here with me and Daniel, if you don't mind a fussy little boy.

"So how many miles did we make today?" Rachel asked, spooning a bite into Daniel's mouth.

"Maybe twelve, if we were lucky." Wade blew on the hot liquid, trying to cool it enough to taste. "We'll make it across the mountains before the first big snow. Still we shouldn't tarry. The sooner we get there, the sooner…"

Wade stopped unable to finish. The sooner they reached Oregon, the sooner he would be leaving Rachel and the children.

Rachel completed his sentence in a broken whisper: "The sooner you'll be rid of us."

Wade glanced up. Rachel's face was drawn tighter than a virgin's on her wedding night. "That's not what I was going to say."

She shoved a spoonful of stew between Daniel's lips. "It doesn't really matter, does it?"

"Rachel, I never meant—"

The sound of sputtering interrupted Wade as the baby blew stew from his mouth, spewing the stuff across the front of Rachel's dress.

"Daniel Hawthorne Cooke!" Rachel exclaimed, suddenly sounding as tired as the child, "That's naughty. You're going to bed."

"Do you need some help?" Wade didn't want her to leave him until they finished this conversation.

"No," she replied, her voice stilted. "I'll be back." With Daniel on her hip, she disappeared into the tent.

Several minutes later, Rachel returned and herded the children off to bed with a determination he'd never seen before. Normally, she let them take their time cleaning up. But tonight she hurried them, telling Grace no at least a half-dozen times when the little girl said she wanted to stay up. The woman was up something, and he could almost guess what had caused the tension he'd learned to recognize around the corners of her mouth. He'd bet his last dollar that it had something to do with Tommy's announcement that afternoon.

With everyone finally settled, she hurried back to the campfire. Sitting across from him, she shifted uncomfortably. A frown fixed itself firmly between her eyes.

"Did Tommy talk to you this afternoon?"

"Yes," Wade replied nonchalantly. He couldn't resist the urge to needle her just a bit. "He wants to breed his mare with Blackjack, once we get settled."

"Did he say anything else?" she asked, her frown deepening.

Wade took a bite of stew and chewed slowly, watching her fume. "He did happen to mention something about a wedding."

"Well, what did you say?" she asked, her voice rising in frustration. "Emily asked me this morning."

Taking his time, Wade scraped the bowl clean. "You make a hell of a stew, Rachel. A lot better than corn bread." The glance she sent him was enough to singe the whiskers off his unshaven face. "I told him we would be honored."

Immediately, he knew it was the wrong response. She puffed up fatter than a Christmas hen.

"I was hoping you would say no. Don't you think we're being hypocritical to stand up with Tommy and Emily when we're not even married?" she hissed.

"He didn't ask me if we were married," Wade rebutted. "If you don't want to do it, then we won't, but I thought it was kind of them to ask us to be in their wedding."

"We'll be a mockery of marriage, standing beside them while they pledge to spend the rest of their lives together."

"Honey, you worry too much," Wade replied. "I like these kids."

Glancing away, Rachel shifted on the bench. "You're shameless Wade Ketchum. We're behaving blasphemously. I should never have agreed to this ridiculous pretend marriage."

"No. I guess I should have left you stranded in Fort Laramie to wait until your cash ran out and you had to prostitute yourself. Then at least you wouldn't be lying to everyone you met. You'd only be whoring instead.

Her quick intake of air was the only sound he heard, until he felt the sting of her palm against his cheek.

Wade reached up and rubbed his smarting cheek. "Hmmm. People should see you hit me more often Rachel. Then we wouldn't be asked to stand up at weddings."

"How could you say such an awful thing?"

"Because it's the truth. And I'm sick and tired of your complaints about the deal we made. No, it's not the best of circumstances, but you're going to reach Oregon.

"I know but—"

"Damn it, Rachel!" Wade jumped up. He rubbed a hand across his face. "I've kept my hands off you for the last three hundred miles. But if you keep giving me fiery kisses and looking at me with those honey stares, I won't…I'm not made of steel."

∽

A week passed before Frank decided the wagon train could halt early one afternoon for Emily and Tommy's wedding. Rachel had seldom seen Wade, but had reflected constantly on their last conversation.

His words had echoed in her head until she wanted to scream. He was right. She had known it for quite some time, but refused to acknowledge the truth, protecting herself from the real feelings that continually plagued her.

It wasn't the pretend marriage that bothered her, rather the fact that she wanted to marry Wade. She wanted to be his wife in every sense of the word.

Wearing a borrowed black suit coat, a white shirt with a matching bolo tie, Wade looked more like a banker than a rough-and-ready gambler. She'd never seen him dressed in anything besides his everyday work clothes. And quite frankly, after seeing him all duded up, she couldn't help but wonder how the man could care about a spinster like herself.

The groom stood beside Ethan and Wade under a makeshift canopy of wildflowers. Rachel stood to the left of Ethan, darting quick glances at Wade. They were a mere three feet apart, close enough that she had to resist the urge to brush a piece of lint from his collar. Close enough for her to smell his cologne. Close enough to stir the rapid beating of her pulse.

Emily floated down the makeshift aisle formed by guests toward Tommy. Candlelight reflected off her best calico dress. Tommy's love shown from his face like a beacon guiding Emily to him. As they came together, the two young lovers shared a secret smile that clogged Rachel's throat and threatened her with tears.

She bit her lip to hold back the cry that welled up inside her. This was what she wanted. This was what she needed. And she wanted this fantasy with no other man but Wade.

"Dearly beloved we are gathered here today…"

The words left Rachel with an unsettled feeling of familiarity. She couldn't help but glance at Wade. His green eyes gleamed in the candlelight, their intensity touching her, swaddling her in a cocoon.

As they stared at one another, she became lost in the sensations of his gaze. No one else existed; only the two of them stood surrounded by candlelight and flowers.

In her vision Ethan spoke to her and Wade, as if they were reciting vows of love and devotion. It was their wedding. She knew at that moment she loved this man. Had probably fallen in love with him long before now, but until this moment couldn't admit the truth.

"Tommy, wilt thou take this woman to be thy wife, and wilt thou pledge thy troth to her, and promise to love and honor, and protect her, in sickness and in health, as long as you both shall live according to the ordinance of God and in the holy bond of marriage?" Ethan asked.

Rachel never heard Tommy's response as she stared at Wade, somehow hearing him answer instead. His emerald eyes seemed to touch her everywhere, and Rachel's skin tingled with awareness, her body flush with its own natural response.

"Emily wilt thou take this man to be thy husband, and wilt thou pledge thy troth to him and promise to love and honor and obey him in sickness and in health as long as you both shall live, according to the ordinance of God and in the holy bond of marriage?"

Rachel swallowed the lump in her throat, her mind automatically crying out I do. She watched as Wade closed his eyes, as if savoring the moment. Could he be feeling the way she was, lost in the realization of the moment?

As the vows were spoken, Rachel could not resist the magnetic pull of Wade's gaze. He looked at her as if he wanted to consume her with his eyes. And she wanted nothing more than to be in his arms. As the ceremony continued, Rachel realized that though the vows had not been spoken, somewhere along the trail, she had stopped pretending to be Wade's wife and had married him in her heart.

Ethan ended the service with a prayer, but Rachel barely remembered the words as she stood with head bowed, reeling with the discovery of her feelings.

She loved Wade.

When the prayer ended, Ethan presented the couple to the waiting crowd, who welcomed them with hugs and congratulatory slaps on the back.

Rachel stood in the background, waiting for some signal from Wade. His face was drawn and tight, but his eyes were hot and intense. She watched as he licked his lips nervously.

They stared at one another, somber and quiet, until Rachel was certain she had misread the message in Wade's eyes. Maybe the wedding hadn't wrung his heart out as it had hers.

"Hey Ketchum, come help us move these tables so we can eat," yelled Homer Jenkins.

"Just a minute," Wade called impatiently to him.

He grabbed both of her hands in his and placed a gentle kiss on each of them. "Ah, Rachel."

His gaze communicated everything Rachel knew he couldn't say, knew he would probably never say. But just the same, she tingled from head to toe. Unawakened areas of her body were suddenly alive with fire and yearning for him.

He kissed her hands again, making her shiver in expectation. "Save all your dances for me. I promise I'll be back."

~

Wade slipped away from the crowd, into the dark cover of night. He watched Emily and Tommy dance to the sounds of the fiddle. Happiness glowed from their faces, brighter than the light of the campfire, and for a brief moment he was jealous.

Rachel sat beside Mary, tending the children. He ached to go to her, be with her, dance with her, but most of all he wanted to take her back to the wagon and make love to her.

Gone was the ugly black mourning dress and in its place was a gown of pale blue cotton that showed off her shapely curves. The bodice fit snugly against her breasts, its high neck edged in ecru lace. She had pulled her hair up into a shower of mahogany curls, loose and flowing, tempting his fingers.

God, what had the woman done to him?

She had changed his life. Loneliness had been his only companion until she'd come along and brought a joy he had been missing. What would he do when she was gone?

Like a fifteen-year-old boy experiencing his first woman, Wade tingled whenever Rachel was near. But his desire for her went beyond bodily sensation. Something about her made him want to put down roots, have a family, make her happy and do whatever it took to keep her by his side. And that surprised the hell out of him.

Did he love her?

All he knew was that during the ceremony, he'd been drawn to Rachel as never before. He'd wanted to cry out, stop the wedding, stop the vows until Rachel consented to be his wife.

If this wasn't love, then he needed to see a doctor. The symptoms were all there, had been there for awhile, but he hadn't wanted to admit to those feelings. He loved Rachel.

Wade glanced at Rachel talking to Mary. He clenched his fists, the thought of leaving her, no matter what the reason, was agony. Damn, this wasn't supposed to happen. He wasn't supposed to fall in love. There was no room for a woman in his life. He had a brother to find, a ranch to start, but the thought of life without Rachel seemed to have lost its appeal.

Across the fire, Rachel met his gaze and smiled. The welcoming curve of her lips drew him to her like a moth to flame. His hands shook whether from fear or joy he didn't know. Right or wrong, he had to be with Rachel.

With certainty in every step, he walked to her, knowing this night would forever change the two of them, for better or worse.

She glanced up at him, her eyes golden in the firelight. "May I have this dance?"

"I thought you'd never ask," she replied, her voice whisper soft, her cheeks flushed.

Rachel followed him as they joined the waltzing couples. The grass made the waltz more a marching drill than a smooth glide, but Wade floated on air. Her soft body in his arms felt like a homecoming. Rachel belonged in his embrace, and when he pulled her close, the smell of lilacs and honeysuckle whetted his appetite. Her scent made him want to put his tongue to her skin and taste her, to see if she was as sweet.

"Where were you?" Her voice was soft in the cool evening breeze. "You disappeared after you helped set up the tables."

Wade didn't know how to tell her the truth. He shrugged. "I had some things on my mind, I had to sort out."

She tensed slightly in his arms. "Weddings can do that, make you think about things you'd rather ignore."

She reached up and brushed a lock of hair from his face, her fingers soft and caressing. He almost moaned. Night after night she'd tempted him until he wondered how much more he could take before he lost all control.

"Rachel," he whispered huskily. "Don't look at me like that.

"Like what?" she asked, widening her eyes.

Wade took a deep breath, trying to ease the pressure building within his body. "I can only take so much. You're driving me crazy."

Like soft bells, her laughter floated on the evening breeze. "How could an aging spinster drive a man raised in a saloon full of women crazy?"

Pulling her closer, he felt their bodies glide against one another. "Easy. Just keep looking at me like I'm desert, and you'll soon find out."

Tilting her head, she studied him. "Apple pie. You remind me of apple pie. Kind of sour until enough sugar is added, and then it's just right." Bands of gold circled the dilated pupils of her eyes, touching him with warmth everywhere.

"You make me feel more like pecan pie, nutty and hard."

She laughed her voice deep and husky. "Why are we talking about desert when we've not even had supper yet?"

Wade knew they were flirting with danger, but he couldn't restrain himself. This was a new side of Rachel, the blooming of a passionate woman, and he wanted to be the gardener.

"To hell with supper. I'm craving something sweet." Wade put his nose against her neck and inhaled. "You smell wonderful." He ran his tongue along the curve of her neck, and she shivered. "You taste better."

"Wade, people are watching."

"Let 'em. I'm past caring."

"What would cure this sweet tooth you've suddenly acquired?" Rachel said, her voice shaky.

"Don't tempt me, Rachel," he warned. "I can't take much more." He put his lips to her temple and sighed against the top of her head. "I can't eat. I can't sleep."

She pushed back in his arms, her warm honey eyes dilated with passion. "Don't you think it's the same for me?"

Her open desire stunned him. "Dear God, what do we do now?"

Rachel cast her eyes down shyly. "What do you want to do?"

"I know exactly what I'd like to do," he replied.

Rachel glanced up into his emerald eyes, glittering with desire and felt as if she were being consumed. Her skin rippled with awareness. A tight spiraling palpitation started in the pit of her stomach, a sensation she often experienced in his presence. If only tonight would last forever.

Closing her eyes, she pushed aside all doubts, her fears; letting her love for Wade fill her completely. She wanted this night with Wade, her candlelight husband.

"Take me home," Rachel said, her voice low and deep. "Take me home and show me how to cure you of this craving."

Wade stopped among the other dancers. "Do you know what you're saying, Rachel?" he asked. "It's one thing to talk about it, but don't tease me."

Her heart pounded loudly in her own ears, but a yearning, a need to be with him silenced her fears. She took a deep breath and swallowed. "I'm ready to go home, Wade."

He pulled her away from the dancing, away from the crowd and into the trees. Darkness wrapped about them like a cloak.

"What about the kids?"

"Mary's been lonely, so she asked if they could spend the night with her and Ethan tonight."

"The woman's a saint!" He swung Rachel up in his arms and began walking to their wagon.

Rachel laughed, the sound echoing nervously in the night. Wade was hurrying her toward their wagon as if he were afraid she'd change her mind and run away. She knew what was going to happen, and she tingled with anticipation.

The path was dark, with only the coals from the campfire to guide them. Long dark tresses at the back of his neck glided through her fingertips. Exploring gently, she ran her fingers along his ear lobe until she found his jaw.

With gentle pressure, she turned his head toward her and kissed Wade softly. He stumbled.

"Rachel, wait, honey," he whispered against her mouth. "I can't think when you do that."

She didn't want him to think, she didn't want to think herself. Because if either one of them came to their senses, they would step back from this foolish chance they were taking.

Reaching the wagon, Wade set her on the ground and pulled her into his arms. "Are you sure this is what you want, Rachel?"

A flutter of fear and eagerness rippled through her. She smiled at the uncertainty in his eyes before turning to climb up into the wagon. Though she appeared calm on the outside, inside she was shaking harder than a baby's rattle.

Glancing back over her shoulder, she said, "Come to bed, Wade."

Without another word, he hastened to follow her. Feeling awkward, she glanced at the pallet they had often shared. This was what she wanted, what she had waited for all her life. Tomorrow would be soon enough to think about regrets.

With the strike of a match, he lit the lantern. Its warm glow filled the narrow confines. Rachel drew the pucker strings of the canvas tight, enclosing them in a sensuous cocoon.

She turned slowly to face Wade. In the tight quarters, he sat upon a cedar chest, his face anxious in the dim light. Gently, he pulled her onto his lap. She wrapped her arms around him, feeling the need to support her shaky legs.

Brushing away the curls that lay on her neck, Wade blazed at path from her shoulder with warm lips. He traced the outline of her ear with his tongue as his hands pulled the few pins from her hair, releasing it.

Threading his fingers through her tresses, he whispered, "You hair is so soft."

Rubbing his cheek against her curls, Wade sought her earlobe with his lips. Rachel squirmed from the tingly sensations his tongue provoked. The experience wasn't unpleasant, more like a tease, sending delicious shivers down her spine.

His warm lips trailed soft butterfly kisses across her cheek, to her lips. There he kissed her softly, his fingers threading themselves through her hair. As he hugged her closer, his lips turned from soft and gentle to strong and demanding, taking her by surprise.

Carried along in his ardor, she ran her fingers through his hair, pressing his head closer to her, wanting more of him, meeting his response with her own urgent need.

His kiss made her hungry for more, aching with the need to be closer to him. Awkward and unsure, but curious at the sensations building within her, Rachel longed to touch him in intimate places, to feel his naked skin, beneath her hands. As yearning stirred between her legs, her awareness increased of a hard pressure against her thighs.

With a gentle stroke, his hand touched her breast, caressing her through her clothes. The urge to arch her back, give him easier access to her flesh, overwhelmed her, yet the need to feel his hand on her naked breast surprised her.

With one hand, she tried to unbutton his shirt, but the button refused to budge. She wrestled with the little disk until finally she tugged, sending the piece of wood flying across the wagon. The clatter against wood, shocked her.

Who was this wanton woman driven to rip open his shirt, explore his flesh?

"Rachel!" he groaned against her lips.

"I'm sorry about your button," she whispered, her voice husky in the darkness.

"Forget the damn shirt," he rasped, grappling with the rest of the buttons and shrugging the unwanted garment from his body.

"Touch me," he pleaded.

She ran her hands across his chest, feeling his nakedness beneath her fingertips. Muscles, hard and firm, warm and silky, flexed at her touch.

Wade reached back and, with both hands, began the tedious task of unbuttoning her dress. Finally, after what seemed like hours, the dress slide from her shoulders the cool night air caressing her skin.

"Turn out the lantern," she said her voice shaky.

"Only because of the shadows," Wade replied as he extinguished the light. "I long to see every naked inch of you."

He pushed the dress down and over her hips until it landed in a puddle at her feet. She continued to sit on his lap, clad only her chemise and stocking feet, her cheeks hot in the darkness.

Lifting her in his arms, he laid her on the pallet occupying the floor of the wagon, then returned to sit on the chest. In the darkened wagon, she watched as he bent to remove his boots, the muscles in his back stretched taut.

When his hands reached for the waistband of his pants, Rachel's breathing almost stopped, yet she refused to look away.

She wanted to see all of Wade.

In one fluid motion, he pushed his pants down, kicking them away. In the darkness, his manhood stood at attention, erect and proud, sending a shiver of anticipation through Rachel.

Kneeling down on the pallet beside her, his skin glowed in the shadowy moonlight. With his fingertips, he caressed the length of each leg as he removed her stockings, leaving behind a tingling trail of sensation.

Reaching behind her, he clasped the strings of her chemise and untied the bow. Fear made her heart pound in her chest, but love soothed the anxious feelings and turned them into desire. The need to touch him intensified as she ran her fingers lightly across his face and lips.

He kissed her fingertips before raising her up to a sitting position. Slowly, he removed her chemise, leaving her totally naked and exposed to his gaze. Though inside she cringed with apprehension, she refused to cower as he looked upon her.

"Oh, God, Rachel. You're more beautiful than I dreamed," he said, his voice husky.

The heat from his gaze made her ache Rachel ache with need. She wanted him next to her, wanted to feel his naked skin against her, wanted him to kiss her until she couldn't breathe.

Wade bent over her breast, closing his mouth around her nipple. She clenched her fists in his hair to keep from moaning out aloud as he lovingly kissed each breast.

The sensations flowing through her were totally foreign and all Rachel knew was she never wanted him to stop. His hand touched the moist, tender spot between her thighs.

She arched her back, crying out loud with need. "Wade!"

"It's okay, sweetness," he reassured her. "You're supposed to feel this way."

No one had told her that making love would be so wonderful. She wanted more, she wanted to feel all of him. She couldn't resist touching him as he slid over her skin.

Gently, she raked her fingernails over his back, pulling him ever closer to her.

Moist with the honey of her arousal, his fingers continued to evoke delicious feelings while his mouth finally found its way to hers. She attacked his lips, needing the feel of him deep inside her.

He positioned himself over her, his knee gently spreading her legs. There was a brief moment of anxiety as he placed his manhood between her thighs.

She tensed for just a second, but he kissed her, until she was so caught up that the pain of his entry caught her off guard.

As he eased his way into her body, she cried out.

"Easy sweetheart. The pain will soon be over," he whispered against her temple as he lay still within her.

What seemed like minutes passed as he murmured softly to her. Finally, she felt him move within her. The pleasure soon began to rebuild, surprising her.

His lips surrounded hers, kissing her until she felt she would suffocate with joy.

An incredible urge to rock him to her made her hips fall into a natural rhythm. He plunged within her, each thrust creating new sensations, all centered in the increasing heat between her thighs.

To Rachel it seemed her body was climbing, reaching, for some unknown destination, building and gathering every feeling in the center of her being. When she thought she couldn't take any more, her world exploded in a shattering release.

Spiraling back to Earth, she cried out his name, just as he, too, exploded within her.

She lay still, her pulse pounding in her ears, her heart swelling with love. The wonder of the moment left her feeling whole, complete and more than a little languorous.

Wade's head lay against her shoulder, his body pressed into hers as his heartbeat slowed and his breathing returned to normal. Rachel ran her hand down the sleek power of his back, loving the feel of him within her. For several minutes, they lay quietly, savoring the moment.

Finally, she asked, "Is it always like this?"

Wade raised up on one elbow, his eyes glowing like green embers in the faint light. He brushed back a lock hair that lay against her cheek. "No. Next time it'll be better?"

Rachel snuggled closer. "How can it get any better?"

Wade laughed and kissed her softly. "The first time is usually painful for a woman. It shouldn't feel that way again."

"I wasn't thinking about the pain," she replied. "I was considering the way you made me feel. Is it always so intense?"

Wade smiled. "Only when it's good, Rachel."

～

In the hours before dawn, Wade awoke to the sounds of the camp beginning to stir. His arm was wrapped around Rachel, her naked body tucked up against him. Holding her revived the joy of making love far into the night, each giving and receiving.

The preacher's daughter had taken him to heights of pleasure, he'd never before experienced. She'd loved him like a wildcat and now she lay curled in his arms, sleeping like a kitten.

Last night, they had teased and flirted about curing his craving, but the morning light found him more in love with her than the night before. This craving was definitely not cured. One sweet sip of her nectar would never be enough.

But to continually drink from the well, would soon find him addicted to the water. And though he loved Rachel with all his heart, he could never tell her.

Speaking the words out loud would only make them permanent, and they had could never last. Rachel deserved a far better man than he was, a man who could provide a home and family for her.

But what a price to pay. To give up the woman who had finally captured his heart.

If he made her his wife, one day she would wake up and realize he could never be the man she wanted. Then she would hate him for not walking away.

Hell, she was going to hate him regardless. No matter what she'd said last night, this morning, she would expect declarations of love. A proposal of marriage. Something he could never offer if he wanted to see her happy.

So what did he do now? The night was over, and the morning sun would soon welcome the day, along with the consequences of their actions last night.

He ran his hand down her arm, across her breasts and stomach to her hip. Satin-smooth skin against his rough fingers, invited further exploration. Even this morning, his body's reaction was swift and sure as she snuggled closer to him, her bottom rubbing against his manhood. Last night had not cured anything. In fact, his feelings were more complicated now than ever before. In the darkness, Wade eased up off the pallet and found his clothes. Long before dawn he left camp, his heart aching with the pain of his decision.

~

Dear Diary,

Last night changed everything. Two months ago I hated Wade Ketchum. But now, more than anything, I want to be his wife. For the first time in my life, I'm in love. This is not the infatuation I felt for Ethan. This much, much stronger.

Even though we're not truly married, I feel as though we are man and wife. So much so that I became his wife in the truest sense last night.

I had never imagined how it could be between a man and a woman. No one told me of the joy I would feel.

Rachel closed the diary and blew out the lantern. She had awakened before the first glint of daylight to an empty wagon. Wade had already left to take care of the stock, though his scent clung to his pillow. She picked up the cushion and hugged it to her, wishing Wade had lingered in the wagon.

Her skin tingled with the memory of the love they'd shared through the night. Never before had she felt so alive, so much in love. The need to see Wade, hug him to her, sent her scurrying out of bed into the cool dawn air.

Though her body was tender in places, her heart was overflowing with happiness. She dressed quickly eager to find him, eager to share this morning – and the rest of her life – with Wade.

As she stepped out of the wagon, a soggy mist slapped her like a wet sponge. The dew-wet grass soaked the hem of her skirt, but Rachel vowed nothing could dampen her spirits.

She stroked the fire, hoping to break the chill as the sun began to lighten the eastern sky with the promise of a new day. Like a giddy young girl, she waited for Wade.

When she could to tarry no longer, she started breakfast, expecting him to walk into camp at any moment. The children returned from Mary's expecting to be fed just like on any other morning. Afterward Rachel was the dishes and packed the tent.

Still no sign of Wade.

Giddiness turned to disappointment, as she hitched the oxen to the wagon. Most mornings, he was back before breakfast. Most mornings, he was underfoot. But this morning, the dawn of their new love, he was nowhere to be found.

Rachel tightened the cinch on the harness to the oxen. The doubts she'd pushed away last night, returned with a vengeance. Last night, he'd never said he loved her. He'd never promised marriage.

Had she imagined the way his eyes glowed when he looked at her, the way his body had responded to her touch? Or could it be he was having second thoughts about making love to her?

Everything was loaded into the wagon: the kids, the cooking utensils, the tent. Other wagons were beginning to pull out, getting a head start. She couldn't wait any longer. It was time to put last night behind her and face the reality of the new day.

She swallowed the lump that seemed lodged in her throat. Disappointment turned into fear.

Rachel climbed up into the wagon. Maybe it was better this way. Had she misread his feelings from the night before? Had it not been a meaningful experience for him?

She grabbed the reins, yelling at the oxen, "Move!"

Chapter Thirteen

Slumped in the saddle, Wade reluctantly rode into camp as the sun slipped low in the sky. A cook breeze grazed his cheeks, and he knew it wouldn't be the only cool reception he'd receive.

This morning, the sight of Rachel's hair sprawling across his naked chest, the feel of his buttocks snug against his groin, had sent him fleeing from the wagon. He had deliberately stayed away all day, trying to sort out his feelings for Rachel.

His thoughts had swirled like a whirlwind, never reaching an end, always coming back to the face he loved. But the facts didn't change. He was a gambler who had a brother to find, and she was a lady.

A sigh escaped him, and he clenched his fists, knowing she was going to hate him for making love to her and never proposing marriage, hate him for walking away when all he wanted to do was stay.

All day, he'd tried to drive the lust from his body by pushing himself to the extreme, though all he'd wanted to do was crawl back into Rachel's bed.

Toby came bounding toward him, grabbing Sadie's reins. "Hey, Wade. Where you been?"

"Hunting," Wade replied. It wasn't totally honest, but it wasn't a lie, either.

"Rachel's been acting kind of funny today," Toby said. "Did you two fight?"

"I wouldn't worry, Toby." Wade swung his leg over his horse. Handing the reins to the boy, he tipped back his hat and swiped his brow with the back of his hand. "I'll check on her."

"Thanks, Wade."

That morning, part of Wade had wanted to ride away and never look back, but he'd known he couldn't do that to

Rachel and the children. Yet he doubted his ability to keep his hands off her for the next six weeks.

Only one part of his anatomy had been doing the thinking last night, and unfortunately, it wasn't the smartest part. Only an ignorant fool would have let things go so far. Tonight, he knew he couldn't let it happen again.

Supper sizzled on the fire, filling the camp with a welcome aroma, while Grace and Daniel chased each other around the tent. Their exuberant squeals were strangely soothing as he watched their childish play.

A dainty slippered foot peeped out of the tent, followed by the rest of Becky, dressed as if she were off to afternoon tea. Daniel's little legs came toddling at full speed around the tent and plowed straight into Becky's peach cotton skirt. He wrapped his grimy hands into the folds of the clean material.

"Don't touch me!" she shrieked as she jerked the tot's fingers from her skirt. Daniel gazed up, his big brown eyes questioning. With a firm grip, she held him at arm's length, away from her clothing. Twisting his body, he kicked out at her until, exasperated, he stuck his tongue out and blew, the sound echoing Wade's opinion.

"Grace!" Becky demanded. "Get this kid away from me."

"Come on, Daniel," Grace called, drawing the toddler away from Becky. "Let's go play somewhere else."

Wade inhaled a deep breath, trying to control the surge of anger Becky always seemed to provoke. "Where's Rachel?"

"She's in the wagon," Becky replied with barely a glance.

"Take the children and follow Toby to the river to feed and water the horses."

"I don't have time," she replied, turning away.

"I'm not asking you, I'm telling you," Wade called after her, not in any mood to argue.

She glanced back at him. "I have plans."

"Your plans just got delayed. Stay with the children by the river."

The look she gave Wade should have singed the whiskers off his face. She stared, as if trying to decide whether to give up or continue her argument. Finally, she emitted a loud groan before she grabbed Grace by the arm. "Get Daniel and let's go."

Wade watched the little procession head, down the path after Toby. Grace turned and looked back at him as if he were punishing her. Daniel's little legs ran to keep up. Wade's heart wrenched at the sight, and he realized leaving them behind would be almost as bad as walking away from Rachel.

But nothing could hurt as much as relinquishing Rachel.

His boots seemed filled with sand as his stride slowed on the final steps to the wagon. He dreaded this first meeting.

The wagon creaked, and Wade watched Rachel crawl over the seat, her back to him. She stepped down onto the wheel, and he reached up to catch her at the waist. The feel of her reminded him of the night before.

She stiffened at his touch. "You're back."

As her feet touched the ground, she whirled around to face him. Her eyes were red-rimmed as if she'd been crying.

"Where have you been all day?"

"Where I am every day, scouting the trail."

She looked at him as if she wanted to wrap her hands around his throat and strangle him. "I missed you at breakfast."

"Too busy. Had to take care of the animals."

He couldn't tell her the tender touch of her slender thighs against his this morning had sent him running. But, dear God, the sight of her now made him want her back in his arms tonight, holding her close for whatever time they had left.

"Supper should be ready in a little while," she coldly replied as she turned and walked to the fire.

"Thanks. I've got to talk to Frank. I'll be back soon."

The woman wasn't ignorant; she knew something was wrong. Somehow her easy acceptance didn't bring the relief he thought he'd feel. It only made him ache worse.

~

The fire sizzled as drippings from the roasting rabbit drizzled onto the coals. Kneeling, Rachel turned the meat on the skewer. She couldn't help but commiserate with the poor rabbit. The morning had left her feeling naked and exposed, while the warm sun had broiled her raw emotions at a slow cook all day.

Brushing back a stray lock of hair, she rose from the head of the fire and, like a limp rag, collapsed into the rocker.

Wade had gone to visit Frank. The children and Becky were down at the river. Being alone was a rare luxury, and for a moment, she leaned her head back and let the peace wash over her.

When he returned this evening, Wade has been as warm as a snowflake on a frostbitten day. The warm lover of last night had disappeared with the dawn, and now, her dreams were evaporating into thin air. She had gambled her heart and virtue. And the gambler had taken his winnings and left the table.

The sounds of footsteps interrupted her peaceful moment. Rachel opened her eyes to see Toby hurrying toward her, a worried frown upon his face.

"Rachel, I can't find Grace," he cried. "We were all down by the river. She just disappeared. I've looked everywhere."

"Where's Daniel?"

"I left him with Mary," Toby replied.

"Good. Grace has to be nearby," Rachel stood up from the rocker. "What were you doing down at the river."

Toby pulled Rachel toward the tree-lined riverbank. "I was watering Wade's horses."

The river's noisy splashing over rocks sped her feet toward the water. "Is Becky searching for Grace?"

"Uh – I don't know where she is. She left me to watch the kids," Toby said as he followed her.

"What was so important that she left you with two little children on a riverbank?" Fear sharpened Rachel's voice.

Toby glanced away. "I don't know. She didn't say."

The river stretched ahead, the water rushing past. She couldn't think about Becky when Grace needed her full attention.

"Where did you last see Grace?" Rachel fought to keep the fear from her voice. Surely, Grace couldn't have wandered far.

"She and Daniel were playing down by the water. I tried to watch them, but the horses needed a rubdown. Last I saw, she was picking flowers near the bank; then she was gone.

"Are you sure she didn't fall in?" Rachel asked, her heart almost stopping at the thought.

Toby's eyes grew large with fright. "I didn't hear a splash or a scream." His shoulders started to shake as tears welled up in his eyes. "I called and called. I ran up the river, all the way to where it curves into the canyon."

Rachel gave him a comforting pat as she tried to rein in her building panic.

"Grace," she called, her voice echoing from the canyon.

The wind whistled through the thick pines, making them rustle, while the river rushed over rocks and around the bend. The echo died into a lonely silence with no response. Her heart pounded in double time as Rachel realized there were many places a child could get lost or hurt.

"Wade will find her," she said in a shaky voice. "Come on, Toby, let's get him."

Picking up her long skirt, Rachel ran to Frank's wagon.

"Wade!" she cried as she rushed into camp.

Long seconds passed before Wade ran around the back of the wagon, a frown darkening his green eyes. "What's wrong?"

She ran to him, her breathing painful. "Grace is missing."

"When did she disappear?" he asked, dropping the shaving tool beside Frank's broken wagon wheel.

"About ten minutes ago, down by the river."

Toby ran up beside her. "I turned my back on her for one second, and she just disappeared."

"I sent Becky down there with you kids. Where in the hell was she?" Wade demanded.

Toby swallowed, his face a brilliant red. "She left."

"Damn!" Wade swore. "I'm going to—"

"Wade," Rachel pleaded. "Not now, we have to find Grace."

"You're right. It'll be dark soon."

Wade turned, his quick stride carrying him around the back of Frank's wagon. The two of them returned at once.

"You go ahead. I'll call the men together. We should find her before dark," Frank reassured Rachel. "Don't worry, Mrs. Ketchum. She'll be okay."

"Thank you, Frank," Rachel said, fear shaking her voice.

"Toby, saddle Sadie and bring her to me."

The boy scurried off, eager to do Wade's bidding.

Wade pulled Rachel toward their wagon. "When Toby gets back, I want the two of you to search along the river. Maybe by the time you search there, the men will be ready to check farther downstream. But I'm not waiting, I'm heading out now."

"Do you think she fell in?" Her heart's wild action squeezed air from her lungs.

He looked over her head. "It's possible."

If Grace had fallen into the river, the swift current would have quickly carried her away. A small child wouldn't last long battling the strong river.

Toby rode atop Sade. He jumped out of the saddle, handing the reins to Wade. Rachel stared. Two months ago, Toby couldn't saddle, let alone ride, a horse.

Wade put his foot in the stirrup and pulled himself into the saddle. He looked down at Toby and Rachel. "We'll meet back here after dark unless we find her earlier. I don't want you to wander from camp. Search for her in this area only." He leaned over the saddle, and squeezed Rachel's hand. "Try not to worry. We'll find her." Wade rode away toward the canyon.

"Come on, Toby. Let's get started. You walk along the shore of the river, and I'll climb up to the top of the hill and look along the ridge. Yell if you find her."

"Rachel?" Toby studied his feet. "When Becky left I should have brought the kids back to camp. I'm sorry."

"It's all right, Toby. Let's just find Grace, then we'll deal with Becky. Grace is probably huddled out of sight, playing with her dolls, forgetful of the time."

Rachel prayed they would find Grace, hidden by the trees or the rocks, playing a practical joke, but she couldn't quite believe it. "I'll meet you at the crook in the river."

"Okay," Toby said as he started off walking along the shore.

Rachel watched him for a few moments, then began the long climb to the top of the hill hugging the river. The canyon sloped gently, with rocky outcroppings and tall pine trees sparse along the sides. Searching in every nook, Rachel climbed to the crest, calling to Grace.

She clambered among the rocks, watching for snakes, looking for any place a child could hide. Panic had risen to her throat.

When the wind blew, she could hear, very faintly, Toby's voice, and every few minutes she shaded her eyes to spot the boy.

The breeze blew the sound of laughter, soft and tinkling like a child's, in her direction. Rachel hurried forward, her determined feet carrying her toward a large, jagged rock. When she found Grace, she would hug her, then give her the spanking of her young life.

Rachel's boots slipped in the soft dirt, and she almost tumbled down the side of the hill, sending rocks rolling and clattering down the hillside.

The laughter came again, emanating from the rocks ahead. Scrambling up the hill, Rachel found a crevice just large enough for a person to slip inside. She wiggled through the opening, certain she would find Grace with her doll. Instead, the scene sucked the wind from her throat.

Ethan and Becky lay entwined together on a blanket, their clothes in disarray.

"Dear God," Rachel gasped as she reeled back in shock. The involuntary words silenced Becky's giggles.

At the sight of her sister, Becky's eyes widened in fright. She jerked up, pushing Ethan off of her, her naked breasts falling out of her unbuttoned bodice.

"Rachel!" Becky screeched. "What are you doing here?"

Shocked, Rachel backed away. "How can you do this?"

"How did you know we were here?" Becky pulled her bodice together, looking smug rather than ashamed.

"I didn't. Grace is lost." Her voice was shaky with anger and a bone-deep fear for the missing child. "While you were out satisfying your lust with a married man, Grace disappeared."

"Wait Rachel!" Becky called to her.

"I have to find Grace before dark. I suggest you leave at once. These woods will be swarming with people searching for her," Rachel warned, hurrying from the scene.

Tears of anger at Becky and Ethan welled up, but Rachel refused to let them flow. She had to think of Grace.

She should have known better than to trust Becky to watch over the children. But she'd never imagined her sister would be this irresponsible.

Rachel rushed from tree to rock in a frenzy of guilt, desperately seeking the child, feeling somehow responsible for her disappearance. The crook in the river where she was to meet Toby loomed ahead, without sight of Grace.

"Rachel," Toby yelled.

She picked up her skirts and ran, hurrying over the rocks, sliding down the hill as she scurried toward him.

"Look what I found," he called, holding up a small brown boot, identical to the ones Grace wore.

"Where did you find it?" she asked, her heart pounding in her ears as she reached his side.

Eyes wide with fright, he pointed down to the swirling water. "It was stuck in the mud, on the bank of the river."

Rachel fell to her knees as she examined the bank. The mud held the indentation of Grace's shoe. Next to that, the bank had a smooth sheen like a slide-mark.

"Dear God, she fell in," Rachel gasped. Fear consumed her, sucking her into a whirring, buzzing vortex. The bile in her stomach rose in her throat. Dizzy, she leaned over and retched in the grass, emptying her stomach until only the pain remained.

Toby knelt beside her, his eyes brimming with tears. "Are you okay, Rachel?"

She pulled him onto her lap, holding him like a small child. Great gulping sobs overcame her while she held onto Toby and cried until no tears were left. But the pain of her loss sat like a heavy weight upon her chest. She'd already lost her father this trip, she couldn't stand the thought of losing Grace.

"Rachel, let's go back and see if Wade found her," Toby prodded.

"She fell in the river," Rachel cried. "She – drowned."

Toby extracted himself from her arms. He grabbed her by the hand and pulled her to her feet. "Let's go back to camp, Rachel. Wade will know what to do."

Like a sleepwalker, Rachel clutched Grace's shoe as he led her from the bank. Her sweet, bubbly child was gone.

~

By the time Rachel and Toby reached camp, the sun had sunk behind the horizon, shadowing the river with darkness.

Mary rushed forward, a worried expression marring her face. "Did you find her?"

Rachel held up Grace's shoe.

Mary gasped. "Where was it?"

Rachel tried to speak, but tears clogged her throat and spilled from her eyes. She shook her head.

"I found it stuck in the mud at the river's edge," Toby replied quietly.

"Dear God!" Mary exclaimed. She wrapped her arms around Rachel, hugging her to her chest. The two women clung to one another. "We can't give up hope, Rachel."

"I'm trying, but that river is so fast. How could she possibly swim in that awful current?"

"Don't give up. Not yet," Mary said, patting Rachel's back.

Dearest Mary. Her best friend, whose husband was fornicating with Becky. But she couldn't think about them right now.

Toby patted Rachel. "Are you okay?"

Rachel nodded, trying to regain her composure. Finally she moved from Mary's arms. "Has Wade come back?"

"No. And the men rode out over an hour ago," Mary said, her eyes tinged with worry, her voice filled with sorrow. "Don't worry about supper. I combined our meals, and I've taken care of everything here. Daniel's been playing quietly."

"Thank you." Rachel stumbled to the rocker, tears flooding her cheeks. She rocked, clasping the tiny shoe, staring into the fire, trying not to wonder if Grace was dead or alive.

Ethan appeared at her side, looking anxious. Both he and Becky had been in camp when Rachel returned. "Mary told me about Grace. I don't know what to say."

Rachel turned her head away from him. She couldn't talk to Ethan right now. She couldn't look at him without seeing him in Becky's arms, and she didn't want to waste energy thinking about them.

"Eat some stew," Mary said to her as she picked up a linen towel and began to dry the eating utensils. "No matter what happens, you need your strength. Toby and Daniel need you."

Rachel had a fleeting thought about her dilemma. How ironic that this woman was offering to strengthen her, when Mary's own world was based on a lie and could be torn asunder any day now.

"I can't. I know I'd be sick." She sobbed. "I wish Wade would come back."

As if her thoughts conjured him up, Wade rode into camp followed by the rest of the men. Their tired, dejected looks answered her most pressing question. What little hope she'd held on to seemed to wither and die.

Wade threw his leg over his mount and slid to the ground.

"I'll take care of your horse, Ketchum, if you want to talk to your missus," Jack Simpson volunteered.

"Thanks," Wade said as he stared at Rachel. Slowly he shook his head and pushed back his hat.

He strode past Ethan and Becky, ignoring them as if they were specks of dust at his feet, before stopping at Rachel's side. Rachel looked at him, fear tripping her heart.

Wade knelt down and wrapped his arms around her. "At first daylight, I'll be out looking again."

"She probably fell in," Rachel said her voice clogged with tears. She held up Grace's boot for his inspection. "Toby found her shoe stuck in the bank of the river."

Wade picked her up out of the rocking chair, then sat back down, cradling her on his lap.

"I followed the river around the bend a long ways. I would have found her body if she'd drowned." He kissed the top of her head, soothing back her hair.

He was right. A tiny flicker of renewed hope sprang to life. "Then where is she? It's dark. It's getting cold. She'll be so afraid."

"She's a tough little girl," Wade reminded her.

"Wade will find her tomorrow, carrying some new animal she wants to keep," Mary said with a smile of fake optimism.

His hand caressed her back with gentle strokes. "She's curled up somewhere, sleeping, knowing I'm looking for her."

"Stop it! At least be truthful," Rachel blurted out. "She could have drowned. She may be dead. We may never find her."

His face looked drawn and tired. "We've got to have hope or go crazy with worry."

"It's late, and we're all tired. If you don't mind, Rachel, I'll take Daniel home with me tonight." Mary picked up the fussy little boy. "Try to get some rest."

"Thank you." Rachel could barely meet her friends gaze.

"You'd do the same for me," Mary replied.

Mary took Daniel by the hand walked toward her camp.

Rachel found Wade's iridescent green eyes full of unspoken worry. "Come to bed. You look worn out," he said.

A lonely, terrifying night stretched ahead, and Rachel needed him by her side. She didn't want to face her fears alone. "How can I sleep with her missing?"

"We have to try so that we'll be alert tomorrow."

Wade lifted her from the rocker and set her on the ground. He kept his arm around her as they made their way to the wagon.

As they passed Ethan and Becky sitting beside the fire, Becky exploded. "No lectures? No scolding? No pointing fingers?"

With a sigh, Rachel faced her sister. "Grace is missing because of you. She could be dead!" She paused, controlling the urge to scream at Becky. "Until I find her, I could care less what you do."

Chapter Fourteen

Dawn was fast approaching as Wade, restless thought of getting up and beginning the search for Grace until Rachel nudged her buttocks against him and he knew why he continued to hold her.

Hours had passed before she'd finally dozed off. And even then, she seemed to sleep fitfully, as if her dreams were more disturbing than reality. Once, she'd sat up, asking how long before dawn, but somehow he'd managed to quiet her, and eventually she'd fallen back to sleep.

But he knew the moment he moved to dress, she would be awake, worrying about Grace. She needed to sleep as long as possible, before facing a day that could be filled with heartache.

"Ketchum!" The still morning air was broken by the sentry's alarmed voice. "Ketchum! Get up. We got company."

Jumping up in the dusky light, Wade stubbed his toe on a box, and swore as he reached for his pants.

Startled, Rachel sat straight up. "What is it?"

"I'm coming Jed. Let me get my pants on," Wade yelled."

"Make it damn quick, man. There's a party of Shoshone warriors out here with your daughter."

"Dear God, they have Grace." Rachel threw back the quilts back and jumped from the pallet. She grabbed the shawl from a hook and threw it around her shoulders, covering her nightgown.

Bumping into Rachel, Wade almost knocked her over as he pulled his pants on over his long underwear. He slammed his feet into his boots, his suspenders hanging around his hips as he crawled out of the wagon, followed by Rachel.

The purple hues of dawn lit the sky, backlighting the early mist with a nightmarish aura. Along the bank of the river, six warriors sat atop their ponies, clad in buckskin.

At the sight of Grace, Rachel ran toward the girl, not heeding the Indian holding the child or her long night rail that whipped against her legs. But Wade caught her, pulling her into his arms, holding her in place.

"Don't move, Rachel. Look at them. Right now, they're as nervous as a skunk in the woodpile."

"But Grace," she choked.

"She's going nowhere, honey. Let Frank and me handle this."

Slowly, he released her shaking body, anxious at letting her go, afraid Rachel would take flight again. Reluctantly, Wade left Rachel's side and joined Frank to greet their visitors.

Jed and several of the men stood back with rifles in hand, prepared to do battle.

Seated in front of a warrior on a beautiful palomino pony, Grace waited a distinct pout on her face. Though mud smeared, the child appeared unharmed. The moment she saw Wade, her small hand went up in a fervent wave and she struggled to get down off the horse. But the warrior held her fast.

Fear rode Wade as he watched Frank speak to the Indians in sign language. The proud warrior signaled back, motioning with his hand to his mouth.

Frank translated. "His tribe is sick and hungry. They want to exchange her for food."

Wade nodded to the warrior in understanding and acceptance. He hurried across the open expanse toward Rachel. Before he reached her Mary and Toby met him, lugging the hind quarter of the elk Ethan had shot the day before.

"Here, Wade, give him this," Mary said as she and Toby handed the wild meat over to him.

Wade wanted to kiss her, but instead he hoisted the meat over his shoulder. "You're a hell of a woman Mary Beauchamp."

She wiped away a tear. "Just get our little girl, Wade."

Hurrying back to the warrior, Wade handed the food to another Indian, and then stood back anxiously, awaiting Grace's release.

The Indian holding her nodded his head, acknowledging Wade's gift. He spoke in a low murmur to Grace before easing her to the ground.

She ran as fast as her short legs would carry her into Wade's arms. The feel of her against him filled Wade with an indescribable joy that had him fighting to hold back tears. He knelt down and squeezed her tightly against him. "Sprite, you scared the hell out of me."

"I was scared, too! I wanted to come home last night, but they wouldn't let me," she said, her voice trembling. "I was afraid they would never bring me back."

Wade couldn't resist kissing Grace on the cheek. "I would have found you. It might have taken me awhile, but I would have kept looking for you until I did."

At the sound of hooves, he glanced up to see the Indians riding against the first rays of the morning sun.

Rachel ran toward Grace and Wade, her night rail pulled up, exposing her ankles. When she reached them, she wrapped her arms around the two, giving them both a hug. "Oh, sweetheart, we were so worried about you. Are you all right? Did they hurt you?"

Grace clung to Rachel. "No. But I was so scared, especially when that big Indian yanked me out of the water. I thought he was going to scalp me and take all my hair."

Rachel eyes skimmed the child as if looking for signs of injury. "I knew you'd fallen in."

"I didn't mean to, Rachel, honest."

"I know sweetheart." Rachel hugged the child to her, thanking God for her safe return.

"My baby fell into the river. I was trying to get her out when my shoe slipped and the next thing I knew, the river grabbed me and took me away real fast."

"How did you get out? Wade questioned.

"That big Indian swam out and got me. Then he took me back to his village. But I kept telling him I had to go home, that you would be looking for me," Grace said excitedly.

Deep relief overwhelmed him. He'd been so afraid they would never see Grace again, so afraid he would find her dead.

Grace took Wade's and Rachel's hands, gripping them as if she never wanted to let go. Holding onto each other, they walked back toward their wagon, with Grace happily chattering.

"I gave that Indian's little girl my baby, since she lost hers. I said you'd make me another one. Will you, Rachel?"

Rachel laughed, sounding more relaxed and carefree than in weeks. "Honey, I'll make you half-a-dozen babies, if you'll stay away from the river from now on."

"I will. That was pretty scary."

Toby bounded toward the three of them, relief etched across his young face at the sight of Grace. "You all right? I looked and looked for you, but I couldn't find you."

Grace ran to him, throwing her arms around his waist. "I waited for you and Wade all night. I just knew you'd come."

"And we would have, Sprite," Wade acknowledged.

Soon the two children were surrounded by people from the wagon train, checking for themselves that Grace was okay. Shaking his head, Wade laughed. "I can't believe they brought her back."

"I'm sure it was in self-defense," Rachel said.

Relief filled him with an overwhelming urge to kiss Rachel. He touched her shoulder, bringing her closer. For a moment they simply held one another. Wade knew he shouldn't, but the need to hold on to something concrete pushed aside his doubts.

Finally, Rachel said against his shoulder. "Something happened yesterday that I have to tell you about."

"What could be more important than a kiss at this moment?" Wade whispered, kissing the top of her head.

She looked up, her eyes dark with worry. "This is serious."

"One kiss, then you can tell me this worry of yours." Wade's lips grazed hers, kissing an invitation for more.

"People are watching." Rachel breathed the words against his mouth.

"So, they'll think we're a happily married couple celebrating the return of our daughter."

He deepened the kiss, savoring the feel of Rachel against him, until she put a hand between them and pushed him away.

"Wade!" she scolded breathlessly.

"It was just a kiss." He smiled at the spots of color on her cheeks.

"Not in front of everyone!" she said, walking away from the growing crowd. "I need to tell you about Becky and Ethan."

Reluctantly he followed her, a wave of uneasiness crawling up his spine. "What about those two?"

The joy of Grace's homecoming disappeared from Rachel's face. "While I was looking for Grace yesterday afternoon, I found them." She looked down at her tightly gripped hands.

Wade didn't have to hear more. Evidently they hadn't learned anything when he'd discovered them fornicating on the hill.

He ran his hand across his face, wanting to wipe out the words he'd just heard. It must have hurt Rachel to find her sister with Ethan. "So, that was her worry last night. That you'd tell Mary about finding the two of them together."

Rachel rubbed her hands up and down against her arms. "I hoped she worried about Grace, but you're probably right."

"I knew about them, Rachel," Wade admitted walking to her side. "Several hundred miles back, I found them together. Ethan threatened to tell everyone about our…marriage."

Rachel's eyes grew wide with surprise. "But that would mean Becky knows about us."

"I don't think so. Ethan sent Becky back to camp before he gave me the ultimatum. My silence for his."

"I told Ethan about us."

"I know."

"But why didn't you tell me?" Rachel asked, clearly exasperated. "Didn't you think I had a right to know about them?"

"I didn't think you'd believe me. I tried to warn you," Wade reminded her.

Rachel glanced down at her hands. "I'm sorry. You're right. It seemed too incredible to believe. I knew you didn't like Ethan, and thought you were trying to cause trouble."

"Honey, I don't need to cause trouble."

"Do you think Mary suspects anything?" Rachel asked.

"What are you afraid of me suspecting, Rachel?"

Mary's sudden approach, with Daniel in tow, caused them both to start.

"How much we're going to hate leaving you in The Dalles," Wade smoothly replied.

"You two have become very special to me. We'll keep in touch." Looking about, she asked. "Is Grace really all right?"

"She'll be okay. She's busy telling Toby and everyone else who will listen about her adventure." Mary's eyes were bloodshot and swollen, as if she'd been crying. For a moment, Wade felt remorse for not noticing earlier how distraught she appeared.

"Are you okay?" he asked, afraid he knew what troubled her.

She squared her shoulders, but couldn't hide the noticeable tremble of her lip. "I'm tired, that's all. I want to give you the rest of the elk. We won't be needing it."

Rachel laid her hand on Mary's arm. "You've been so helpful these last few days. Why don't we combine our meals tonight? The elk won't go to waste, and we can celebrate Grace's return."

"I don't know, Rachel. I'm truly tired."

"You won't have to cook dinner. Besides, you cooked for me last night and watched Daniel. No wonder you're tired today."

"Okay, I'll stew some dried apples and bake biscuits."

Wade couldn't help but wonder if they could celebrate with the knowledge of Ethan and Becky between them. Only Mary was in the dark regarding her husband, and from the look of her, he thought she, too, knew the truth.

"Speaking of food, I'd better get dressed and fix us something to eat so we can get going."

Mary handed Daniel over to Rachel. "I'll see you tonight."

Walking past the thinning crowd of onlookers, Mary went by Becky who stood beside Grace. Becky chose that moment to bend down and hug the child, looking over at Rachel and Wade.

Rachel quickly turned away. "I can't talk to her right now. Anything I say will only sound bitter. Maybe later I'll be able to speak to her without saying things I'll regret. But not now."

"Regret! Isn't it obvious the woman has no feelings?" Wade clenched his hands at his sides.

"Even Becky has feelings. But they're all centered around herself," Rachel replied. "What do you think we should do about Becky and Ethan? Somehow we've got to stop them."

"Honey, they're two grown adults, old enough to make their own choices," Wade counseled. "We can't stop them."

"Well, I can't just sit by and watch them destroy my friend. I have to do something."

"Are you prepared to tell Mary? Are you ready for Ethan to tell everyone we're not married?" he whispered.

∼

The late afternoon sun edged lower in the sky as Rachel set up camp with Grace playing at her side. Digging a small pit, she laid twigs and dried leaves inside, then struck flint against stone. A spark jumped, and the leaves smoldered. Fanning the smoke, she waited for the twigs to catch fire before she added the larger limbs. It was nice to use wood again, instead of the buffalo chips they'd used for so many miles.

The twigs crackled and popped, smoldering as she added the dried branches and hung the meat on a spit to roast. Smoke drifted across camp, blowing with the ever-changing wind.

All day, Becky had been as nervous as a sinner on Sunday morning. Several times she'd attempted to speak with Rachel, but each time Rachel had walked away, not ready to discuss the latest misdeeds with her wayward sister. She knew sooner or later they would have to talk. But not now. Not tonight.

Right now, all she could think about was Mary, the friend who had become more of a sister than Becky had ever been. If Rachel told Mary, Ethan would sacrifice her reputation by telling everyone of her pretend marriage to Wade.

"Are you all right, Rachel," Grace asked.

She held out her arms for the little girl, who slipped into her hug. "I'm fine, sweetheart."

"You seem sad," Grace said, an anxious note in her voice.

"I'm just tired. I didn't get much sleep last night, worrying about my little girl."

Grace's eyes grew round. "You won't let them get me again, will you, Rachel?"

The question tugged at her heart. "Not if I can help it."

Arms loaded with a pan of hot biscuits and a pot of apples, Mary strolled into camp. "Has Wade come in yet?" The circles under her eyes had grown larger and darker as the day waned.

"He's helping Toby with the horses," Rachel said, wondering what she should say to her friend.

"How long before supper is ready?"

"As soon as the men come in, we'll dish it up," Rachel said, noticing the tight lines around Mary's lips.

"What's wrong?"

"Ethan's late again," the other woman responded dully.

"We can wait awhile," Rachel said. "I still need to have Toby find Bec—" How could she be such a fool? Ethan was late, and she hadn't seen Becky in hours.

Mary drew in a shaky breath, her bottom lip quivering. "I meant to bring a jar of peach preserves with me," she said. "I'll be right back."

Whirling away, Mary almost ran back to her own wagon. Why would the mention of Becky upset her, unless she already suspected the truth?

In that moment, Rachel knew her conscience would not give her a moment's peace until she told Mary what she'd found. Since Grace's return, she had struggled with the knowledge that telling Mary would mean sacrificing her own good name. She would be an outcast from the rest of the train, but Mary's friendship meant more than the opinion of anyone on this journey.

Tension eased from Rachel as Wade strolled into camp. Grace ran as fast as she could, her tangled curls bouncing on her shoulders as she launched her body into Wade's arms.

Wade released Grace, but held her small hand in his as they walked into camp. His emerald gaze captured Rachel, holding her prisoner as his look seared her. Her breath caught in her throat before she reluctantly broke away from his stare.

"You finished early, "she croaked, passion clogging her throat.

"With two currying the horses, it didn't take long," Wade replied as Toby strolled in behind him. "Where's everyone else?"

"Mary went back to her wagon for a moment. Ethan hasn't come in yet, and I don't know where Becky is."

"Oh," Wade said, his lips turning down.

"Would you check on Mary for me, please?" Rachel asked, uneasy with the way her friend had left camp earlier.

"No need," Mary called, walking back into the firelight. "I've brought back the last of the peach preserves."

Rachel glanced at Mary. Her nose was as red as her eyes. "Thanks," she said. "As soon as Ethan comes in, we'll eat."

"No. We're not waiting on Ethan any longer. Everyone else is here, so let's go ahead," Mary replied, placing the jars of preserves on the wagon's toolbox.

"But Becky's not here," Grace insisted.

Rachel quickly tried to cover up the child's protest. "We're not waiting on her any longer, either."

"Good," Wade said. "The smell of Mary's hot biscuits has my stomach rumbling."

Rachel handed out plates as everyone filed past the food set up on the wagon's toolbox. The roasted elk was cut into thin slices, the biscuits were hot and fresh with apple or peach preserves and relish on the side.

Though the elk was tender and succulent, Rachel couldn't seem to get the meat past her throat. She picked at the slices, pushing them around on her plate; wondering where Ethan and Becky were, outraged at their flagrant disappearance.

Finally, Wade asked the question that hung over the group like a gathering thunderstorm. "Did Ethan say where he was riding out to today?"

"He didn't tell me," Mary replied. "He disappeared soon after Grace returned this morning."

The sound of giggling drew Rachel's attention from the conversation. "Finish eating, you two. You need to get to bed."

"Can't we stay up for a little while?" Toby asked.

Rachel rose to her feet and began to clear the dishes away. "No. It's been a long day."

"Let's get these dishes cleaned up; then I'll help you get the children to bed," Mary said, rising to her feet. The food on her plate had been shuffled around and picked at, too.

"Thanks. But why don't you sit by the fire and rest. It won't take me a minute."

"I can't just sit and do nothing, Rachel." Mary wrung her hands. "I'll put the children to bed, and you wash the dishes."

"Deal."

For the first time since they'd joined up together, Wade dried the dishes while Rachel washed. "I think we have to tell her," Rachel whispered.

Running the towel across a plate, Wade acknowledged, "I'm not too sure she doesn't already know."

"She's definitely suspicious."

"Are you willing to risk everyone finding out about us, for Mary's sake?"

Rachel closed her eyes, pain pounding in her temples. "I can't live with this knowledge anymore, Wade. My conscience will not give me any peace until I tell her the truth."

Wade sighed. "I was afraid you were going to say that."

"How are you going to feel about everyone finding out we're not married?" Rachel asked, wishing he would put an end to her unmarried state and say the words she so longed to hear.

"I don't like it one damn bit. But I like Mary. She deserves to know the facts, not Ethan's lies."

Rachel scrubbed the dishes with a force that reflected her frustration. "I have to tell her, no matter what it does to us."

"I know," Wade said, his voice full of resignation.

Strolling back from the tent where she'd put the children to bed, Mary called, "You two are whispering like conspiring thieves. Whatever are you talking about?"

The answer stuck in Rachel's throat. Now was the time to confess, tell Mary the truth. But the words lodged in her throat were not to be released, for the guilty pair strolled into camp. Mary's expression, already tense, tightened. Her lips thinned at the sight of Becky and Ethan standing side by side, their clothes slightly rumpled.

"I knew I'd find you here." Ethan walked over to Mary, a big smile on his lips. He acted as if strolling in with another woman was an everyday occurrence.

"Did you forget about our celebration dinner?" Mary asked, her tone polite yet distant.

"No. I rode further than I realized, and I just got back. But I did find Becky along the way." Ethan's face wore a mask of innocence that made Rachel physically ill.

Stepping around Ethan, Becky walked over to the box where the food was stored. "You've already put everything up?"

"Supper was an hour ago." Rachel tried to control the trembling in her voice. "Where were you?"

Becky's glance could have started a fire. "Out."

Like a proud warrior, Mary announced, "I'm going home." She started across the encampment, her head held high, her eyes brimming with tears.

"Wait, Mary," Rachel cried. She couldn't let her friend suffer any more indignity. "There's something I need to say."

Mary turned around, and Rachel could feel all eyes focused on her. Secrets and suppressed desires hummed about them like insects, making the air thick with tension. She twisted the dish towel in her hands and glanced at Ethan and Becky. Ethan appeared to hold his breath, while Becky glared at her.

Mary stood patiently waiting, her face taut and drawn.

"You know, don't you?" Rachel's hands shook. "You know that my sister is committing adultery with your husband."

"Yes, Rachel, I know," Mary said, her voice dull.

"Rachel!" Becky cried, rushing toward her sister.

Blocking her path, Mary pushed Becky down into the rocker. "You're not the first one. But you are the last."

Stunned, Becky remained seated, her mouth gapping.

Ethan hurried over to his wife's side. "You know I love you, Mary. How can you believe such lies?"

Like burning coals, Mary's eyes raked him. "Ethan, I'm not going to listen to your foolishness anymore. I've overlooked your women in the past. I've listened to your promises for the last time. No more."

"But, Mary—"

"Stop!" The woman's voice shook with anger. "From the day we were married, you've been unfaithful. Tonight, the two of you come back into camp with your clothes rumpled, and the smell of Becky clinging to you; then you expect me to believe lies?"

"I'm your husband, Mary. We'll always be together."

"Wait a minute!" Becky declared. "What about our plans?"

Mary clasped her arms. "Get your things out of my wagon. You're not welcome in my bed any longer."

Ethan didn't even look at Becky. "I'll make it up to you, Mary. I'll never do it again."

"Save your speeches for Becky. You'll cheat on her, too. You've fooled me for the last time."

Mary turned and proudly walked from the campfire. Rachel ached to go after her, check on her, make sure she was really all right. But somehow she knew her friend needed time alone to clear her thoughts and deal with the idea that she and Ethan would no longer live as husband and wife.

Ethan didn't follow his wife. Neither did he take a seat next to Becky. They sat worlds apart, staring into the fire.

"You shouldn't have told her, Rachel." His voice held a menacing tone that Rachel had never heard before.

"I think you're confused, Ethan. You shouldn't be cheating on your wife with my sister. Not only have you sullied your name, but my sister's as well."

Becky jumped up, hands on her hips. "Oh, Rachel. It's always been Ethan and me. Papa sent Ethan away when he caught Ethan kissing me. Not you. Me!"

Rachel glanced at the two of them, stunned. "All this time I thought Papa sent Ethan away because he caught him kissing me, and it was really because of you?"

"Papa warned me not to tell you. He wanted to protect you."

Silence filled the camp as Rachel realized just what a fool she'd been. As the information slowly penetrated, she asked, "If you loved Becky, then why did you marry Mary, Ethan?"

"I didn't plan on finding Becky again. It just happened. In the meantime, I'd met Mary. Things were working just fine until you managed to louse it up. But I'll get Mary back."

Barely able to look at her sister, Rachel asked, "How can you think he loves you when he just said he's going to get Mary back? Do you really think he can be faithful to you?"

"He would have stayed with Mary until we reached Oregon. There our life would begin. I know how to make him happy, and she doesn't," Becky smugly replied.

Rachel's heart ached over Becky's irresponsible behavior. "You deserve one another. And it's obvious Mary deserves better."

Ethan stood, his face turning red. "I think you're forgetting something. I know all about you and Wade."

A look of confusion crossed Becky's face. "Know what?"

The truth was coming out about herself and Wade, and though she dreaded the scandal, it would be a relief to be rid of the lies. "The wagon train wouldn't accept us unless one of us was married. So I persuaded Wade to pretend to be my husband for the length of the trip."

Rachel watched as her sister's eyes grew large and Becky's hand flew to her mouth. "You're not really married?"

"No," Rachel admitted, her chin rising.

Becky laughed, her voice loud in the still night air. "My angelic sister is fornicating with a man who is not her husband, after all the times she warned me about the sins of the flesh."

"At least my man isn't married to someone else," Rachel replied quietly.

"You told Mary about Becky and me, I think it only fair I tell Frank about you and Wade."

Ethan's smile revealed just how wicked the man really was. Not for the first time that day, Rachel wondered how she had ever thought she loved this man.

"You do and you'll answer to me," Wade said from the shadows.

Ethan laughed. "I'm not worried. But if I were you, I'd be concerned about Rachel's good name, about Frank forcing you to marry her. It'd be a shame if you were trapped in your own game. Forced to go spend the rest of your days together."

In two steps, Wade reached Ethan. He grabbed a handful of Ethan's shirt, yanking him off the bench. His fist cracked against the side of the preacher's jaw sending him sprawling onto the ground. "I've wanted to do that for the last five hundred miles."

Becky screeched and flew to Ethan. She brushed her hand tenderly across his cheek, glaring at Wade.

"Are you crazy?" she exclaimed. "Why did you hit him?"

"For trying to blackmail me," Wade said, as Ethan stared up at him from the ground, a trickle of blood trailing from his lip. "And for threatening Rachel."

Reaching into her pocket, Becky withdrew her handkerchief. She blotted the blood on Ethan's rapidly swelling lip.

Wade growled in warning, "Tell anyone you like about me and Rachel, but just remember one thing. After everyone finds out about the two of you, who do you think they're going to believe. Rachel and me or Becky and you?"

Rachel touched Wade's sleeve, her eyes brimming with tears. "I've had my fill of this. Let's go to bed."

Wade turned toward her and offered her his hand. She looked at it without expression, but put her fingers on his.

Leading her to the wagon, he helped Rachel up the wheel and over the seat. Quickly, he climbed up after her.

Inside, Rachel lit the lantern and sank down on the cedar chest, her face showing she was wracked with grief.

He didn't know who he wanted to hurt the most, Becky or Ethan. "I guess by tomorrow we'll be the gossip in camp.

Rachel bowed her head, her body sagging. A tear rolled down her cheek, followed by another. "Why is this happening? First Grace, now Becky and Ethan. What will happen next?"

Bent over like an old man to keep his head from rubbing the top of the wagon, Wade crept to Rachel's side, then sat on the chest and pulled her onto his lap. He held her in his arms while her tears cleansed her tired spirit.

"It's been a tough couple of days," he said. "But the important thing is, Grace is okay, and Mary will be, too.

"But how could Becky do this?" Rachel sobbed. "Mary's my friend. And they hurt her so badly."

"You're not responsible for what Becky did." Wade brushed his hand across her back in a comforting gesture.

"But Mary will never be able to look at me without thinking of what my sister and Ethan did to her."

Rachel shivered. "I want to believe you, for she has no one, Wade. No one but us. We have to help her."

"And we will," Wade promised.

"How could my own sister do such a terrible deed?" Rachel's tears were accompanied by little hiccup sounds.

"What makes your family any different from everyone else's?" Wherever people are, you find good and evil. And we never know when evil will reach out and touch us."

Swiping at the tears with her fingers, Rachel gazed at him quizzically. "I'm surprised to hear you say such a thing, Wade Ketchum. The next thing I know you'll be quoting scripture."

"Don't count on it, honey, though being raised in a whorehouse, you see people do all kinds of strange things."

She leaned her head on his shoulder. "How could I have been such a fool, Wade? To trust Ethan, to believe in him."

"You're a trusting person, Rachel. Sometimes you'll get burned." Wade rubbed the back of her head, her hair soft to the touch. "When Ethan was courting you, do you remember how he treated Becky?"

"Becky was only thirteen years old."

"Old enough, honey."

She grimaced. "Poor papa. No wonder he hated Ethan. And to think I grieved over the man for years. And Becky knew I grieved. I feel so deceived, by both Ethan and my sister."

"Do you still care for Ethan?" The question slipped from Wade's lips.

"Heavens, no!" She paused a moment, and then whispered, "You're the only man I care about, Wade."

Moments ticked by, while Wade sat holding Rachel in his arms, neither one speaking. They simply held one another, giving and receiving comfort while he tried to think of anything other than the fact that Rachel was in his arms. He tried to deny the words she'd whispered.

Finally, Rachel asked, "What will we say when Ethan and Becky tell everyone we're not really married?"

Wade sighed. "The truth. It seems to be the best place to start. Are you worried about it?"

Tilting her head back, she gazed at him, probing. The lantern's glow turned her eyes a warm amber, filled them with a heat that seeped through him and burned away the day's evil.

After what seemed like hours, she said, "I'm tired of worrying about what others think. I only know how I feel."

Holding her, Wade wanted to speak all the words she longed to hear. He knew she waited for his declaration of love, waited for him to ask her to be his wife, to protect her good name from the gossip. He wanted to defend Rachel.

Deep in his heart, he knew he should tell her they were never meant to be. But the words wouldn't come. A tug of war raged inside Wade. He wanted her for himself. He needed her tonight more than she needed him.

He bent, drawing her to him as his lips sought hers in a thirsting quest.

Like an accomplished seductress, Rachel kissed him back, wrapping her hands through his hair, pulling his lips closer to her own. Their mouths merged into a growing frenzy.

Rachel put a hand between them and pushed away. Her breasts rose and fell with the raggedness of her breathing. "Make love to me, Wade." Her voice deep and husky. "Take me in your arms and help me forget the terrible events of the last few days.

His lips crushed hers in a desperate effort to silence the voice inside his mind that insisted he could never marry her. He feared this would be his last time in her arms, the last time before they were torn apart.

He wanted only to think about the pleasure he received in Rachel's embrace. He wanted every moment possible with her before she kicked him out of her bed and her life forever.

She pushed away from him, and he was certain she meant to stop their lovemaking. Instead, she reached down and turned off the lamp, enshrouding them in darkness. His lips claimed hers once again, while his hands sought her breasts.

The rough cotton against his hand sent his fingers to the buttons at the back of her dress. His lips never left hers as he unfastened the buttons, while she hastily did the same for him. His hands were steady, concealing the feverish tide racing through his body. Calmly he eased her dress down over her shoulders and breasts, abandoning it around her waist.

Slipping the shirt down his back, she ran her fingers along his naked skin, sending shivers of delight rippling through his body. Craving her touch, he could not deny that need any more than he could refuse his need for water.

The strings of her chemise beckoned him, the bow promising a gift-wrapped delight. He tugged on the drawstrings, untying the bow and pulling open the cloth, until her firm breasts lay exposed to his sight. The temptation to pluck each nipple gently with his lips was not to be resisted. Bending his head, he tasted the tender orb, rolling it around on his tongue. Rachel arched her back in heated response, and he pushed the chemise to her waist.

He lifted her from his lap and laid her down on the blankets, pulling the dress and chemise down her sleek hips and legs. Only her petticoat remained, and he quickly

dismissed the garment along with the others. Spread upon
the pallet, she gazed up at him, her eyes dilated with heated
passion.

Quickly, he shucked his pants and boots, and joined her
on their makeshift bed. Naked, flesh to flesh, they lay side
by side, enjoying the touch of their bodies. She was
smooth, he was rough. She was soft, he was hard. She was
silk, he was stone.

Her fingers traced down his spine to his buttocks and
then pulled him closer to her. With feather light kisses, she
touched his eyes, his nose, his lips and whispered, "Do
what you did before. Chase away my fears, make me feel
that tonight will never end."

The words stung him like a barbed arrow. "Tonight will
always be with us," he whispered against her silky hair.

He moved down her throat, his lips trailing soft kisses
and raising goose bumps on a path to her nipples. He
swirled his tongue around each rising point, nipping them
with his teeth. She tasted like honey, moist and sweet.

Her hands explored his naked thighs until she reached
his manhood. Wrapping her fingers around him, she gently
stroked.

Disbelief held Wade still; then he encouraged her by
moving her hand up and down in a satisfying motion. All
concentration fled as he reveled in her loving attention.
Gradually, he regained control enough to return the similar
satisfaction and placed his hands between Rachel's thighs.

Finding the nub between her legs, teased her until her
moans filled the wagon. Honey flowed over his fingers like
sweet nectar as she writhed against him.

He kissed her mouth deeply, with the promise of sweet
passion to come. Clutching his hips, she tried to pull him to
her, but Wade resisted the quick satisfaction she sought.

Rolling over onto his back, he pulled her along with
him until she perched astride him. Grasping her hips, he

raised her over his rigid manhood, groaning as she took him inside. She answered his thrusts, meeting his upward motion, riding him with eager need.

He was lost. The past was forgotten, the future suspended. Nothing mattered but the pleasure this woman demanded and delivered with each stroke.

Rachel consumed him. The smell of her, the taste of her, overpowered him, filling his lungs with her very breath of life until he wanted this moment to be suspended forever.

Wade felt more alive than he had in all his twenty-nine years. She was heaven, she was earth and she absorbed him with a passion he had never experienced before.

While he wanted to hold back forever, to suspend this moment as long as possible, his body overcame him, sending him crashing into a stunning climax. A Rush of tenderness flowed over Wade as he clutched Rachel to him. For a moment, they lay quietly, waiting for their breathing to return to normal.

What had living been like before he'd found Rachel? Somehow it seemed she had always been in his life. She was as much a part of his yesterdays as she was of his tomorrows.

But the realty was, she was never meant to be a part of his tomorrows.

Chapter Fifteen

"Rachel, are you awake?" Mary called.

Rachel turned over, her hand bumping into a wall of steel, male flesh, and muscle. Sunlight peeked through the pucker strings of the drawn canvas at the end of the wagon.

"Yes, Mary, I am."

Opening fully, her eyes collided with the emerald green of Wade's. The heat from his gaze made her sizzle with the memories of their lovemaking the night before.

But Mary's voice brought the vivid recollection of Becky and Ethan's betrayal and of their threat to tell everyone the truth regarding her and Wade's marriage.

Mary spoke rapidly. "I hate to bother you, Rachel, but Toby is sick and Grace says she isn't feeling well either."

Sitting up, Rachel wrapped the blanket around her. She crawled to the opening and stuck her head out the drawn canvas.

"What's wrong with Toby?" Concern smote Rachel along with the cool morning air. "That boy never gets sick."

Mary stood outside the tent, holding Daniel, her face drawn and tight. She appeared to have aged twenty years since the night before.

"His head hurts, and he feels warm to the touch. He didn't want to bother you since you weren't up yet."

The sun peeked over the eastern horizon, and Rachel realized it must be after six. The long night of lovemaking had led her to oversleep in Wade's arms.

Rachel scanned the still camp. "Where's Grace?"

"In the tent. She has the same symptoms." Mary frowned and shifted Daniel to the other arm. "At first, I thought they were playing ill, but they're not. Something's wrong."

"I'll be right out, Mary. In the meantime, maybe you should keep Daniel away from them." She searched for her underclothes in the strewn garments that lay about, discarded.

Shifting through the mess, she turned to find Wade pulling on his pants. "What's wrong with the children?"

"I don't know. But Mary seems concerned." Rachel found her chemise half-hidden under Wade's shirt. Feeling self-conscious, she pulled the garment on.

A frown creased Wade's forehead as he slipped on his shirt. "About ten days ago we passed a wagon that had a case of measles. You don't remember them getting near it, do you?"

"I don't think so." A splinter of fear threaded its way down Rachel's spine.

Pulling on his boots, he grimaced. "Let's hope it's nothing."

She turned her back and slipped on the black cotton mourning gown she had worn almost every day for the last two months.

As she turned around, she noticed Wade sitting on the chest, completely dressed, staring at the pallet where they had spent the night exploring each other's bodies.

He looked up at her and cleared his throat. "I'll check on Toby and Grace before I get too busy today. Frank wants me to ride point, so I don't know when I'll be in again."

With a sinking feeling, Rachel realized that while Becky and Ethan did their dirty gossiping, he would be out blazing the trail, oblivious to all the hurtful comments. She would be the sole target of whispers and snubs.

She stood up, locking eyes with Wade. "So I'll be left to deal with all the questions about our marriage.

"Of course not. But Frank asked me last night to ride point, and I agreed." Wade grabbed his hat and pushed it down on his head. "Don't worry about Ethan and Becky. We'll talk to Frank tonight."

Leaning down he gave her a quick kiss on the lips. "I'll see you later."

Briskly, he retreated. Did all men run this hot and cold, or was it just Wade? One moment, he was her passionate lover, leading her to expect his declaration of love, and the next he was withdrawn, with no show of feelings for her.

Last night, he'd spoken no promise of marriage, no whispers of love. In fact, when she'd said he was the only man she cared for, he had said nothing. But, last night, she'd believed his physical response proved his unspoken love.

This morning she wasn't so sure.

Climbing out of the wagon, she held her skirts up to keep from falling. Mary and Wade stood by the tent, whispering.

Joining them, she asked, "Are Grace and Toby okay?"

Mary's eyes were swollen, her nose was red as if she'd been crying. "I don't think so." She held a handkerchief up to her eyes and dabbed at them. "I have something to tell the two of you. " Her bottom lip quivered. "Ethan, is gone along with my horse, Nellie. And I haven't seen Becky this morning, either."

Rachel opened the tent and peeked inside to see Grace and Toby lying on their pallets, resting. They looked up at her, their eyes dull with pain.

The tent was now without all of Becky's belongings.

"Her bedroll is missing, and her trunk is open and empty," Rachel called out behind her before going in to check on the children. She couldn't help but feel if the two were gone, their disappearance would be a blessing.

But before she could think about Becky, she had to check on the children. "What's wrong, Toby," she asked.

"I ache all over and my head hurts," the boy said.

Rachel put the back of her hand to the child's forehead. The boy was hot, his cheeks flushed. "I think you should rest in the back of the wagon today."

"Oh, Rachel. I'll feel better in a few minutes. I want to go riding with Wade."

"If you feel better this afternoon, you can walk. But this morning, I want you riding inside the wagon," Rachel said. She reached over, touching the back of her hand to Grace's forehead, and found the same symptoms.

"Grace, the same goes for you."

The child lay listless upon her bedroll. "All right."

Her easy acquiescence alarmed Rachel. Grace wasn't feeling well if she didn't argue about being confined.

Exiting the tent, Rachel found Wade pacing anxiously. "How are the kids?"

"Mary's right. They're running a fever. I'll keep them in the wagon today."

Wade frowned and shook his head. "I better go check and make sure we still have horses."

He hurried off toward the animals. She still felt irritated at Wade's response. Though he played the perfect husband to everyone else, she wanted to hear him voice his true feelings. She needed to hear him say he loved her.

Rachel held out her arms for Daniel, who eagerly went to her. "I have to tell you I'm ashamed of my sister."

"It's not your fault. And the blame isn't entirely Becky's. Ethan made his choice." A single tear marked Mary's cheek.

"Oh, Mary. What can I do to help you?" Rachel felt helpless as she watched Mary's tears increase.

"Don't let this come between us. Continue to be my friend," she whispered in a broken voice. "Right now, you're all I have."

How could life be so unfair? Mary deserved to be happy, she deserved a good husband and children. Ethan wasn't worthy of the love of a good woman like her.

But Mary was strong. She would get over Ethan's deception. Though the future appeared bleak now, one day she could still find happiness.

Rachel hugged her friend with her free arm.

"You're more like a sister than Becky has ever been. I'll always be here for you."

Mary's shoulders shook with sobs.

When her tears had subsided, Rachel asked, "You still want to go to The Dalles?"

As she stepped back, a small smile emerged on Mary's face. She gave a queer laugh. "I can go anywhere I please now, can't I."

"You can do whatever you want," Rachel replied.

Mary drew her shoulders back, her face resolute. "I'll reach Oregon without Ethan."

∼

The last three days, Rachel had watched the children grow continually worse as she and Mary battled against their high fevers, runny noses and coughs. If this was war, they were slowly losing the battle.

As Rachel stirred a thin broth, the heat from the fire curled the loose hair around her face in disarray. With little or no sleep the last few days, she felt drained, unable to face any more problems or squabbles with Wade for the moment.

He sat across the fire, his legs stretched out, his arms crossed behind his head. But there seemed to be an edge about him tonight that was previously missing. From the time they'd realized the children's illnesses were serious, Wade had been remote, as if his thoughts were elsewhere.

"How are Toby and Grace?" His deep voice was warm and pleasing. Their differences of several days ago seemed petty and insignificant now, yet she worried he would never propose.

Rachel tucked back a stray lock of hair from her braid and heaved a deep sigh. "Toby appears better, Grace's fever is still high and Daniel has been fussy and feverish all afternoon. If it's the measles, all three are coming down with them.

His eyes were tender as he stared across the fire at her. "You look exhausted." The look made her want to crawl on his lap and let him hold her until she felt capable of nursing the children once again.

"I'll be fine. We have apple preserves and biscuits left if you're hungry. Or I'll fix you a bowl of broth."

"Making yourself ill won't help the kids." He sat up straighter on the bench. "Let me help you care for them."

Wade seemed sincere, yet his face was drawn, and he appeared tense and nervous. It was almost as if he wanted to help, but was afraid to. But afraid of what?

"Mary is worn out from assisting me and dealing with the loss of Ethan," she said considering the possibility of his help. "I still have to feed Daniel and Grace."

"Give Daniel to me. I'll feed him," Wade said reluctantly.

As irritable as Daniel was, Rachel figured he would send Wade packing.

"Why don't you feed Grace?" she suggested.

He lifted his chin and met her gaze, with a steady stare. "I know how to take care of babies."

Wade's odd reaction piqued her interest. "How did you learn about babies while living in a brothel?"

He scowled. "I took care of my two brothers and sister."

"You mother raised four of you in a cathouse?" The moment the question slipped off her tongue, she regretted her curiosity. His family was none of her business.

"No. I was the only one who lived in the brothel with my father. We all lived in a house in town until my mother died."

"I'm sorry," she said. "I never should have said that. But I had no idea your mother had died when you were so young."

"I was twelve." He paused while the information settled over her. "When mother died, she asked me to take care of Michael, Sarah and Walker."

Rachel didn't know what to say. "How nice to have a big family. Do you get to see them often?"

His features tightened, and the lines around his mouth grew taut. "Except for Walker, they're all dead." His voice dropped to a lifeless monotone. "Died a year after my mother."

The spoon in Rachel's hand almost fell into the soup. Dead. They were all dead, except for a brother. For a moment she felt dizzy watching the broth swirl around the inside of the pot. How young he'd been when he'd lost almost everyone he loved.

"You've seen so much death. How painful for you at such a young age." She wanted to rush to his side and wrap her arms around him, comfort him; but she sensed that Wade would resist any consolation from her.

"I managed," Wade replied gruffly.

"When did you lose Walker?"

"I haven't seen him since he was five." Wade paused, clenching his fist. His voice became harsh and strident. "After Sarah and Michael died, my father turned Walker over to an orphanage, where he was adopted.

She stopped stirring the broth, unable to comprehend the cruelty of such an act. "Your father gave him up? But why?"

Wade shrugged. "Pa got into debt and sold the house to save the saloon. I was old enough, to help with the business. Walker was too young to work, so Pa gave him away."

The horror of his father's action washed over Rachel, leaving her sickened.

"Pa knew how to run a saloon, but his heart was cold enough to give a boy frostbite. So you see I have lots of experience with children, both good and bad," he said, his voice flat.

"That's why you didn't want anything to do with the children when we first met," Rachel said quietly. "It wasn't because you disliked them; you were afraid of becoming attached to them."

He closed his eyes, his voice so soft she had to strain to hear him. "Maybe. When I look at Grace, she reminds me so much of my sister, Sarah, my chest near bursts with pain."

"The only person I've lost to death was my mother, and now my father. But to watch a child die..." Rachel sensed the tears building behind her eyes.

"They were so ill, and I was young and stupid. I didn't know what to do to help them. I prayed for help to come. Only death showed up."

"What happened?" Rachel asked, afraid of the truth.

The bleakness of his eyes echoed a boy's devastating loss. "I held them in my arms and slowly watched them die. Then I laid them down and cursed your God."

For a moment Rachel was stunned. Until she realized that young Wade had been severely hurt. She brushed dampness off her cheek. "I understand why you would feel that way."

"I was thirteen years old and everyone I loved had been taken from me." Wade's voice rose. "I wanted to die with them."

It was all Rachel could do to walk slowly to Wade's side and simply lay a hand on his shoulder. She wanted to hold him against her breast, smooth the lock of hair from his face and wipe away his pain.

Instead, she settled for a comfort he might accept. "What happened was horrible. But it wasn't your fault."

"Try telling that to a thirteen-year-old kid." Wade took a deep breath. "It's still with me."

"And always will be." Returning to the fire, she scooped the steaming broth into bowls. His words wrenched her heart, yet they explained so much about his reactions to the children, even to herself. "You can't change what happened. Knowing the man, I'm sure the boy did the best he could."

He didn't respond. She sensed his withdrawal, as he suddenly realized how much he'd revealed.

"I'll be back," she promised, as she carried the bowls to the tent. Wade had to find forgiveness within himself.

A moment later, she returned, holding a fussing Daniel, whom she promptly thrust into Wade's arms.

"Your mother obviously trusted your skills in caring for your brothers and sister. It's time you put them to use."

The astonishment on Wade's face as she left him holding a crying Daniel proved she had done the right thing. At this moment, the baby and the man needed each other to heal.

~

A baby's insistent crying seeped into Wade's subconscious, waking him from a sound sleep. He knew immediately the cries came from Daniel as he reached over, patting the quilt beside him, realizing Rachel had never come to bed.

An uneasy feeling of déjà vu and fear crept over him. Quickly, he dressed and left the wagon, crossing the short distance to the tent in the darkness.

This was the time of night when shadows came alive and death stalked the earth. Hair prickled along his neck, and he was struck by an urgency to hurry to reach the shelter, to reach Rachel.

Jerking back the flap of the tent, he was confronted by his worst nightmare. Toby's skin was speckled with a rash that seemed to connect in red blotchy patches. Grace lay listless, her eyes closed, each breath a wheezing, gasping struggle.

Daniel fussed as Rachel laid cold clothes against his flushed body. Wade felt he had stepped back in time. The faces were different, but the symptoms were the same.

"Christ, why didn't you call me," he demanded as he rushed to Rachel's side.

She glanced up at him, her eyes red with fatigue. "I've been a little busy."

Standing beside her, he asked, "Where's Mary?"

"In bed. Earlier, Daniel wasn't this bad. She was exhausted, so I sent her to bed." Her voice was tired and anxious.

Picking up one of the damp clothes from the bucket of water, Wade twisted out excess moisture before laying it against the baby. "Didn't you think I would help?"

Tears glistened in her eyes. "I didn't have time to get you. Toby's been taking care of Grace, while I tended to Daniel."

Putting the back of his hand against Daniel's forehead, Wade exclaimed, "His fever is too high. We've got to get it down."

"Don't you think I know that? What do you think I've been trying to do?" Rachel sounded almost hysterical.

Wade ignored her outburst. The memory of Sarah's fever climbing until she became unresponsive spurred him into action. He picked up the bucket she'd been using. ""I'll get cold creek water; then we'll bathe him."

"You're not putting this baby in icy water. The damp cloths I'm using will bring the fever down." She continued her unceasing vigil.

"How long have you been using the cloths on him?"

Pushing back a stray lock of hair, she said, "I don't know. Since before everyone went to bed."

"It's close to dawn, Rachel. His fever is only getting worse. If we don't bring it down, it could kill him."

"But ice water!" Her eyes pleaded with him. "It could make him sicker."

"What kind of chance do you think he has now?"

Rachel glanced at Daniel who had stopped fussing. His eyes rolled back into his head as he lost consciousness. In horror, she watched as his limbs began to twitch and jerk. She picked him up, and held him close.

"Do something, Wade!" she cried, her voice full of panic. "Help him."

"We've got to cool him off!" Running out of the tent, Wade hurried to the creek and filled the bucket with water flowing from the mountains. He'd seen a doctor do this to a whore's child to bring fever down, but the man had also used chunks of ice. All Wade had was the cold creek water.

Stepping into the tent, he set the bucket down on the ground and took Daniel from Rachel's arms. The twitching and jerking had stopped, but still the tot lay listless, his eyes closed.

As Daniel sank into the ice water, his body jerked sluicing cold water over his limbs. He awoke with a start and began to cry, yet he didn't fight them. His body shook and his lips turned blue.

Wade spoke gently to the baby, trying to calm him, but Daniel wailed, tears running down his face.

Kneeling beside him, Rachel ran a soothing hand across the baby's brow. "Is he getting cooler?

"His body feels cooler, but I don't know if the fever has broken," Wade replied, cupping the cold water and running it down Daniel's naked body.

"You can't leave that baby in there much longer," Rachel cried, her voice rising with anxiety.

"Just another few minutes," Wade responded. "Get a dry blanket ready."

He wanted to leave Daniel in longer, but knew Rachel could not endure seeing the baby suffer, even though what they were doing should bring the fever down. She picked up the blanket she had wrapped Daniel in earlier.

"Give him to me," she demanded.

"It's barely been five minutes. Give it a little longer," Wade said, sponging the baby's heated skin.

"His lips are blue, and he's shivering to death. Give him to me now!" she insisted.

Wade handed a wet dripping Daniel to Rachel.

Wrapping him tightly in the blanket, Rachel sat on the pallet and began to rock. Soon, Daniel's lips returned to a normal tone, his cheeks seemed to have more color, yet he lay lethargic upon Rachel's breast.

After an hour, Wade whispered, "Does he feel warm?"

Rachel laid the back of her hand against the sleeping baby's forehead. "He seems cooler."

Picking up the lantern, Wade held it high above Daniel's head. In the glow of the lantern, faint red spots could be seen forming on the toddler's head and neck. Wade reached down and felt the boy's forehead to reassure himself, the fever had cooled.

Daniel's skin felt warm to the touch, but not the burning hot like before. Still, Wade waited another hour and then checked the boy again. This time the baby's skin felt normal.

A feeling of euphoria overwhelmed Wade, giving him a sense of victory. They'd cheated death from taking another child. Though he'd lost the battle before, this time he had been victorious. A weight he'd carried around for years seemed to lift from his shoulders.

Kneeling beside Rachel, he wrapped his arms around her and Daniel. She laid her head on his shoulder. The feeling of intensive relief was almost too much to bear. Tears sprang to his eyes, and he quickly wiped them away.

"You saved his life, Wade," Rachel whispered against his shirt. "I was losing him, and you brought him back."

Wade gently rubbed the baby's face. "Thanks, but it wasn't me. Maybe your God has other plans for him, too."

Rachel kissed his cheek. "Thank you."

The flap to the tent jerked open, and Mary stepped in. "I woke up and had to come check on the little ones. Are they all right?"

"I think they're going make it," Rachel whispered.

Have you had the measles, Mary?" Wade asked.

"I think so," she replied.

"Good. The children all have them."

Mary leaned over and checked each child. Grace's breathing had evened out, and she appeared to be sleeping normally. Toby, over the worst, was sound asleep also.

"I think they're better."

Rachel let out a tired sigh. "Thank God."

Reaching down, Mary plucked Daniel from Rachel's arms. "I'll stay with the children now. You two go back to your wagon and get some sleep. You look worn out."

"No. I don't know if Daniel is over the worst yet," Rachel protested.

"He's sleeping soundly, Rachel. If he wakes up, I promise I'll call you." Mary flapped a hand at them. "Go on now, both of you. I'll be right here if they wake up."

Wade helped Rachel rise. "Come on. You haven't slept."

Wearily, Rachel stepped on the wheel of the wagon and climbed under the canvas covering, with Wade not far behind her. The pallet lay stretched across the floor, the indention of Wade's body clear on the blankets. Reaching behind her back, she began to undo the buttons of her dress until Wade's fingers pushed hers aside to finish the tiresome task.

For the last two days, he had been withdrawn, distant. But tonight a new side of him had come to light, a vulnerable Wade who had suffered as a child.

And to think he had been thirteen at the time, alone with a heartless father. It was a wonder his good heart had survived?

With her back turned to Wade, Rachel slipped out of her dress and eased her nightgown over her head. She lady down on the pallet and pulled the blankets up around her.

Yanking his boots off, he laid them close to their bedding. He finished undressing and joined her.

A sigh escaped from Rachel. "I was so afraid, tonight. If we'd lost Daniel, after losing Papa only months before..."

Wade rolled over and wrapped his arms around Rachel, pulling her against him. "The fever broke. I think he'll be okay now."

"How did your brothers and sister die?" she asked.

"Measles."

Rachel turned in Wade's arms until she was facing him. Her hand reached up and caressed his face as she realized how fearful tonight must have been for him.. "Tonight was..."

"Just like when my brother and sister died, he finished.

Rachel placed a soft kiss on his lips. "Thank you for helping me tonight. Daniel would have died without you.

~

Rachel stretched her legs, colliding with the hard muscular strength of Wade's thighs. She rolled over, laid her head against his chest, and snuggled up against him. She felt splendid this morning. The relief of Daniel's fever breaking, and the memory of Wade confiding in her about his family had left her feeling everything would be fine.

She kissed his cheek, her lips nuzzling him with feathery kisses. One green eye, then the other, opened to gaze at her in sleepy surprise.

"You're wide awake this morning," he said, before his lips claimed hers for a kiss that left her insides quivering.

"Good morning to you too," she replied. "I wish we could spend the day in bed. We could look for each other's ticklish spots."

Wade pulled her tightly against him. "The thought sounds inviting, but you'd never go through with it.

"You might be surprised." She traced his mouth lightly.

His lips curled in a half-smile. "You're not going to get up and check on the children this morning?"

Rachel frowned. "You're right."

"Besides, we don't want to be left too far behind the others," Wade reminded her.

"I know, but the thought was nice."

"Being in bed with you is more than nice," he said kissing her earlobe.

She giggled and dodged his grazing lips. He made her feel like a young girl, but gratitude made her speak seriously. "Thank you for saving Daniel last night, and for telling me about your family. It helped me to understand.

He pulled her down on his chest, wrapping his arms around her. "You're welcome."

She relaxed in the warmth of his embrace, feeling secured and loved. After last night, she understood Wade's reactions much better than before. Still, she wondered about his intention to locate Walker. "Since we left Fort Laramie you haven't said much about finding your brother. Have you given up?"

He toyed with a loose curl. "No. Sooner or later, I'll find him. He's the only family I have left, and I want to see him. Maybe even go into the ranching business with him."

"But you could search forever without success."

"I'm not giving up." He sounded determined. Her fingers caressed the soft bristles of hair on his chest. She understood his need to find his brother, but what about their life together? What about the love they felt for one another?

He'd never mentioned love. He'd never said anything about staying with her. Surely he didn't still mean to leave her and the children once they reached The Dalles.

Rachel could no longer stand the pretense, she could no longer wait to hear the words she hoped Wade would say. And she could no longer hold back the words that filled her own heart.

"I love you," she whispered in the predawn chill.

The silence stretched on while Wade absorbed the information he had known, but refused to acknowledge. He loved Rachel in return, but that knowledge would stay with him until his dying day if he had anything to say about it.

Telling her he loved her would only make it that much more difficult when he had to leave. He knew that time was quickly approaching. And it was already getting to be hell.

"Don't you have anything to say?" Rachel asked, her voice rising in panic.

"No."

She rose on her elbow and looked down at him. "Doesn't what we've shared together mean anything to you?"

Pain ripped at his heart. How could he deny what she meant to him without hurting her severely? If only he could tell her that she'd made his life whole for the first time, that he would spend the rest of his days missing her, wanting her.

"It's not that simple, and you know it, Rachel," he replied, his reply terse.

"You're not answering me," she said, her voice cracking. "Am I just another of your whores?"

Wade tensed, his voice rising in an angry whisper. "Don't you ever call yourself a whore! You'll always be special to me, but you and I both know that you're not the man for me."

Rachel jumped up, from their bed. "What are you saying? How could you make love to me and then just leave?"

"I'm doing what's best for you," Wade replied, unable to lie about his feelings.

She snatched up Wade's pants, his shirt and underwear. Her hands shook as she flung them at him. "How can it be best for me when you're breaking my heart? I can decide what's best for me, thank you. Get out of my wagon. Get out of my life."

"Rachel—"

"If I'm just another of your women, I don't need you anymore." She turned her back on him as she stared to dress.

Wade stood. Why couldn't she see he acted out of love for her? She would come to hate him if he married her, more than she did at this moment.

Quickly, he yanked on his clothes. As he pulled his boots on, he reminded her, "We're a hundred miles from The Dalles. Maybe I should leave now."

"I should have known a gambler like you could never fall in love."

But he had. She was his sunshine, his joy. But he loved her enough to give her what she needed, a good man who could provide her with a secure home.

"You're no different than Ethan."

No, he wasn't like Ethan. But she needed a husband who was a better choice than a wanderer like himself. "You'll feel different later, Rachel. You may even thank me one day."

"How can you do this Wade?" Her voice broke. "I thought I meant something to you."

"Don't ever trust a gambler, sweetheart." You never know when he's wearing his poker face."

Rachel stumbled over to the trunk and jerked open the lid. She dug around inside until she found her coin purse. Pulling out a wad of bills, she quickly counted four hundred dollars. She shoved the bills into his hand.

Wade let them drop to the floor. "I don't want your money, Rachel."

Picking up the bills, she stuffed them in his shirt pocket.

"Take your money and get out now!" she yelled at him. "Our deal is finished. I don't need you anymore."

Bent over like an old man, he crawled out of the wagon into the early morning light. Dear God, what had he done?

Chapter Sixteen

The noonday sun caressed Rachel's face, its radiance warm against her skin, but the rays couldn't penetrate the ice encasing her heart. She prayed something would make Wade come to his senses, realize the worthiness of their love and return to her. But with each passing mile her hope dimmed, and she knew she was alone.

Around noon, the children finally penetrated the fog that had descended on her with Wade's departure. Stopping to feed them a quick lunch, she watched the wagons roll by, knowing she should get ready to roll again. But she couldn't find the strength to move another mile.

Putting her face in her hands, she let the tears she had kept damned all morning flow down her cheeks, in rivers of pain. In the blink of an eye, Wade had left, taking her heart as a souvenir, along with the four hundred dollars due him according to their agreement. Why she had thought she could hold him would forever be a mystery.

But she had foolishly responded to his lovemaking, giving herself to him like a young bride, surrendering her heart and her body, though he had never spoken the words she longed to hear.

She sat with her back to the wagons rolling by, her face hidden. In her anguish, she failed to hear Mary approach. "Rachel, what's wrong? Are the children worse?"

Rachel dried her tears, wondering how much she should tell her friend. "No, they're in the wagon, feeling much better."

"Then what's wrong?"

Her bottom lip trembled with suppressed emotion, and she felt as if she were dying a slow, painful death with each breath. "Wade's gone. I told him to leave this morning and he did."

Mary sat down, tucking up her dusty skirt. "Wade left?"

"Yes." Tears clogged Rachel's throat.

Mary shook her head perplexed. "Where did he go?"

"I don't know." But she did know. He had chosen his old life, gambling and whoring in every saloon he could find, leaving her as easily as if she were one of his soiled doves.

"Come now, Rachel. He'll be back by the time we make camp tonight." Mary gave her a quick hug. "Wade loves you."

A sob escaped Rachel as she shook her head. "No, Mary. You don't understand. This whole trip has been nothing but a farce. I'm not the person you think."

A frown gathered between Mary's eyes. "Rachel, what do you mean?"

Rachel twisted her hands together. "It's just that…" How could she explain the desperation of being left behind in Fort Laramie? Could Mary understand she had been faced with only bad choices?

"Whatever you're trying to tell me can't be that bad." Mary's eyes were soft with sympathy. "I've known you long enough to realize what kind of person you are."

"How could you? I've lied to you and everyone else I've met." Guilt lay like the oxen's yoke, across her shoulder.

"Lied about what?" Mary looked perplexed.

Rachel extended a hand. "This is a long story, and for you to understand, I have to start at the beginning."

"I'm listening," Mary said, squeezing her fingers.

Leaving nothing out, Rachel explained how she had met Wade, and she revealed the bargain they had agreed upon. Mary's face was a kaleidoscope of reactions, reflecting everything from sympathy to shock as Rachel confessed the truth regarding her marriage.

When she finished, Mary patted her hand. "I don't know what to say." She paused as if searching for words. "I have to admit I'm surprised. But you had no choice. You couldn't go back. You lied only to save yourself and the children. If you'd stayed in Fort Laramie you might have had to prosti—"

"Instead, I prostituted myself to Wade. I sold myself for a trip to Oregon," Rachel whispered.

"You made the best decision you could have in a bad situation, Rachel!" Mary reprimanded. Her voice turned softer. "If you lay with Wade, I know it was because you loved him and expected him to marry you proper."

"But he didn't Mary."

Mary put an arm around her friend. "I don't know what to say. You, of all people, know I'm not very good with men. It could be he's not ready to you or himself that he loves you. But I find it hard to believe he's ridden out of your life forever."

Bitterness welled inside Rachel. "He got what he wanted from me, and now he's gone back to his gambling, while he looks for his brother."

"Maybe," Mary acknowledged, pulling a handkerchief from her apron pocket, handing it to Rachel, "But sometimes you have to lose the ones you love before you realize how precious they are."

"That may be true with most folks, but not Wade. He didn't love me, so he won't be coming back, Mary." Rachel thought her heart would shatter with the pain. She dabbed at her eyes. "Until today, I never knew how much it hurt to love."

"Amen to that," Mary said, standing, and pulling Rachel up with her. "Come on. The afternoon is ebbing away, and we don't want to get too far behind."

Rachel sniffed. "You're right. But it seems odd that we're three weeks away from The Dalles, with no man between us."

Mary gazed sadly at Rachel. "I never thought I'd end the trail alone, without my man. But I'm not going to quit now."

Rachel's voice trembled. "Wade agreed to leave before we reached The Dalles, but not this soon. And then, somewhere along the way, I began to think he would always be by my side."

~

Damn her! Wade sat on the cold, hard ground. , chewing on the piece of beef jerky that was his supper. For the last week, he'd followed the wagon train, unable to leave, yet not really sure why he couldn't ride away. Every day, he kept just out of sight, but watched Rachel and the children.

And every night, when he camped nearby, the smell of Rachel's cooking would tempt him unmercifully while he sat eating hardtack without the luxury of a fire or a cup of coffee.

He slid down until his head rested against the hard leather saddle. Hell, who was he kidding? She didn't need him! She was the one who had asked him to marry her, take her to Oregon. And now, after all they'd been through, she'd thrown him out in the cold, just because he thought it was in her best interest to find someone else.

Who knew where he would be right now if he hadn't fallen for her plea. Sure, he'd been broke at the time, but her four hundred dollars was the hardest money he'd ever earned. Physical labor didn't leave a man all shredded inside, like he felt right now.

Wade slapped at a mosquito buzzing around his face. You'd think the cold temperatures at night would freeze the little buggers. The past months with Rachel had softened him. He wasn't used to bedding down with only his blanket to keep him warm, eating cold hardtack, doing without home-cooked meals.

But most of all he'd forgotten the quietness of being alone. How, in the stillness of the night, his own heartbeat could be the loneliest sound in the world. He missed feeling the soft roundness of Rachel's backside snug up against him, hearing the pleasant sound of her breathing and feeling the silkiness of her hair tickling his cheek.

But he'd get used to being alone again. After all, he had four hundred dollars he was a free man and tomorrow morning he would pack his horse up and ride as far from Rachel and the children as he could push three horses in one day. Yet the thought of leaving made him anxious. What if she needed him?

A raindrop splattered on his face and ran inside his collar. Another drop hit, then another, until they fell in a steady rhythm. He pulled his ground cloth over his blanket and huddled against the hard ground, seeking warmth. Damn, he hated rain.

Wade rolled over, pulling the ground cloth over his head to keep off the downpour. He shivered. The rain was freezing. It would be a long, lonely night filled with thoughts of a warm, dry wagon and Rachel by his side.

~

Wade sat atop Sadie and looked across the valley at Rachel and Mary's camp. The early morning sun had chased away the clouds from the night before, and a cool north breeze dried the earth. The temperature had dropped; the next rainstorm would bring snow to the mountains.

From atop the peak on which he sat, they looked like moving dolls. He was close enough to confirm they were safe, but too far to distinguish their features or hear their voices.

Now, seventy-miles away from The Dalles, he watched Rachel struggle with harnessing the oxen. It was a painful reminder of the day he'd found her. Funny how a chance meeting with a half-pint woman had changed his life.

He watched Toby help her lift the harness and slip it over the oxen's heads. If the woman wasn't so stubborn, he would be hitching her wagon instead of watching. He would be doing the chores that required a man instead of a half-grown boy.

But he found the anger of the last few days hard to revive, and if the truth were told, he felt nothing but emptiness. A void he'd never known existed until Rachel.

The urge raged inside Wade to ride down and kiss her until she cried out his name. But he sat, hat pulled low over his forehead, watching her load up the wagon.

He couldn't remember a time in his life when he'd felt more miserable. His old way of life no longer appealed. Being free to come and go didn't give him the same pleasure as spending time with Rachel. Even the thought of searching for Walker no longer obsessed him. Walker was a grown man now, probably with a family of his own, while Wade once again faced life alone. The thought disheartened him as never before.

Rachel helped the children into the wagon to start the day's journey. My family. My woman.

The realization shocked him, yet after a moment's reflection, it felt so right. The words held a sense of belonging that he could never remember experiencing, not even with his mother and father.

He loved Rachel and was tired of fighting himself, worrying whether he was right or wrong for her. He'd loved her even before they made love. Even though he wasn't the man for her.

To hell with the right man for Rachel!

Right or wrong, Wade was the only man for her. He wanted to spend the rest of his days with Rachel by his side, and not on some foolish chase, searching for an elusive dream of a brother he hadn't seen in years. What he wanted was in front of him.

He no longer wanted to live like a nomad. For the first time, the desire to put down roots and stay in one place seemed inviting. Rachel deserved a home, and he was just the man to give her one.

As the sun burned away the morning fog, his mind cleared. He knew what to do to secure their future. The four hundred dollars she'd given him was an opportunity calling out to him.

With little more than a week before Rachel reached The Dalles, he had time to put his suddenly conceived plan into action, a week to prove to the woman he loved how much he wanted them to be together. He knew he had one last chance to win her heart.

With a last glance at Rachel as the big oxen pulled the heavy wagon away from the campsite, Wade wished her godspeed.

Then he turned his horse towards The Dalles. She'd have a surprise waiting at the end of the trail, a surprise he hoped would make her willing to take a second chance with him.

∼

Rachel pulled the wagon to a stop in front of the church where her father would have preached. The building looked new, its white exterior freshly painted.

Four narrow windows graced each side of the structure and a chimney stood at either end. A picket fence enclosed an area out back, where four smaller houses sat. It looked perfect for a school or an orphanage, and would have been ideal for her father. The thought saddened her even more.

"We're here, Rachel!" Mary exclaimed as she ran to the wagon. "Can you believe we made it?"

Rachel stared at her friend. "No, I can't."

For the last week, Mary had done her best to lift Rachel's spirits, when all Rachel wanted was to be left alone with her misery. She knew she should be more excited, but she felt old and tired.

"Come on. We should be celebrating."

Rachel leaned against the wagon, her joints aching with fatigue. "Maybe after I rest for a while, I'll feel better."

She'd done a lot of thinking in the last week, and wondered how she was going to keep the children with her and support them without a husband. She had discussed opening a boardinghouse with Mary's help, yet somehow the thought wasn't appealing.

The children scrambled out of the back of the wagon, exuberant with their arrival and eager to explore their new home. She was relieved to see them so happy, since the days following Wade's disappearance had been full of questions and sadness.

"Come on, Rachel," Mary urged. "Let's go see the church."

A tall, thin man with wavy blond hair stood in the doorway of the chapel. He was dressed conservatively, with his shirtsleeves rolled up, suspenders holding up his khaki-colored pants.

This must be Ben, the man who would have been her father's assistant. He was handsome for a preacher. But he didn't have Wade's stubborn jaw or flashing green eyes, and then she doubted he liked to drink whiskey or sing "Buffalo Gals" at the top of his lungs, either. Even though she knew it was wrong, at this moment she would have

loved to hear Wade's baritone rendering one verse of that
barroom ditty.

The man hurried toward them, a welcoming smile upon
his face. "Welcome to the Westward Mission. Can I help
you?"

Rachel climbed down from the wagon. Regret made her
steps slow as she approached him. When she reached his
side, she glanced up into dark-blue eyes, dreading the
explanations. "I'm Rachel Cooke, and this is my friend,
Mary Beauchamp."

His eyes widened at the mention of her name.
"Welcome to The Dalles. I've been expecting you and
Brother Cooke." He looked around Rachel as if searching
for her father.

"I'm afraid I have bad news for you. My father was
killed by the Pawnee before we reached Fort Laramie,"
Rachel's voice choked with emotion. "Our…entire wagon
train was wiped out, except for my sister, me and three
children."

Rachel began to shake as reaction to everything that
had happened over the last six months overwhelmed her.
Tears cascaded down her face.

Ben froze, momentarily in shock. "Dear God." He
clasped her hand in his. "It must have been a terrible
journey for you."

Rachel used her free hand to wipe the tears from her
eyes.

His face was full of concern as he watched her. "Why
don't you go inside the chapel for a few moments to
compose yourself?"

The idea of slipping within the church was too tempting
to resist. She needed a few minutes to gather herself and
decide where to go from here.

Ben opened the door for her and gestured inside. "Go
on. I'll take care of things out here."

As she stepped into the dimly lighted church, her eyes took a moment to adjust to the darkness. The serenity of the chapel was soothing, its peaceful atmosphere a balm to her overwrought nerves.

In the muted light, she saw something moving – a man. From the back, his physique reminded her of Wade, but she quickly brushed away the thought. It couldn't be Wade. He had left her, choosing freedom over love.

As the shadow turned to face her, her breath caught in her throat. The man who had haunted her dreams for the last hundred miles stood before her, hat in hand.

Chapter Seventeen

"Wade," Rachel exclaimed, staring at him, her stomach churning with elation and fear. It took every bit of self-control she possessed to keep from flinging herself into his arms. She grabbed a pew for support, her heart pounding. "Why are you here?"

"I need to explain some things to you," he said, his voice tense, his eyes dark. "Will you come for a ride with me?"

The thought that he'd returned for her sparked a flicker of hope in her chest, which faded as she recalled he didn't love her, wouldn't marry her. He must have come for another reason. The brief moment of elation was quickly replaced with despair.

Mentally and physically exhausted, she didn't need to subject herself to another heart-wrenching scene with Wade. "I don't think that's a good idea."

The man had a lot of nerve, to come plunging back into her life after leaving her on the trail with three children. Yet the sight of his beloved face fed a deep need. Bleakly, she suspected she would always love him.

"I know I've hurt you, and you have no reason to trust me. But I want a chance to explain things. Then, if you never want to see me again, I'll go away."

Wade stood before her, twisting his hat. His face was intense, his cheeks taut; tempting her to risk heartache once more. The pain of his leaving festered like an open wound, but she couldn't bear to see him walk out of her life just yet.

She was so tired, yet part of her wanted to hear what he had to say. Still another part wanted to walk out the door. But why had he traveled all this way, and what could he explain? Could she turn him away without knowing – for the rest of her days – what he had to say? Curiosity fought her trepidation.

"I promise, Rachel, I don't mean to hurt you anymore," he said quietly, his expression sincere.

He'd already broken her heart, what more could he do? One last ride with Wade before they would be through. One last conversation before he left her life for good.

Reluctantly, she said, "All right."

Wade closed the short distance to take her by the elbow. "Then let's go. We'll have to hurry to get back before dark."

The fall sun shone down on them as Wade helped Rachel into the wagon. Once on the seat, she couldn't refrain from asking, "Where are you taking me?"

"Just wait," he replied.

The wagon bounced through the small town, the roads rutted and muddy from a recent rain. They drove alongside the Columbia River, following it along the cliffs and through the pines, occasionally glimpsing the churning water below.

She was in heaven, and she was in hell. The last three weeks had stretched forever without him. Beside him now, she longed to seek the comfort of Wade's touch. Yet she remained distant, touching him only when the wagon jostled them together.

"Did you find your brother?" she asked, curiosity overcoming her reluctance to speak.

"Nope. I found something much greater," Wade replied.

Considering his need to find Walker, his statement seemed odd. What could mean more than his family member?

They rode among hills green with pine trees and oaks, golden with fall foliage. But Rachel couldn't appreciate the beauty of this new land. Her mind was focused on the man beside her.

No matter what he showed her, no matter what he said, she didn't need any more heartache than he'd already caused. She must move forward, yet she couldn't seem to picture life without Wade. No matter how hard she tried, he appeared in every thought she had about the future.

She scolded herself. Today would be their final chapter, an ending without a proper beginning. In fact, everything about their courtship had been entirely improper. Yet somehow it had felt so right.

After thirty minutes of bouncing over bad roads, she asked, "How much longer?"

He kept his gaze fixed on the road. "That's why I said we had to hurry. It's at least an hour from town."

"Can't you give me a hint about where you're taking me?" The need to end this ride filled her voice with frustration.

He looked at the road ahead. "Patience, Rachel. It'll be worth it, or at least I hope you'll think so."

She crossed her arms, trying to calm her unsteady nerves. With each passing mile she wondered, if he made some sort of attempt to crawl back into her bed could she resist him? She didn't know if she had the strength to withstand him. One touch, and she could be lost to the sensations only Wade evoked.

He shifted nervously as their gazes met. "Did you have any trouble the rest of the way?" he asked.

She glanced at him, eyebrows lifted with disdain. "Mary and I did just fine. We're talking about opening up a boardinghouse."

"Oh," Wade said, with a strange catch in his voice.

They rode for the next few minutes in silence. She sat beside him, her emotions warring, wondering if this trip would ever end. Wondering if she would ever feel like the girl who'd left Tennessee.

Pulling on the reins, he slowed the oxen. "We're almost there. It's right around this bend."

Rachel shot him her best imitation of a bored expression, trying to restrain her curiosity. "Good. I need to get back to the children and Mary."

Wade clucked to the oxen, and they trudged around the bend. She tried not to appear eager, yet she couldn't help but crane her neck to see what lay ahead.

As they turned onto a narrow dirt lane that had recently been cleared she noticed a rough wooden arch over the road. Closer, she read the sign: Love's Last Gamble.

They passed beneath the painted words before jolting down the dirt road. "What's this?" Rachel asked puzzled.

Ignoring her question, he pulled the wagon to a stop in a lush meadow sprinkled with pine trees. In the background, the hills gleamed golden in the autumn sky.

He set the brake, jumped down and helped Rachel alight. They walked side by side, not touching, away from the wagon.

"Remember that four hundred dollars you paid me before I left?" Wade said, looking across the countryside.

Rachel stared at him, baffled by his question. "Yes?"

"After I left that morning, I spent the next week following you and the children."

She gasped as she realized, Wade had been close by.

"I tried to leave." To go find my brother. But Walker didn't seem important. As I kept vigil over you, I realized you and the children had become my life, my family.

He turned to face her, his eyes clouded with anxiety. For the first time, she felt as if she were looking into the very depths of Wade's soul, that he was offering her, this brief glimpse, but seemed terrified of what she could see.

"I suddenly knew that a brother that I hadn't seen in sixteen years couldn't take the place of the love I had found with you."

Rachel felt her heart stop. He had returned for her after all! Time hung suspended as she tried to gather her wits.

"Finally one morning, after being miserable all night, I realized I wanted you and the children to be with me always."

"Oh, Wade!" Rachel said, her voice barely above a whisper as she realized what he could say next.

"I have a lot of price, Rachel. I kept trying to make you think there was a better man for you because I had nothing to offer. Even though I loved you, and giving you up nearly killed me, a man has to provide for his family. That's when the four hundred dollars you'd shoved down my shirt suddenly came in handy. I realized what I could do with the cash."

He took a deep breath, picking up both of her hands in his. "I love you, Rachel and want to spend the rest of my days with you by my side. Will you please be my wife?"

Tears clouded Rachel's eyes. She wrapped her arms around him. "I'd given up hope of ever hearing you ask."

"I'm not rich. But I promise I'll be by your side until my dying day." Wade's eyes overflowed with love.

Whatever reservations Rachel might have had disappeared. If she knew one thing about Wade Ketchum, his word was better than gold. "Do you really think all that matters? I love you, not your possessions. Of course, I'll be your wife."

"You deserve a man who can provide better for you," Wade said as he turned to glance out at the land. "I couldn't ask you to marry me without being able to give you a home."

"That doesn't matter to me."

"But it did to me." He paused. "This land isn't much, but it's a start. I love you, Rachel. I'll never leave you again."

"I couldn't stand it if you did," she said. "I need you by my side each day. Wherever you go, I go."

Wade wrapped his arms around her, his lips brushing hers for a kiss that promised so much more.

"What about Walker? Will you ever look for him again?" Rachel asked when she could get a breath.

He nuzzled her neck, trailing kisses to her lips. "No. I'll always wonder about him, but I have my family now."

His mouth lowered to hers in a kiss that took Rachel's breath away and left her blood pounding. All thought receded, fading into the flush of passion Wade evoked. Until this moment, she had no idea how much she'd missed the strength of his embrace, the taste of his lips.

They broke apart, his breathing ragged. "Are you still in a hurry to get back?"

"Not now!" A giggle escaped her lips as he held her close. "Wade, why did you name our ranch, Love's Last Gamble?"

"Because this was my last gamble, and I did it for love."

"I like that."

His kiss claimed her. "Take me to heaven the way only you can."

Rachel sighed against his lips. "My pleasure, Mr. Ketchum."

Thank you for reading!

Dear Reader,

Thank you for reading *A Hero's Heart*.

This was my second historical romance, and in 1996 it was a finalist in the Romance Writers of America's prestigious Golden Heart Contest. Originally, it was published through a major New York publisher back in 1999, then for a while it was available exclusively as an eBook, and now I'm excited to have it in print once again! Whew, time certainly brings many changes!

If you feel so inclined, please leave a review of *A Hero's Heart*. Reviews from readers have the power to make or break a book.

Yours in Drama, Divas, Bad Boys, and Romance,
Sylvia McDaniel

Books by Sylvia McDaniel

Contemporary Romance

Standalones
The Reluctant Santa
My Sister's Boyfriend
The Wanted Bride
The Relationship Coach
Her Christmas Lie
Secrets, Lies, and Online Dating
Paying for the Past
Cupid's Revenge

Anthologies
Kisses, Laughter & Love
Christmas with you

Collaborative Series

Magic, New Mexico
Touch of Decadence

Western Historicals

Standalones
A Hero's Heart
A Scarlet Bride
Second Chance Cowboy

The Cuvier Women
Wronged
Betrayed
Beguiled

Lipstick and Lead
Desperate
Deadly
Dangerous
Daring
Determined
Deceived

Scandalous Suffragettes
Abigail
Bella
Callie
Faith

The Burnett Brides
The Rancher Takes a Bride
The Outlaw Takes a Bride
The Marshal Takes a Bride
The Christmas Bride

Anthologies
Wild Western Women
Courting the West
Wild Western Women Ride Again

Collaborative Series

The Surprise Brides
Ethan

American Mail Order Brides
Katie

About the Author

Sylvia McDaniel is a best-selling, award-winning author of historical romance and contemporary romance novels. Known for her sweet, funny, family-oriented romances, Sylvia is the author of The Burnett Brides, a western historical western series, The Cuvier Widows, a Louisiana historical series, and several short contemporary romances.

She is the former President of the Dallas Area Romance Authors, a member of the Romance Writers of America®, and a member of Novelists Inc. Her novel, A Hero's Heart, was a 1996 Golden Heart Finalist. Several other books have placed or won in the San Antonio Romance Authors Contest and the LERA Contest, and she was a Golden Network Finalist.

Married for nearly twenty years to her best friend, they have two dachshunds that are beyond spoiled and a good-looking, grown son who thinks there's no place like home. She loves gardening, shopping, knitting, and football (Cowboys and Bronco's fan), but not necessarily in that order.

Look for her the first Tuesday of every month at the Plotting Princesses blogspot, and be sure to sign up for her newsletter to learn about new releases and contests. Every month a new subscriber is entered into a drawing for a free book!

She can be found online at: www.sylviamcdaniel.com or on Facebook. You can write to Sylvia at P.O. Box 2542, Coppell, TX 75019.

Looking for a new book to read?

<u>Check out Secrets, Lies, and Online Dating!</u>

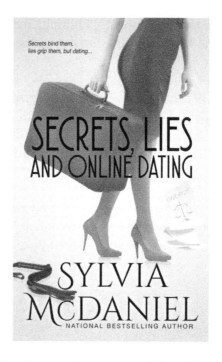

One lie changes the course of three lives...

When Marianne Larson uncovers a truth about her marriage, she sets out to change the course of her life, finding herself along the way. But that journey doesn't come easy as her mother and daughter decide to take a ride of their own – a ride that just might change all of their lives.

While discovering secrets, lies, and the truth about men & dating, three generations and three very different personalities recreate their lives and strengthen their female bond. But what they find might just be what they knew all along...

Sneak Peek into Secrets, Lies, and Online Dating

Marianne Larson stood before the apartment door of her husband's latest fling with his two suitcases in hand, determined, scared, and mad as hell. Birds twittered happy songs in the early spring afternoon in North Dallas, but it could have been a death dirge for all she cared.

Like an overcooked steak, she felt fried, burnt to a crisp –she was emotionally done. She had finally let go of the idea that marriage is forever. Each breath she took felt like a fifty-pound bowling ball resting on her chest.

Marianne dropped the two bulging suitcases onto the concrete walk and waited for the constable to step out of sight. She shoved her blonde hair away from her face, yanked back her shoulders, and lifted her shaking fingers to the doorbell.

Her new life was about to begin.

A shadow filled the peephole, and hushed, panicked voices echoed from inside the apartment. She recognized her adulterous, soon-to-be ex-husband's voice. The door opened as far as the security chain allowed.

A blonde woman peeked through the gap with a too-wide, fake smile. Marianne blinked in disbelief at the girl's thigh high boots, clinging thong, and bustier. A leather whip was still in her hand, the perfect accessory to her dominatrix outfit.

"Marianne! What a surprise."

For a moment, Marianne stared, stunned, before hysterical laughter bubbled up from deep within her. She recognized the girl from the company picnic, but leather? Whips?

At her laughter, the girl's russet eyes darkened.

"Yes, a surprise for both of us. I never knew Daniel was into…" Marianne stumbled over the word "…games." She gathered her wits. "I brought Daniel his clothes."

The woman's dark eyes widened. "Here? Whatever for?"

"Look, I know Daniel is inside. His BMW is in the parking lot. You're not the first one to climb on top of him while earning a promotion, though I see you have a unique way of securing your advancement."

Daniel's reddened face appeared in the doorway, his body hidden by his dominatrix. "Marianne, what are you doing here?"

"Bringing you your clothes."

Marianne gazed upon her college sweetheart, her heart void of the love it once held. Daniel shoved his lover aside, slid back the security chain, and yanked the door open.

"Honey, you know this means nothing."

The view of her husband with a leather choke collar around his neck and a leather thong clinging to his loins brought uncontrollable laughter spewing from her like a fountain. How could she not have known that he was into sexual games?

The constable standing to the side muffled his snicker.

"You're right. Your cheating means nothing anymore."

Daniel flinched.

She handed the bulging suitcases to the man she'd once loved.

"Here are your things," Marianne said, trembling from nerves, though she'd never felt more certain in her life. "And Constable Warren has something for you."

The constable stepped into the breezeway. "Are you Daniel Larson?"

"Yes?"

The officer shoved the paperwork into Daniel's hand. "Consider yourself served."

"Marianne?" Daniel questioned, his voice rising as he tore open the envelope. "What the hell is this?"

"It's called a divorce. You've cheated on me for the last

time."

His dark eyes widened as he scanned the contents of the document.

Daniel lifted his shocked gaze to her. "You can't be serious! You locked me out of our home?"

"Yes. I'll see you in court," she said, wanting to escape before the scene turned ugly.

Craving something more western?

Check out _Desperate_

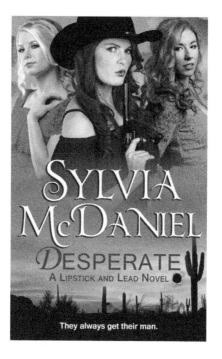

In 1880 Zenith Texas, the McKenzie sisters, Meg, Annabelle and Ruby find themselves penniless after the death of their father. When the bank threatens foreclosure, the women realize they need a way to support themselves. They have three options; marriage, women's work or... following in their papa's footsteps.

After her failed proposal of marriage, Meg McKenzie, turns to her dream of being a seamstress and discovers it's not all it's cracked up to be. Sweet and practical Annabelle McKenzie gives waitressing, a whirl, but soon wandering hands shove her out the door. The youngest of the McKenzie sisters, Ruby has her rose-colored glasses tarnished when she discovers cleaning houses can be hazardous to her virtue.

Spectacularly fired from their traditional jobs, they have no choice but to follow in their father's footsteps – bounty-hunting.

Sneak Peek into *Desperate*

"I don't believe you. My sister was not charging boys to kiss her," Meg McKenzie said, standing in the field of her small East Texas family farm in her father's hand-me-downs.

Her sister's schoolteacher stood in front of Meg with her arms folded, her expression filled with contempt, her nose wrinkling up in disdain.

This was her fourth trip out to the farm this year. Surely by now, the schoolmarm had grown accustomed to the smell of manure that permeated Meg's clothing. Certainly, she knew Meg worked the farm alone, which was not for the faint of heart, and most definitely, she had to know Meg could barely tolerate the woman who wasn't much older than herself.

Meg closed her eyes and wished for the thousandth time she lived the life of a normal young girl. With a living mother and a father who spent time at home. That she had a life of dancing, pretty dresses, and young men courting.

When she reopened her eyes, Meg recognized the poke bonnet and a bustle beneath the teacher's skirt from the last catalogue Papa had brought home. The woman was wearing the latest fashion. Fashions Meg longed to design. Fashions Meg wanted to wear. Fashions that would make Meg feel like a woman, rather than an ugly hoyden.

"She was kissing boys," the woman repeated. The schoolmarm's reddening cheeks and narrowed eyes bespoke of the temper she seemed barely restraining as she confronted Meg about Ruby's bad behavior.

At nineteen, Meg felt too young to be the responsible parent of a fifteen-year-old. And her sister, Ruby was definitely more than one person could handle.

"I'm sorry, Meg. I know you've had to raise this child without much help from your father, but I can't have her coming back to school. She's a distraction in the classroom," the refined woman told Meg, her parasol shielding her from the hot midday sun.

For a moment, Meg wanted to reach out her hand to touch the silky fabric of the woman's dress. But knew that would be wrong. Yet she longed to know what such rich material felt like.

They stood in the pasture where Meg had been hoeing as she prepared the spring garden for planting. Mud coated her work pants, she smelled of animals and sweat, and her hands were calloused and rough from time spent working the land. This was not the life she wanted for herself. Meg dreamed of being a woman who had few responsibilities and wasn't accountable for the care of the farm and her two sisters. She didn't want to be a parent.

And Ruby seemed to stay in trouble. "My sister may not have had a mother to raise her properly, but she's been taught that girls don't chase boys."

"She wasn't chasing them, Meg. She was charging them a nickel a piece to kiss her," Miss Andrews said, her parasol held tightly in her gloved hands.

Meg couldn't help herself; she laughed. Not even Ruby would be foolish enough to do something so naughty. "I don't believe you."

Miss Andrews placed her hand on her hip and almost snarled at Meg. "I would never have found out about it, if the line hadn't gone clear around the building. I caught her in the act of kissing Jimmy Brown."

"Oh," Meg said, her brows drawing down into a scowl. Could Ruby have been so stupid? At first, Meg couldn't believe what the teacher was telling her, but when she thought about it, Ruby was at a stage in her life when she seemed intrigued with boys. "I'm sure she has a perfectly good explanation for her behavior. I'll talk to her."

The teacher took a step towards Meg, a frown on her

scholarly face. "I'm sorry, but that's not good enough. She would have graduated next month anyway. Let's just say she'll receive her certificate showing she completed school in the tenth grade. I don't think I can teach her anything else." The woman lowered her voice, muttering under her breath, "She might be able to teach me some things."

"She's a kid. A girl who's curious," Meg said, defending her sister. Yes, Ruby was troublesome, but she was not a bad girl, just someone perplexed about the changes going on in her young woman's body. Ruby was highly intelligent, easily bored, and often mischievous if left to her own devices.

The schoolmarm raised her brows in an insolent way. "Well, she's training the students in a subject that neither boys nor the girls in my classroom need to learn at this time in their life."

A rush of fury tightened Meg's chest at the contempt she sensed from the schoolmarm. All of her young life, Meg had been dealing with the prejudice of people like the schoolmarm, who didn't understand that Meg wanted to act and dress like a woman, but because of her situation in life, she dressed like a man. It wasn't a choice, but a necessity. And now it seemed as if that injustice was reflecting on Ruby.

With a toss of the hoe, Meg walked up to the teacher. "Okay, Miss Andrews, Ruby will no longer be attending your classroom. I'm sure that will make your life a little easier."

"Most definitely, since this is my fourth visit to your place this year. I'll have more time to spend on students who are not so...social."

Rage bristled Meg's insides, and her Irish temper roiled at the not so subtle reference to Ruby's antics. How dare the woman belittle her sister? Ruby could cause trouble, but still, she was a McKenzie, and Meg would protect her sister and the family name with her dying breath. "Maybe if your lessons weren't so boring, Ruby wouldn't be involved in seeking outside stimulation."

The woman gasped. "If your sister would study rather than spending her time kissing young men, then I wouldn't need to come out here. Good day, Meg."

Meg reached out and grabbed the woman's dress, her muddy hands clasping the material. It felt smooth and shiny and oh, so wonderful. The schoolmarm was in a hurry, and the material ripped, falling away from Meg's hands.

Oh, dear. She hadn't meant for that to happen; she'd only wanted to feel the material.

"Get your dirty hands off my dress," the teacher said, taking a step back.

A smile lifted the corner of Meg's mouth. She'd been rude, but the woman had deserved it, though she hadn't meant to mar the lovely dress or the beautiful material.

Meg shouted after the woman, glad to see her leaving.

Made in the USA
Monee, IL
12 March 2022